Billie Templar's WAR

www.kidsatrandomhouse.co.uk

Also by Ellie Irving:

For the Record

ELLIE IRVING

Billie Templar's WAR

THE BODLEY HEAD
London

BILLIE TEMPLAR'S WAR
A BODLEY HEAD BOOK 978 0 370 33199 7

First published in Great Britain by The Bodley Head,
an imprint of Random House Children's Publishers UK
A Random House Group Company

This edition published 2012

1 3 5 7 9 10 8 6 4 2

Copyright © Ellie Irving, 2012
Illustration © Sarah Coleman, 2012
Pink shoe photograph © Getty Images
Boot photograph © istockphoto

'Singin' In the Rain' Words and Music by Arthur Freed and Nacio Brown © 1929
Reproduced by permission of EMI Music Publishing Limited, London W8 5SW

The Random House Group Limited supports the Forest Stewardship Council (FSC®),
the leading international forest certification organization. Our books carrying the FSC label are
printed on FSC®-certified paper. FSC is the only forest certification scheme endorsed by the leading
environmental organizations, including Greenpeace. Our paper procurement policy can be found at
www.randomhouse.co.uk/environment.

MIX
Paper from
responsible sources
FSC® C016897

Set in 13/19.5pt Bembo

RANDOM HOUSE CHILDREN'S PUBLISHERS UK
61–63 Uxbridge Road, London W5 5SA

www.**kids**at**randomhouse**.co.uk
www.**totallyrandombooks**.co.uk
www.**randomhouse**.co.uk

Addresses for companies within The Random House Group Limited can be found at:
www.randomhouse.co.uk/offices.htm

THE RANDOM HOUSE GROUP Limited Reg. No. 954009

A CIP catalogue record for this book is available from the British Library.

Printed in Great Britain by Clays Ltd, St Ives plc

For all the Billies with family
in the Armed Forces.

CHAPTER ONE

Don't you just hate it when you get into a fight, and it's really not your fault, but nobody believes you, and your auntie sits in the headmaster's office glowering after he called her when she was in the middle of getting her hair dyed because she *hates* being a redhead even though the brilliant companion in *Doctor Who*'s ginger? And here I am, trying to tell Mr Law that I didn't start it, but he's not bothered. In fact, he's fuming. There's a little vein bulging out of his neck.

'Now, listen here, Billie,' he says, and his eyebrows knit together like they've been superglued. Actually, they might have been — I've never seen Mr Law look at me *without* his eyebrows knitted together. 'This is the third scrape you've got into this term.

And while I do appreciate your home situation is' – he looks across at Kirsty as he searches for the word – '*challenging*, this fighting has simply got to stop.'

I look up from my scuffed school shoes. 'That's what I keep saying,' I cry, pleased that at last someone has started to pay attention. 'It's been going on for years, and even though the Coalition government have said troops will be withdrawn by—'

Mr Law raises a hand to stop me. 'Not *that* fighting, Billie. You.'

'Oh,' I say softly.

He picks up a folder with BILLIE TEMPLAR, 6H written on it. Great. My very own folder. Mr Law frowns as he thumbs through it. 'An incident involving Charlie Walters on the twenty-eighth of May—'

'He started it!' I blurt out, and the vein in Mr Law's neck looks like it's in a disco-dancing competition.

'On the eleventh of June,' he continues, ignoring me, 'Matilda Midgely suffered two grazed knees.'

'She started it!' I say, but Mr Law snaps shut the folder.

'And now this,' he thunders on. 'Of all the things to do. What were you thinking?'

I fold my arms. 'She started it!' I mumble.

'She's the midday supervisor!' Mr Law draws himself up to his full height and rubs his temples. His black hair's going a bit grey, even though he's younger than my dad. 'You've been uncharacteristically quiet,' he says to Kirsty.

Kirsty wrinkles her nose, and all the freckles join up to make one big patch. 'I don't know what you want me to say. There are only so many times I can tell her.'

Mr Law sits back down behind his desk and nods. 'I know. You're doing your best with her.'

'I am *here*, you know,' I say. Though when Mr Law fixes me with his piercing brown eyes, I wish I wasn't.

'What would your dad make of all this, Billie?' he asks softly. 'Arguing. Being abrasive to other children. Fighting for no reason.'

I swallow hard. He's only blinking gone and got me there. Mr Law knows my dad would be disappointed in me. *I* know Dad would be disappointed in me. And fighting's just top of the list why.

Mr Law lets out a long sigh. 'I guess it's detention then,' he says. 'Again. You can start this afternoon.'

Just as I'm thinking, *Well, isn't this marvellous? Isn't this just tickety-boo fan-tas-tic?* Kirsty pipes up.

'We've got an appointment this afternoon,' she says. 'Can it be Monday?'

Mr Law frowns.

'Hope Springs,' Kirsty adds.

He obviously knows what she's going on about, because he nods and says, 'Fine. Detention for the whole of next week.' Then he looks as if he's had an idea. 'On second thoughts,' he continues, 'I know the manager. I'll give him a ring, see if Billie can help out while she's there.'

'Oi!' I protest. 'While I'm where?'

'Billie,' Kirsty snaps, 'mind your manners.'

'Exactly,' Mr Law says. 'Hopefully she'll pick up manners. And patience. And she'll learn to respect others.' His face brightens as he thinks of something else. 'She can make tea and chat to the residents – that sort of thing. And if it is a' – he looks to Kirsty again – 'permanent arrangement, the residents could be a wonderful influence on her. She could help out more often.'

Residents? Where's he sending me? Oh God.

They call *prisoners* 'residents' these days. I saw it on *Look North*.

'Please don't put me in jail,' I shout. 'I can't go in the clink!'

Mr Law and Kirsty look at me in surprise for a moment. And then they both burst out laughing, though Mr Law tries really hard to turn his laugh into a cough.

'Seriously,' I say, 'I won't fight any more, I promise.' I'm desperate. Then I remember what they always say on *EastEnders*. 'I'm not going down!' I cry. 'It was just one little scuffle. You can't make me do time for that.'

Mr Law exchanges a glance with Kirsty. 'It's a nursing home,' he says.

'What? For old people?' I say, surprised. 'You want me to hang out with a load of old people?'

Mr Law nods.

'But old people are odd,' I say, 'and they forget things all the time, and they need help getting out of their chair, and they fart and pretend it was the dog, which Nana May's always doing, even though we haven't *got* a dog, and they say things like:

It'll never happen in a month of Sundays, which just goes to show how odd they all are, because there's no month that is full of Sundays, and—'

Mr Law glowers at me again, so I shut up. 'The Board of Governors are always telling me I should do more to encourage pupils to get involved in our community,' he says. 'So here goes. You need to realize that there's more to life than fighting, Billie.'

I start trying to tell him about the war again, but Mr Law holds up his hand to stop me. 'I mean,' he says, 'you have to learn to be a team player.'

I frown at him, but he just says, 'Help out at Hope Springs today, or it's detention for a whole month' – he laughs – 'Sundays or otherwise.'

'You just said a week!' I cry.

'Take it or leave it,' he says matter-of-factly.

I look to Kirsty, but she just shrugs at me, being her usual unhelpful self.

'Fine,' I sigh. But then I think of something else. 'Wait – why are we going to Hope Springs anyway? Is it to do with Nana May?'

Mr Law gets up and ushers me and Kirsty out of his office. 'I'll let your aunt explain.'

★

The talk with Mr Law means I'm late back to class after lunch, and everyone turns to stare as I walk over to my seat. Andy Nelson gives me this smirk, like he knows I got into trouble. Everyone knows. It didn't help that Mrs English, the midday supervisor whose shin accidentally got caught on my foot, shouted, 'They may as well make you a plaque for that seat, you've sat on it so many times,' as Mrs Hussein bundled me off to sit outside Mr Law's office.

Mrs Hussein looks up from her desk in the corner of the classroom. 'It's Golden Hour, Billie,' she says. 'You can work on your project if you like.'

Golden Hour's all right for everyone else. They can paint or finish their project work, as Mrs Hussein puts classical music on the radio, and lets us do whatever we want while she catches up on her marking. But I use the time to write to my dad, and all the lying and making stuff up is exhausting.

I sit down at my desk, and take out the letter I've been working on for the last couple of days.

Dear Dad,

Lots of news to report this time. I had tea at Linda's last night, and I taught Fur Ball a new trick with some wool. She can now jump three metres in the air, which is brilliant!

I'm thinking of going on 'Britain's Got Talent' — we'd be the only eleven-year-old-girl-and-six-year-old-cat combo, I bet.

I hope everything is OK. You said that it was especially hot out there last month, so I hope you remember to put extra sun cream on, otherwise you'll get as burned as the time we went to Great Yarmouth, when Mark and I buried you in the sand and forgot to put sun cream on you, and your back went all blistery and you couldn't move for a week. Remember? When Mum was there.

I pick up my pen and cross out that last bit. Dad doesn't like me talking about Mum. No one does, really, and I don't want to upset him. He's got more than enough on his mind, what with trying to stay alive and not get shot and all.

I try and think of something else exciting to say, because I really want to cheer him up. Trouble is, nothing exciting happens to me, and it's probably best not to mention the midday supervisor. But I'm sure Dad doesn't want to hear about stuff like Fur Ball, because it's pretty boring, actually. I want to give him something worth fighting for.

Before I can start thinking of new tall tales to tell, there's a cry from the next table, and the entire contents of Sarah Knowles's pencil case scatter to the floor.

Sarah ducks down and starts picking up crayons and pencils. They're all chewed and most of them are broken. Andy Nelson looks over at his mate Sabrina Mitchell and the pair of them hold their noses and go, 'Eeeeeeewwwwww!' The rest of blue table giggle – but quietly, so Mrs Hussein doesn't hear over the violins blaring from the radio.

Sarah's scraggly mousy hair covers her face, but I can see she's gone bright red. Her hands are shaking.

'Wet yourself again?' Andy taunts her, and everyone

laughs as he and Sabrina wave their hands under their noses to waft away the smell of wee.

I don't say anything, but I go over to help Sarah. I have to bite my lip to stop my eyes from watering, because Sarah Knowles really *does* smell a bit.

Sarah looks at me dead gratefully as I pick everything up. 'Thanks,' she mutters. I shrug my shoulders. It's not Sarah's fault she only has one school uniform. It's her mum and dad's job to buy and wash her clothes, isn't it? Kirsty may not be my mum, because I haven't got one any more, but at least she knows how to use a washing machine.

I go back to my seat and Mrs Hussein switches off the radio and claps her hands. 'Right, everyone,' she says, and moves to the front of the class. 'This year's carnival . . .'

Everyone stops what they're doing and practically runs to sit on the carpet in front of her. 'What day's the race, miss?' Sabrina Mitchell asks.

'The last day of the summer term is Tuesday the seventeenth of July,' Mrs Hussein replies. 'The race will take place the Saturday that week and the king chosen then. The carnival will be the day after, Sunday the twenty-second. Which gives you plenty of time to work on your carnival costumes.'

I stick my hand in the air. Mrs Hussein glances at me, then quickly looks away.

Sabrina Mitchell pipes up again. 'My dad's started going to the gym. He's determined to win the race.'

I waggle my hand around. 'Uh, miss,' I say.

'He'll have to beat mine,' Andy Nelson tells her. 'And there's no way he'll do that.'

I stand up to try and get Mrs Hussein's attention. 'Mrs Hussein,' I say loudly.

She turns to me. 'Sit down, Billie,' she says, 'and stop mithering me.'

'But—'

'Sit down,' she says sharply.

I can't believe it. Why is she being so mean? And why are we even having a conversation about who will win the race?

'Yeah, sit down, Billie,' Andy sneers at me. 'It's got nothing to do with you.'

'What are you talking about?' I hiss as I sit down on the carpet again.

'Billie Templar,' Mrs Hussein cuts in. 'I've told

you to be quiet. Do you want to go back to Mr Law's office?'

I shake my head, but my cheeks are going red. 'No, miss, it's just—'

Mrs Hussein interrupts me again. 'Billie,' she says, but her voice is softer this time, 'that's enough.'

She turns to the rest of the class. 'You'll need to pass the information on to your fathers, and then get practising. Only one of them can be crowned Merchant Stanton's carnival king.'

I've had enough of this. What's a person got to do to get a word in edgeways round here? 'Well, we all know who that'll be!' I yell.

The whole class turns to stare at me. Mrs Hussein readjusts her headscarf. 'And who's that, Billie?'

I look at her like she's lost her mind. 'My dad, obviously.'

Next to me, Andy Nelson laughs. 'You're such an idiot,' he whispers so Mrs Hussein can't hear.

'We'll be needing a new king this year, Billie,' Mrs Hussein says quietly.

'Why on earth would we?' I reply. Ever since Dad got a new army post and we moved to Merchant

Stanton we've won the father-and-child three-legged race. Meaning my dad, Don Templar, the fastest, bestest racer in the world, gets to be the carnival king.

I fold my arms across my chest. 'Dad and me have won the last four years in a row,' I say firmly. 'I don't know why anyone else bothers to turn up, to be honest.'

This time, the whole class laughs at me. My cheeks get hot again. 'What?' I say, though I'm practically yelling, I'm so annoyed at everyone. 'What *possible* reason would there be for us not to win this year? Hey? Anyone?'

Mrs Hussein clears her throat. 'Your dad's not here, Billie.' She gives me this look, almost like pity. 'He's not coming back for the carnival.'

Everyone shuts up at that.

I open my mouth to say something, but nothing comes out. Mrs Hussein ploughs on. 'He's off fighting for Queen and Country,' she says. 'He's a very brave man, and our thoughts are with him, and all the troops.'

She goes back to talking about fancy dress again,

but I'm not really listening. My mind's whirring.

'Not home for the carnival?' I say eventually. The thought had never even crossed my mind.

Mrs Hussein stops talking and looks straight at me. She shakes her head. 'No, love,' she says. 'Your dad's on tour for a few more months yet. You know that.' She turns to the rest of the class. 'Now, homework for the weekend . . .'

Before I can say anything else, the smell of wee drifts under my nose. 'If it's any consolation, my dad's not entering the race this year, either,' Sarah Knowles whispers to me. It isn't.

Just then the bell rings, and everyone scrambles to their feet and runs to get their coats and bags.

As Mrs Hussein shouts out something about spellings, I slowly stand up and walk back to my desk. Before I know it, I'm the only one left in the classroom. 6H are a speedy lot, that's for sure.

'Billie?' Mrs Hussein says, looking up from her desk, where she's packing her things away. 'Come on, it's home time.'

I bite my lip. I knew Dad was going away for a long time, but I just thought . . . I mean, it's the carnival. He's *always* here for the carnival. We've never not done it before. 'I forgot he wasn't coming back,' I murmur. 'Do you think he *could* come back, just for this?'

A car horn honks in the car park, and Mrs Hussein gestures for me to pick up my things. She holds the door open and ushers me outside, stepping out after me. 'I don't think so, love,' she says, shutting the door. 'I'm sorry.' And she strides off into the car park.

Fat lot of good 'I'm sorry' is. Where does 'I'm sorry' ever get you?

'Dad's *always* the carnival king,' I whisper.

But there's nobody left to hear me.

CHAPTER TWO

I'm standing outside Hope Springs Retirement Home with Kirsty and Nana May, because this, Kirsty told me, is going to be Nana May's new home. She's a bit of a handful, is my nan. She's dead funny – even when she doesn't mean to be. She's comes out with things like, *Turn your tripod off when I'm talking to you*, when I'm listening to music. She's been living in the little bit at the side of our house that used to be the garage – until Dad put in a washbasin and a handrail so Nana May didn't have to use the stairs – but things have changed since he went away. A couple of weeks ago, Kirsty got a call in the middle of the night because Nana May had been found dressed in her bathing costume and slippers,

16

dancing on top of the old Second World War tank Mr Clewson bought on eBay and keeps in his front garden. Now everyone thinks it's Best All Round if she comes to live here.

Hope Springs doesn't look as nice as its name suggests – at least, not from the outside. One of the front gates is off its hinges, and the patch of lawn beside the concrete drive has gone all yellow. There's an apple tree, but its branches are withered and leafless. The care home's three storeys high and has a little attic room at the top. I count one, two, three, four boarded-up windows, and the green paint on the front porch is peeling. It looks like a run-down B&B.

Kirsty's still mad at me, and as she leads Nana May up the front steps I skulk behind. We walk through the porch and then the front door, and Kirsty heads towards reception. Me and Nana May hang back.

'Nana May?' I ask as soon as Kirsty's out of earshot. 'Do you know if Dad can come back before his tour's over?'

'What's that, love?' Nana May replies. She doesn't look at me; her eyes are sweeping over the drab carpet and gloomy corridor, trying to make out what's going on.

'Dad,' I say. 'Is he coming back for the end of term, do you know?'

'Do you know . . .' Nana May repeats slowly, and I lean forward in anticipation. 'Burton's haven't had sticky toffee pudding on their menu for ages,' she finishes eventually.

I let out a sigh. 'Have they not?' I ask – but I've got other things to worry about than the local café's line in desserts.

Kirsty heads back towards us, accompanied by a tall man in a sharp suit. He shakes our hands enthusiastically. 'Welcome, welcome,' he says. 'My name's Brian Stephens. I'll be giving you the grand tour this afternoon.' He frowns as he looks around. I follow his gaze to the peeling paint on the wall. 'We're waiting to hear from the council about a grant.' He smiles, almost apologetically.

Nana May just beams at him. I'm not entirely convinced she knows what's going on. She's probably still thinking about pudding.

Mr Stephens looks at me and narrows his eyes

a little. 'It's Billie, isn't it? I've had a phone call from Mr Law.'

I don't like the sound of this.

'Why don't you head in there and ask for Derek while I show your nan and aunt around?' He jerks his thumb to a door off the corridor. 'You're just in time for supper.'

I check my watch. It's ten past four.

Kirsty nods at me. 'Come on, Mum.' She and Nana May start the grand tour while I trudge off along the corridor.

Call me crazy, but standing in a dining room watching old people try and eat their tea while one old man bangs on about Hitler and another keeps taking his false teeth out and leaving them in the gravy boat is *not* my idea of fun. Especially when you've just been told your nan's moving in because she's a danger to herself, and your dad's not coming home for the Merchant Stanton Carnival.

I go round pouring tea into everyone's mug. There's an empty space at the far corner of the dining table. 'Shall I do this one?' I ask Derek, the head carer, holding the teapot over the mug.

He looks over, but before he can answer, everyone starts giggling. 'You're having a laugh, aren't you?' the old man with the false teeth cries. Though because they're currently floating in the gravy, it's more like, 'Yoravinalaffrntyoo?'

An old woman with hair as red as Kirsty's pipes up next to him. 'The Lord of the Manor never deigns to eat with us,' she trills.

Derek frowns at her. 'Mr Featherstone always takes his tea in his room,' he explains.

I shrug my shoulders. 'Shall I take it to him, then?'

Everyone bursts out laughing again. Honestly, it's like a blinking sitcom round here. An unfunny, boring, smelly sitcom.

'He never has visitors,' the old woman whispers. 'Thinks he's above it.'

'Literally,' the old man next to her cackles. 'He's on the top floor.'

The teapot's practically empty so I wander into the little kitchen to refill it. A young nurse is in there, buttering a bread roll. She puts it on a tray, along with a slice of quiche and a bowl of salad.

She picks up the tray and heads out of the kitchen. I shove the teapot on the counter and follow. 'Is that for Mr Featherstone?' I ask.

She nods and carries on down the corridor.

'Derek asked me to take it up to him.'

The nurse looks at me in surprise. 'Are you sure? Mr F wouldn't want that.'

I shrug. I don't *quite* know why I'm doing this, but I'm curious, like. I want to see who Nana May's going to be living with. I reach out to take the tray, but the nurse hesitates. Just then, a tinkling sound comes from round the corner and she looks at me in horror. 'Mr McIntyre!' she cries. She shoves the tray at me and races off. 'Not again!' she yells, rounding the corner.

Framed pictures of countryside scenes hang on the walls up the stairs as I make for the little attic room at the top. My stomach growls and I try not to look at the bread roll. It's practically calling out to me. I knock on the door.

'Leave it outside,' Mr Featherstone grunts after a moment.

And to think Mr Law wanted me to learn manners.

I slowly open the door and peek inside. An old man, smartly dressed in grey jumper and beige slacks, sits on the single bed, staring down at a blue envelope and a little black comb in his lap. I don't reckon Mr Featherstone's used the comb though, because he's got shockingly messy hair. It's white and sticks out, a bit like the picture I once saw of Albert Einstein. Maybe this Mr Featherstone's a mad scientist too.

'What part of "Leave it outside—"?' Mr Featherstone starts – but he stops when he sees me. 'Who are you? Are you . . . *visiting*?'

'Something like that,' I reply. I walk into the room and have to duck because the roof slants on one side. It's got a skylight, and there's a little window looking onto the front lawn. I plonk the tray down on the chest of drawers beside the bed.

Mr Featherstone just grunts at me. 'You can go now,' he mutters.

I guess the others were right about him. 'You're welcome,' I say, not without sarcasm. Honestly, I reckon Mr Law needs to come and see this for himself. I turn to leave, but then I spot a framed black-and-white photo above the little washbasin in the corner of the room. 'That's a Supermarine Spitfire,' I blurt out before I can stop myself. I lean in for a closer look at the aeroplane. 'It was designed by R. J. Mitchell and first flown in nineteen thirty-five.' I know this because Dad told me. There's a framed picture of the same plane on the wall of *his* bedroom – Grandad Templar was in the RAF but Dad didn't fancy flying, so joined the army instead, and I'm always getting him to tell me about it. At least, I did when he was here.

'Nineteen thirty-six,' Mr Featherstone corrects me.

I turn round and see that he's peering at me in surprise. 'You sure?' I ask.

He nods. 'I was around then,' he replies. 'Were you?' His grey eyes twinkle a little and I realize he's making a joke.

I laugh. 'Yep,' I reply. 'I just look good for my age.'

Mr Featherstone opens his mouth to say something, but then my stomach gives an unearthly growl. I clutch it and try to stop staring at the tea tray. He raises his bushy white eyebrows at me. 'Hungry, are we, lass?'

I nod and feel my cheeks go red, 'cos it's a bit embarrassing, like.

Mr Featherstone looks me over for a moment and then nods towards the tray. 'You can have the roll, if you like.'

As I grab the roll, I notice that the letter on his lap says AIRMAIL; the little black comb has gold letters running up the side spelling GRANDAD.

'Ta, guv'nor,' I say after I've wolfed the roll down practically in one. 'That's what they say on *EastEnders*,' I explain, seeing Mr Featherstone's confusion.

He frowns. 'You don't watch that rubbish, do you?'

'When Mark and Kirsty are out and I've got the house to myself, I sometimes watch the omnibus, even if I've seen all the episodes anyway,' I tell him.

Before Mr Featherstone can reply, Derek blunders into the room, wiping his hands on the trousers of his dark blue nurse's uniform. He starts when he sees me. 'Billie . . . ?' He purses his lips. 'I'm so sorry, Mr F, I didn't know she was up here.' He narrows his eyes at me. 'Have you been eating his tea?' He's seen the crumbs round my mouth.

I turn to Mr Featherstone in panic.

He looks Derek over. 'I keep telling you not to call me Mr F,' he says after a moment.

Derek adjusts his glasses, distracted. 'It's a term of endearment,' he replies. 'You're Mr F in Room F.'

'It's disrespectful,' Mr Featherstone mutters. 'Even the Pope called me Mr *Featherstone*.'

It takes me a second to register what he's just said. Clearly he's less 'mad scientist', more just plain 'mad'.

But Derek calms down and sighs. 'Mr Stephens is looking for you,' he says to me, less angry with me now.

Mr Featherstone gives me a tight smile and I sneak out of the room.

Mr Stephens is in the corridor, his arm entwined with Nana May's. 'Your aunt had to go,' he says. 'She asked me to send you home when we were done.'

I remember that it's Friday and check my watch. 'Did she go to her Zumba class?' I ask.

Mr Stephens shrugs his shoulders. He hands me Nana May's arm. 'We've had a lovely look round, and I think she'll be very happy here.'

Will she now, I think. I pat Nana May's hand.

It's dead wrinkly, with brown liver spots all over it. 'Come on, then,' I say softly. 'Home, sweet home.'

I walk with Nana May past Mr Marsh's farm, through Eddington fields and round the back streets of the Cobsworthy Estate. We play the cloud game 'cos the sky's so clear and blue. 'Look!' I point at a thin cloud scudding by. It's shaped like a triangle, with two wisps on either side. 'An alien spaceship!'

Nana May smiles. 'Or a trampoline.' She doesn't quite get the game, even though, with this heat wave, we've been playing it practically all summer.

As we walk along the cobbles on Fairfield Lane, I notice something odd. There are loads of cars parked outside number seven. Tons. There are three on our driveway, and two parked up on the pavement.

And then my stomach turns over and my throat goes completely dry as one thought pops into my head.

Dad.

Something's happened to Dad.

I push Nana May up the drive, weave her between the cars and race to our front door. I fumble with the key in the lock, then burst through the door and into our front room.

Everyone turns to stare at me as I stand there, panting, trying to get my breath back.

Oh God. Kirsty's perched on the sofa, definitely *not* at her Zumba class. She's got her arm round Mandy. Mandy's married to Steve, Dad's best friend. Next to them on the sofa is Jade, their daughter. She's my age, but almost twice the size of me. Standing by the sofa next to them is Trish, who's going out with Ed, Dad's second best friend. And there are four other women watching the telly, all of them married to soldiers in Dad's regiment.

And they're all crying.

Oh God. Oh God. Dad's dead. That's it. He's only gone and been blown up.

Nana May heads into the front room as Kirsty gets up and comes towards me.

'What's going on?' I say — though, to be honest, I don't want to know the answer. Not if it's what I think it is.

Kirsty gives me this sad little smile as she says, 'There's been some bad news.'

'It's Dad, isn't it?' I blurt out.

Kirsty looks over her shoulder at Mandy, then back to me. 'It's Steve,' she whispers. 'There was a roadside bomb.'

'Is he dead?'

Kirsty shakes her head. 'No, but it's pretty bad. He's severely injured.'

'And Dad?' I say. There's a lump in my throat. I almost can't get the words out.

Kirsty strokes her hand over my messy ponytail. 'He's fine, sweetie,' she replies.

Relief floods through me in waves. He's fine. Dad's OK. But then Mandy starts crying again and I feel really bad. I like Steve. Every time he sees me he gives me a fireman's lift. Perhaps it's because he can't lift Jade any more.

'They called me when we were at Hope Springs,' Kirsty explains. 'I thought I'd get here before you came home. Was everything OK with Mum?'

I nod absent-mindedly and figure it best not to mention Mr Featherstone. Mandy takes a call on her mobile and goes off into the kitchen to talk. Jade trots along after her. The rest of the ladies huddle together and whisper so that Mandy can't hear.

'I just want my Ed to come home,' Trish sniffs, perched on the edge of the sofa. 'I've not slept for weeks, worrying.' Everyone nods in agreement. She thinks for a moment. 'And I need some shelves put up,' she adds.

'I can't work the DVD player,' someone whispers conspiratorially. 'I've been dying to watch *The Only Way Is Essex*.'

Trish raises her eyebrows in surprise. 'You can watch that on normal telly, you know.'

'I can?' the lady replies, and immediately looks brighter.

Everyone looks at the last woman in the group. She doesn't say anything.

'Lou?' Trish asks her. 'Why do you want your Pete home?'

Lou thinks for a moment. And then another moment. She opens her mouth to say something, but then shuts it again. She shakes her head. 'Nope, can't think of anything.'

My head feels a bit dizzy listening to all this, so I take a deep breath. 'Is Mark in?'

'He's in his room,' Kirsty says. 'Best leave him. Your dad's going to call in a bit.'

My heart leaps into my mouth. 'Dad's calling?' Dad hardly ever calls, because they don't always have a good signal, and they can't go worrying about getting near a phone mast when they're trying not to get shot.

Kirsty nods and then motions to all the women in our front room. She lowers her voice. 'Couldn't be a star and make this lot a brew, could you? I'm on tissue patrol.'

What is it with making blinking cups of tea today?

As I head towards the kitchen, Mandy and Jade come back and sit down on the sofa. I sneak a look at Jade. I should really say something to her, but what? *Sorry your dad's badly injured, but actually I'm really pleased that it's not mine?* That's terrible. I can't say that. So instead, I don't say anything. Even though she's looking dead miserable.

In the kitchen I flick the switch on the kettle and listen out for the phone. I try to think of more exciting things that I can tell Dad when he calls. And by 'tell' I mean 'lie'.

'Got any custard creams?'

Jade's standing in the doorway. Her eyes are all red and puffy from crying. Her dark hair's scraped into a plait, which she chews away at. Always obsessed with eating, even at a time like this.

'Uh . . . I don't know,' I say. 'We're not really fans.'

'Oh,' she says, clearly disappointed. 'It's just that they're me and my dad's favourite biscuit.'

I can't think of anything to say to that, except, 'I reckon we might have bourbons,' and I take a quick look in the cupboard. There are a few crumbly ones left at the bottom of the packet, so I hold those out to Jade. She takes them gratefully.

Neither of us says anything for a minute; it's just silence. Well, silence and the sound of Jade crunching a bourbon.

'I'm really sorry about your dad,' I say eventually.

Jade stops crunching and looks down at the floor. 'Thanks,' she mumbles.

The switch on the kettle flicks up, and as I pour water into mugs, I rack my brains for something else to say. What do they always say on *EastEnders*? *He was a good bloke*, and *I'm here for you, mate*, and

If you have been affected by any of the issues in tonight's programme, please call our helpline.

Just as I'm about to speak, our phone rings. 'I'll get it!' I yell, and run out into the hall like a madwoman.

I pick up the phone so violently I almost yank it off the wall. 'Hello?'

Silence.

'Dad? Hello? Dad, can you hear me?'

There's a bit of crackling down the line. A couple of beeps. More crackling. And then, 'Billie?'

'Dad!'

'All right, love?' Dad says, though he sounds all distant.

'You're not dead, then,' I say, and after a three-second time delay Dad laughs. He's got such a brilliant laugh, my dad. It's really deep and booming. It suits him because he's as big as a bear. 'Strapping', Linda once called him. He doesn't laugh often, Dad, but when he does it makes you light up inside, because you've told a really good joke that he thinks is ace.

'No, love,' he replies. 'Not dead. How are you?'

I panic a bit at that. I haven't thought of anything

exciting to tell him – I was too busy finding crumbled biscuits for Jade.

'Uh . . .' I say, trying to push all thoughts of detentions and care homes and midday supervisors out of my head.

'How's school?' he asks.

'It's . . . OK,' I manage to stutter. 'It's nearly over.'

There's another couple of beeps. 'Billie, love, go and fetch Kirsty for me,' Dad says. 'The signal's playing up – I've not got long.'

Just then another thought pops into my head. With everything that's happened today, I'd completely forgotten about it.

'Dad?'

'Aye?'

'What about being king?'

More crackling down the line. 'What?' Dad says. 'I can't hear you. What about what?'

'Merchant Stanton Carnival,' I say. 'You know, the three-legged race.'

Dad makes this noise down the line – like he's sighing. 'What about it?'

I speak really quickly to get it all out in one go.

'Will you come back for the race so that we can win and you can be the king again? You know, like you always are?'

Dad makes another noise. It's *definitely* him sighing. 'Billie, I've not got time for this. Go get Kirsty.' He sounds different. Angry, almost.

'But, Dad—'

'*Now*, Billie,' Dad interrupts. 'Just do it.'

I put the phone down on the little table and head into the front room. 'Dad wants to speak to you,' I say to Kirsty, but even as I'm saying it, I realize that my voice sounds all shaky.

Kirsty comes out, picks up the phone and shoos me out of the way, but I hang around by the stairs where I can still hear her. 'All right, Don,' she's saying, 'I'll do that.' And then, 'Yep, yep, all right,' and 'I already said yes.'

I hover around, because I want to speak to Dad again. I need a definitive answer about this king business, if only so I can wipe the smug smile off Andy Nelson's face come Monday morning.

'Can I speak to him?' I say, but Kirsty waves me away with a flick of her hand.

I hop from one foot to the other. If Nana May wasn't currently dozing in an armchair, she'd say, *Patience is a virtue*, like she always does, but she's not awake and I'm not patient.

'Come on,' I say to Kirsty. 'Let me speak to Dad again.'

But just then I hear everyone in the front room wailing and crying even louder.

Kirsty raises her voice to make herself heard over the din. 'It's on the news,' she says to Dad. 'They're all here.' And then, 'I'll put him on.'

She cranes her neck and shouts up the stairs. 'Mark! Pick up! It's your dad.'

I edge forward to the phone table. 'Just let me speak to him while Mark's—'

But Kirsty shoos me away again. 'It's Mark's turn,' she says. 'And then Mum'll want to talk to him.'

I ignore her anyway and pick up the phone. 'Dad?'

But there's nothing. Not even beeps. I hold the phone out to Kirsty, confused. She holds it to her ear for a second, and then replaces it back in the cradle.

'Signal must have gone,' she says matter-of-factly,

and heads back into the front room to get more tissues for everyone.

I don't want to go back in there. Not with everyone crying.

Instead, I head up the stairs and stop outside Mark's room. I hear the same music he always listens to coming from inside. Blinking drum and bass. It drives Kirsty and me mad.

Maybe Mark would know if Dad really isn't coming home for the carnival, or if Mrs Hussein was just making it up to be nasty to me because I also accidentally kicked *her* in the shins when she was taking me to sit outside Mr Law's office.

I knock on the door.

After a moment Mark opens it a crack, a towel around his waist. His brown hair's all sticking up in tufts and he's still got flecks of paint in it from work, despite his shower. He's dead muscly, Mark. Not like me. Dad says I've got hollow legs because I'm one of the skinniest in my class, even though I eat Chinese and shepherd's pie and chocolate and stuff. Not as much as Jade, mind. He's quite good-looking too, Mark, I suppose. He's not got spots or anything like a lot of eighteen-year-olds. Sabrina Mitchell's older sister's best mate's been after him for ages.

'Can I come in?' I ask.

'Not now, Bill,' Mark says. 'I'm getting changed.'

'Did you hear about Steve?'

Mark nods.

'It's bad, isn't it?'

He nods again. 'Yeah. He's a good bloke.' Just like in *EastEnders*.

There's no easy way of asking this, so I just come out and say it. 'Did Dad say anything to you about the race,' I ask, 'before he left?'

'What?'

'Or about being king? You know – the carnival.'

Mark gives me this quizzical look, like he thinks I'm the most stupid person in the world. 'I think Dad's got other things to worry about, Billie.'

And then he shuts the door.

I'm left on the landing. The sounds of the TV and the chatter from the front room drift up the stairs. I really don't want to go back down there.

Instead, I make for the door at the end of the landing. It's Dad's room, but Kirsty's been sleeping there since she came to look after us when Dad went away. I guess Dad must have known how much time Mark spends in his room and wanted someone else to cook my tea for me. If you can call beans on toast and ordering Chinese 'cooking'.

I push the door open, and a strong whiff of perfume hits me as I walk in. 'Midnight Blue' – Kirsty's favourite.

I head over to Dad's chest of drawers, glance round to check no one can see, and then pull open the third drawer. I know exactly where to look, but I have to be careful not to leave anything out of place. I pick up an old frayed army jacket of Dad's, put it on the bed, and return to rummaging in the drawer.

And there it is.

It's a picture of Dad standing outside our old house with a pint of beer in his hand. In front of him, with a shaggy haircut and dungarees, is Mark. He only comes up to Dad's chest, so he must be about seven or eight. And standing next to them is a beautiful woman with long black hair; peering out under her fringe are lovely blue eyes – as blue as the sea. She's holding a baby in her arms. That's me, I reckon, 'cos the baby's got a tuft of blonde hair and green eyes, just like me. Except I've got more hair now, like. Kirsty always says she'd kill for long blonde hair like mine – then she wouldn't have to spend a fortune at the hairdresser's. I always wished I had long black hair and blue eyes, though, like Mum. Maybe she wouldn't have left then.

Dad doesn't know I know it's here, but looking at the picture makes me happy. Everyone's smiling in it – even Dad, and he doesn't really smile much, so it must have been a nice time. Either that or he'd had more than one pint of beer. But somehow, even though I can't remember being there, I reckon it's because we *were* all happy.

I wish we could be that happy now. I'd buy Dad a million pints of beer if Mark wasn't in his room all the time, desperate to get his own flat, and Mum was living with us, not somewhere up north, and Dad was back home, not off in the army, probably about to be blown up like his best friend.

I stumble over to the bed and sit down. My head feels light, and my bottom lip starts twitching. The photo goes all fuzzy as my eyes fill with tears, and I blink quickly to make them go away. But it's not working, because now the tears are running down my cheeks and sploshing in drips onto the photo.

I wipe my face with my sleeve and give a big sniff. As I put the photo down on the bed next to me, my fingers find the fraying edges of Dad's jacket. I pick it up and hold it against me. It smells of smoke and aftershave, just like Dad.

What if he doesn't come home? I suddenly think. *What if I never see him again? What if he never gets to play the king?*

Then I see it. In the inside crease of the neck of the jacket, Dad's written the words *Don Templar*. I start to laugh, because that's exactly what he does to all my school clothes. Not *Don Templar*, obviously, but *my* name. Next to *Don Templar* are the words *Her Majesty's Armed Forces*, again written in Dad's handwriting.

Hang on a sec—

My mind starts going like the clappers then, and I'm thinking all kinds of thoughts. But one in particular sticks out. I think back to what Mrs

Hussein said in class about Dad being away on tour. About how he was off fighting 'for Queen and Country'.

'Her Majesty's Armed Forces' means they're the *Queen's* Armed Forces. And if they're the *Queen's* Armed Forces, then the *Queen* has control over what they do and where they go and who they fight.

And if the Queen's in control of the Armed Forces, then the Queen can send my dad home.

That's it!

I leap off the bed like I've sat on a pincushion, because this, officially, is the best idea I've ever had. The Queen can send my dad home! It's *her* army; she can do what she likes with it.

So I just have to get the Queen to let my dad off fighting so that he can come back home safe and sound and not get blown up by a bomb – or Improvised Explosive Device, as they're called – like Steve did. And best of all, he can come back and we can do the three-legged race and win, just like we always do. Father and daughter. Billie and Don Templar versus the world. Or, at least, versus the other dads of Merchant Stanton. And Dad will be the carnival king, just like he always is, and nobody – not even Andy Nelson or Sabrina Mitchell or Mrs Hussein – can say otherwise.

I'll just get the Queen to write a note to excuse him from fighting – like Kirsty did once to excuse me from PE because I'd had a curry and spent half the night on the toilet, and she didn't think me swimming in the junior pool the next day was a good idea.

It's so simple, I can't believe I've not thought of it before.

I scoop up the photo, and I'm shaking a bit because I'm so excited, but I have to be careful to put it back in the drawer so Dad doesn't know I know about it.

I run to my bedroom and shove Dad's army jacket under my pillow. Then I run past the drum and bass blaring from Mark's room, and leap down the stairs two at a time. I even start humming, I'm that excited.

This is going to be the best Merchant Stanton Carnival ever.

CHAPTER THREE

I burst into the front room, and stop dead in my tracks as everyone turns round. I'd kind of forgotten they were all there, to be honest, and now Mandy and Jade and Kirsty and everyone else are looking at me with puffy red eyes.

'Are you humming?' Kirsty mouths at me.

I'd forgotten about that. I guess bursting into a room full of crying women and singing 'God Save the Queen' isn't the best thing to do when you've just heard your dad's best mate's been blown up.

Then I notice what Jade's doing. She's sitting on the sofa with our laptop balanced on her knees. For goodness' sake – how am I meant to email the Queen if Jade's playing *Moshi Monsters*? I can hardly move her – *Sorry, Jade, I know you've had a terrible shock, and the fact that your dad might never be the same again sucks, but can you just budge over, because I've thought of a way to make my dad come back?* I can't say that.

I turn round to get to the phone, but Trish is hogging it now. So I can't phone the Queen, either.

At least not here.

'I'm going round to Linda's,' I say to Kirsty, and head towards the front door. Linda lives next door and is dead mumsy, even though she's no one's mum, 'cos she cooks my tea sometimes and lets me watch *EastEnders* on her massive plasma TV, even though she says I should 'stay true to my Northern Roots' and watch *Corrie*. Linda's got a really nifty computer too, which Dad installed for her. It's got a screensaver of Fur Ball on it. She's ginger and covered in hair. Fur Ball, obviously, not Linda. Linda's got dead curly brown hair and wears a lot of ethnic jewellery – turquoise necklaces and jangly bracelets, that sort of thing. She's always nicely dressed too – though she doesn't go to the pub with Dad and his army mates any more, because her condition's got worse.

'Don't mither her,' Kirsty says, looking up. 'It's a stressful time and it's given her a bit of a turn.'

I let out a big puff of air. There's nothing for it – I'm going to have to write. Pen and paper, the old-fashioned way.

'I think I'll go to bed,' I say.

Kirsty gives me a funny look. 'Are you sure? It's only seven.'

I nod.

'And you've not had your tea,' she says. 'There's beans on toast if you want.'

I shrug my shoulders. 'I'm OK,' I say. ''Night.'

Everyone in the room murmurs their goodnights to me, and I head up the stairs.

'Billie?'

Kirsty stands at the bottom of the stairs, looking up at me. She's biting her lip. 'I know it's been a tough day,' she says, leaning back and shutting the door so the others can't hear. 'Finding out about Hope Springs. Now this. But your dad's going to be all right, you know.'

I beam at her. 'I know he is,' I say. 'Goodnight.'

Kirsty gives me another funny look, like she thinks I'm up to something, but she doesn't say anything. I have to stop myself practically skipping up the stairs and giving the game away. For some reason I reckon it's best to keep it quiet for now. Just until the Queen replies, like.

Bright and early the next morning, I'm up and dressed and standing in front of the post box at the corner of our road. I tried to phone Buckingham Palace this morning, but Kirsty was on the phone to one of her boyfriends, and I wasn't sure if the Queen would be in on a Saturday. She might be off doing a big shop. I tried email, but it was a general enquiries address, and I know they're just going to fob me off with an automated response, so I figure a letter's my best bet. Especially if it's addressed directly to the Queen.

I take the letter out of the envelope to check for spelling mistakes. This is what I came up with last night:

Dear Your Majesty,

My name is Billie Templar. I am eleven years old. I live in Merchant Stanton near Leeds, which is all right, but it's not as nice as Buckingham Palace, I bet. Anyway, I know you're really busy, what with being Queen, and all the tiaras and jewels and dogs you have, but I have a favour to ask you.

Please can you send my dad home from the war? He's been out there for the last eleven weeks. But his best friend got blown up today, and I don't want him to get hurt, so please can you excuse him from the fighting?

I know you've a lot to do, so I've made it a bit easier – I've included a note for you already. I copied it from one of the letters my auntie wrote to my teacher excusing me from PE. I'll not go into why – it's not that pleasant. You just need to sign it.

By the way, I wasn't sure if you prefer to be called 'Queen' or 'Your Majesty'. I need to look that up on the Internet, but I can't get there at the moment because Jade's hogging it.

Also, I've included another envelope for you to reply to me in, but I haven't got a spare stamp. I figured you'd have some. Or just put one of your passport pictures on the corner of the envelope, and it should get to me. Then I'll send it to my dad, and he can show it to his boss, and he'll be home in time for the Merchant Stanton Carnival, which won't be as good as Kate and Wills' wedding last year — it's not a bank holiday or anything — but it's normally good fun all the same.

Thanks very much. I think you're a good queen, and I quite like Prince Harry!

Billie Templar

I put the letter back in the envelope, lick it and seal it shut. This is it. I give the envelope a quick kiss and then, taking a deep breath, shove it in the postbox.

Now all I have to do is wait.

CHAPTER FOUR

With everything that happened yesterday, I left my school bag at Hope Springs when Mr Stephens thrust Nana May at me and told me to go home, so I head back there. I'm not fussed that my spellings homework's in it, but I'd best do it; then I can concentrate on waiting for the Queen to get back to me, and on practising the three-legged race for when Dad does come home. You can't win four years in a row without a bit of practice, you know.

As I walk up the drive of Hope Springs, there's a lot of noise coming from round the back. It sounds like cheering.

All the residents are standing by a minibus. Derek's trying to herd them on in an orderly fashion, but it's a bit chaotic. There's loads of them waiting around in warm coats, despite the glorious sunshine. Some are in wheelchairs, with blankets covering their legs. One man shuffles along wheeling an IV pole, with a drip attached to his nose. He's wearing his dressing gown and slippers, but no one seems to mind.

'What's going on?' I ask.

One of the elderly women beams at me. 'It's our day out.' She grins, clearly massively excited. 'We're off to the seaside.'

I frown. There isn't any seaside near us. 'Where's that, then?'

Derek clenches his jaw in despair. He's trying to get one old man to stop kicking the tyres of the minibus, while another is unzipping his trousers as if he's about to have a pee. 'Can't stretch to the seaside, I'm afraid,' Derek says through gritted teeth, trying to grapple with the man's zip. 'We're taking a nice trip to the River Aire.'

Now, I may not be good at geography, but I know that's only four miles away. 'Hardly a "day" trip, is it?' I ask.

'It is when it takes all morning to get there,' Derek sighs. 'Come on, everyone,' he cries. 'Get on the minibus!'

Another two carers come out of the back of the care home and help round up the rest of the residents.

My eyes scan the group. 'Where's Mr Featherstone?'

The old man with the IV pole snorts at me. 'Doing what he always does . . .' He tries to climb onto the minibus, but his drip pole gets stuck in the doorway. 'Staying in his room, moping.'

Derek gives him a shove, and the man stumbles forward up the steps, then glares at him, but Derek's too stressed to notice.

I leave him to it, and head through the back door into the care home. It's nice and peaceful inside now it's almost empty. Though it seems pretty soulless, and I'm worried about Nana May coming here. The walls are grey and bare. The furniture looks stiff and old. The carpet is a faded orange, covered in stains.

I collect my school bag from reception. My stomach rumbles because I didn't have any breakfast, what with being too excited about posting the letter, so I wander into the little kitchen area, hoping to find biscuits or cake or something to snack on.

But someone's already there.

Mr Featherstone's hair is just as wild as it always is; he's standing at the counter with his back to me, leaning over the kettle. He's stood up dead straight, like he's got a rod up his back. Dad does that, because that's what they teach you in the army. Except Mr Featherstone's shoulders are a bit hunched over, what with being old. He's trying to lift the kettle over the mug to pour water in, but he's shaking a bit. After a couple of rubbish attempts, he puts the kettle down and flexes his hands. They're all gnarled and knobbly and raw, like he's been scrubbing them with bleach or something.

'So you do come downstairs sometimes, then?' I say.

Mr Featherstone spins round, and I swear the corners of his mouth twitch when he sees it's me. 'Sometimes,' he replies. 'When everyone's out.'

I nod. 'They said you were a recluse. So's Linda. She's got OCD.'

Mr Featherstone raises an eyebrow. 'Don't you ever stop talking?' he sighs.

'Why aren't you on the day trip?' I ask.

Mr Featherstone snorts at me. What is it with old people snorting all the time? Don't they know it's rude and unpleasant and that stuff might fly out of their nose without them realizing? 'Being squashed on a coach with a bunch of idiots singing "The White Cliffs of Dover" and eating soggy egg sandwiches is not my idea of fun,' he mutters, flexing his hands again.

I frown at him. 'They're not idiots,' I say. 'They seem nice. Especially that chap with the pole.'

Mr Featherstone sighs again. 'Believe me, they're all idiots.' His face darkens, like he's just had a flash of memory. 'You'd have to be to live here,' he adds under his breath. But I catch what he's said.

'My nana's coming to live here,' I say, folding my arms.

'More fool her,' he replies, and now he's positively scowling. He shoves the mug and spoon to one side and heads out of the kitchen.

'Why do you have to be so grumpy?' I blurt

out before I can stop myself. Mr Featherstone just shuffles out into the corridor.

Well, I'm not having this. I don't care if he *does* know about bread rolls, or about Spitfires and standing up straight, like Dad. How dare he be mean about Nana May?

'Do you know what?' I say to him, and I push past and turn round so that we're face to face. Well, my face to his chest, because I'm not as tall as him, but there you go. The main thing is, I'm facing him. 'I'm going to tell my dad about you, and when he gets home, he's going to come round and sort you out, because nobody should be that rude, especially about my nana. And my dad's in the army, so he knows what he's doing when it comes to a fight.'

Mr Featherstone stops for a moment. 'Gets home from where?' he asks.

'The war,' I reply.

He looks at me curiously. His silence starts to annoy me, like he thinks he can just be rude to anyone without having to apologize, and I'm having none of it.

54

'He'll be home in a few days,' I say. 'I know that for a fact.'

Mr Featherstone still doesn't say anything but sets off down the corridor again.

'He's being sent home personally,' I say – and, all right, I might not know that for a *fact*, but Mr Featherstone doesn't *know* I don't know. 'By the Queen.'

Mr Featherstone stops dead in his tracks, and I'm following so close behind that I bump into him.

'The Queen?' he repeats.

I nod.

'She's sending him home personally?'

I nod again.

And then Mr Featherstone's face breaks out into a broad grin and he starts laughing. It's just a giggle at first, but then a big laugh booms out, and before I know it, he's wiping tears out of his eyes. 'That's the best thing I've heard all day,' he says.

I stamp my foot. 'It's true,' I say, and I'm mega, super annoyed that he's not taking me seriously. 'It's not a laughing matter.'

He doesn't stop laughing. 'That's funnier than

the time the Prime Minister tried telling me a rude joke,' he hoots, trying to catch his breath.

'I wrote her a letter this morning,' I continue, ignoring his mad claim, 'and all she's got to do is sign it, and she'll send my dad home.'

He still doesn't stop laughing.

'Oh, for goodness' sake!' I turn and start walking away. 'No wonder no one likes you here.'

As I'm storming off up the corridor, wanting to get as far away from him and his nastiness as possible, Mr Featherstone coughs. Then he gives a big sigh. I spin round to see what he's doing and he gestures towards the common room.

'Come with me.'

We sit in two stiff armchairs near the window.

'You've written a letter, you say?' Mr Featherstone asks.

I nod. 'Directly to the Queen. She'll probably get it first post Monday.'

Mr Featherstone lets out another snort. 'You obviously don't know the Royal Mail,' he mutters. 'When *I* was Chief Executive of the Royal Mail . . .'

I frown at him as he goes off on another of his mad stories. 'I'm not sure it's going to work,' he says after a moment.

'What do you mean?' I ask in surprise.

'I mean,' he replies, 'the Queen has a personal assistant to answer all her letters. One of her ladies-in-waiting. She doesn't do it herself.'

I think for a minute and then eventually shrug my shoulders. 'So? Her assistant can give her the note to sign.'

'Do you know how many letters and requests and invites and cards and thank-yous the Queen gets each and every day?' Mr Featherstone asks.

'Doesn't matter,' I reply. '*My* letter's important. She'll get it.' read up to here.

'I wouldn't be too sure,' he answers. Neither of us says anything for a moment. Then Mr Featherstone gives a long sigh. 'You're sure you want to ask the Queen?'

'She's the only one who can send Dad home,' I say. 'It's her army.'

He nods. 'Very well. But if at first you don't succeed, try, try again.'

'What's that meant to mean?'

'It means be more proactive,' Mr Featherstone replies. 'If it means that much to you, if you feel you *have* to get the Queen to send your dad home, then go and ask her yourself.'

Just then, Derek walks past the common room. He does a double-take and his eyes practically bulge out of his head when he sees me and Mr Featherstone chatting. 'Mr F?' he asks in disbelief. 'You're in the common room!'

'No flies on you,' Mr Featherstone retorts gruffly.

I look at my watch. It's only half twelve. 'What happened to the day trip?'

Derek's face darkens. 'Don't ask,' he mutters.

Mr Featherstone starts to get up out of the chair. His hands try to grasp the arm rests and his face contorts with pain. He puffs and pants. Derek comes over, but Mr Featherstone shoos him away. 'I can manage,' he huffs.

Derek stretches out his arm. 'Just let me help—'

'Leave. Me. Be,' Mr Featherstone says through gritted teeth.

Derek backs off and we just watch as Mr Feather-stone eventually, stubbornly, struggles to his feet.

'Are you staying for lunch?' Mr Featherstone asks me over his shoulder. 'It's never as good as the Michelin restaurant I used to own, but it's not bad.'

But I'm not really listening. His words of wisdom replay in my mind: *If you feel you have to get the Queen to send your dad home, then go and ask her yourself.* I grab my school bag and leap up out of the armchair. 'I can't.' I grin at him as an idea starts to form in my mind. 'I've got too much to do.'

And with that, I leg it out of the room, out of Hope Springs, through Eddington fields and all the way home. How's that for three-legged race practice!

CHAPTER FIVE

I'm on my knees on my bedroom floor, pulling out the piggy bank I keep stashed under my bed. It jingles, and my heart sinks – it doesn't sound like there's much in there.

Eighteen pounds and fifty-seven pence, to be exact. How's that going to get me to Buckingham Palace? It'd barely get me to Wakefield.

I can hear Kirsty faffing around in Dad's room, and I have an idea.

'Kirrrrrr-steeeee?' I say in my most politest, bestest voice as I knock on the bedroom door.

'Ye-e-ess?' she replies, like she knows I'm after something. She's still in her dressing gown, even though it's lunch time, and she's got black rings round her eyes because she didn't take off her mascara after she and Trish and Lou had a bottle of wine last night.

'You know how much you love shopping . . .' I say, my mind going a million miles an hour as I work out how to go about this. 'For shoes and bags and stuff?'

'Ye-e-e-ess?'

'Well, where do you reckon the best place to go is?'

Kirsty thinks for a moment. 'Leeds Victoria Quarter?'

Not what I had in mind. 'Think further afield.'

'Sheffield's Meadowhall?'

'Think Christmas,' I say, starting to feel a bit impatient with how thick she's being. 'Think Christmas lights and late-night shopping.'

Kirsty looks tired. 'Where's this going, Bill?'

'I was thinking . . . as a treat, like' – I try to judge what she's thinking – 'we could go shopping in London to get our Christmas presents this year.'

Kirsty sighs. 'We don't need to think about this now.'

'But I wanted to go next weekend.'

'For Christmas presents?'

I shrug, trying to act casual. 'Beat the rush,' I say.

'Nice idea,' Kirsty laughs, 'but it's a bit out of our price range.'

I knew she'd say that. Now I go in for the kill. 'I know, but I just figured we needed a bit of cheering up. What with Steve and everything.'

Kirsty looks at me, and then sighs again. 'I'm sorry, love, I just can't stretch to that.'

'Maybe Mark could help?' Even as I'm saying this, I know it's ridiculous. The last time I asked Mark for money – for Kirsty's birthday present three months ago, in fact – he looked at me like I was an idiot and gave me this lecture about how he works so hard because he needs money for a deposit on a flat, and he needs to move out and stand on his own two feet, and he's not a kid any more. Which basically meant no.

But I can't give up. 'Well, what if *I* had the money? Would you come with me?'

Kirsty narrows her eyes at me. 'Where are you going to get the money for that? You're looking at about fifty quid for coach tickets, and that's before we worry about money for presents.'

I shrug my shoulders. 'Just promise you'll take me.'

Kirsty moves over to the chest of drawers and picks up her pack of face wipes. She looks at me in the mirror as she slowly removes last night's make-up. 'We'll see,' she says after a moment.

Good enough for me!

I'm walking the corridors of Hope Springs with my arms full of boxes of old toys and clothes and books and jigsaw puzzles and posters. I've had a totally mega genius idea: all the residents are as old as my nana, which means they must have grandchildren themselves, and what do grandchildren like getting? Presents! So I'm here for the second time today, this time to flog whatever I could find lying around my room.

And it seems to be working. So far I've sold an old Take That poster and a *Blue Peter Annual* for £4.60, which the old lady thought was a bit steep, but I managed to convince her it was because of a new poster tax they've introduced, and I'm only trying to cover my overheads – and *Inflation's gone up, hasn't it, love?* which is exactly what they say on the market stalls in *EastEnders*. Plus some old guy gave me two quid for an old Barbie doll, even though one of its legs was missing. He was a bit blind, though, so I don't reckon he'll notice.

But it's still not enough — not if I need at least fifty quid.

But just as I'm knocking on the door of Room M, Derek spies me and comes marching over. 'What are you doing, Billie?' he demands.

I smile at him over the top of a box. 'Helping out,' I reply.

He folds his arms across his chest and waits for me to explain. 'I'm helping the residents with their Christmas shopping,' I tell him. 'You know, to beat the rush.'

He peers into the box and frowns at my old cardies and skirts. 'What could they possibly want with these?' he says, which is a bit rude. 'In July?'

A crash from inside Room M diverts Derek's attention, so I head up the stairs to Mr Featherstone's little attic room. The sound of someone shouting blares from the telly inside. 'I know that voice,' I say, pushing the door open. 'That's Phil Mitchell.'

Mr Featherstone's sitting on the bed, his eyes glued to the telly in the corner. 'Shush,' he whispers. 'He's about to beat someone up for not giving him his money.'

I smile. Clearly he listened to my raving about *EastEnders* after all.

'Thought I heard someone gabbing downstairs.' He frowns at me. 'Let me guess. You need more of my expert advice.' He takes in all the stuff I'm lugging round.

I think back to the black GRANDAD comb he has. 'Would you like to buy a toy? It's all top-quality stuff.'

Mr Featherstone rifles through a carrier bag I've tucked under my arm. 'I'm all right for a barking toy dog, thanks. I've already got a signed one from Lassie. Well, chewed more than signed, but still.'

I roll my eyes. 'I didn't mean for you,' I say. 'For your granddaughter. Or your grandson.'

Mr Featherstone recoils like he's been stung. He takes a moment to catch his breath. 'Why would they want this tat?'

I smile because I think he's joking. 'All right, Grandad,' I reply.

He's not joking. 'Don't call me that,' he snaps back.

Honestly, I think he *must* be mad – I've never seen someone go from being sort of nice to being nasty so quickly.

'Just get out!' he thunders.

'Wait!' I protest, but he's struggling to his feet to switch off the telly.

'OUT!' he bellows.

Well, that's just brilliant. I had this fantastic money-making scheme that was going to get me to the Queen – which was totally Mr Featherstone's idea in the first place – and here he is being all nasty and grumpy at me.

I spin on my heel and head out. 'Fine,' I yell. 'No wonder you haven't got any friends. You're horrible!'

Derek is hurrying up the stairs towards me. 'I'm done,' I shout at him, my cheeks red. 'Just be sure to tell Mr Law that I helped when I was here. I did my bit. I was a team player!'

I glance at Mr Featherstone. 'Unlike some. You've probably been alone your whole life you're so mean. I'd hate to have a grandparent like you.'

He slams his door with such force the door frame rattles and a bit of ceiling plaster comes down.

I think a bit and then I shout at his door, 'And I don't want my nana to come and live here with mean people like you. I wouldn't be seen dead in here again.'

And I think a bit more and shout, 'Not like you lot. You'll all be seen dead in here sooner or later. Sooner, probably, because you're all dead old, and you're all going to die soon anyway!'

And my face feels all hot, and I'm running out of breath, and I know I'm shouting mean things, but I don't care. And I don't realize until I've finished shouting that the old man with the drip pole has come out of Room M, and he's staring at me with a really sad look on his face, and now I feel really mean for saying that everyone's going to die.

So with that I head home.

There's nothing for it. I've only got £25.17 altogether, which is nowhere near enough, so I'm just going to have to dip into my super-secret savings. The savings I haven't told anyone about, they're so super secret. Under my bedroom window there's a floorboard that came loose when I was eight and had a bit of a tantrum because Mark wouldn't let me watch *CatDog* on Nickelodeon as he wanted to see a Leeds United match. I jumped up and down in my room, and one of the floorboards wiggled loose. That was the day I first got the idea for my super-secret savings, because that was when I decided to start saving for my super-secret trip.

I prise up the floorboard quietly, because Kirsty's having a lie down in her room, even though she only just got up, and pull out an old ice-cream tub.

And from it, I count out £37.50, which is what I've managed to save in three years of birthday and Christmas money. And £37.50 plus £25.17 gives me . . .

£62.67! Which is totally enough to go to London and see the Queen and ask her to send my dad home. Cracking!

And I'm so excited I forget Kirsty's trying to be all quiet and restful, and I bound into her bedroom. 'I've got it!' I shout with joy. 'We're off to London!'

Kirsty props herself up on her elbows. 'What?'

I wave all the money at her. 'Look! I can buy the tickets!'

Kirsty frowns. 'What have you been up to?'

'It's all legit,' I reply before she can start going on. 'I worked really hard for it all. I promise.'

She sighs. 'I can't take your money, Billie.'

I stick out my lip a bit and try to look all sad. 'All right,' I reply. 'It's just that I've been thinking about Dad since Steve got blown up, and I wanted to get something nice to send out to him – something to cheer him up, you know – and I figured you've been really good at looking after me, and might like a nice trip out, and it's a once-in-a-lifetime offer, really, so—'

Kirsty holds up a hand to stop me. She's obviously picked that up from Mr Law. 'Fine,' she says, rolling her eyes. 'We'll go next weekend, if you want. A one-off.'

I really want to throw the money up in the air and dance under it as it rains down on me like they do in the movies, but I can't run the risk of mislaying any pennies, so I just grin and run out of the room.

'I'll get everything booked,' I yell as I pound down the stairs towards the laptop.

CHAPTER SIX

Waiting all week for the weekend to come is like waiting all year for Christmas. It takes for ever. And I'm anxious for it to hurry up, because as each day goes by, I get more and more worried about Dad.

There's been some sort of hold-up with flying Steve back to England to start his treatment, so we've had loads of upset people round the house. I don't mind too much, because Trish brought chocolates one night, and I managed to sneak at least six before Kirsty ordered me to hand them round.

But all the crying about Steve just makes me more determined to go through with my plan. I've not heard back from the Queen yet, and a small part of me worries that Mr Featherstone's right – either the Royal Mail's being really slack, or the Queen's personal assistant hasn't shown her my letter yet. Either way, I know I *have* to go to London. I have to visit Buckingham Palace and see the Queen in person.

After what feels like endless nights, and endless days of taunts from Andy Nelson and Sabrina Mitchell about how their dads are going to win the three-legged race and be the carnival king – which is totally stupid, because only one person can win it anyway – it's finally Saturday.

I'm up dead early. I had a bath last night so that's one less thing to do this morning, and I'm even wearing a dress I haven't got out since Dad's cousin's wedding last year. It's a bit fancy and a bit pink and a bit tight, but there you go. I'm sure the Queen'll be impressed. If I breathe in.

Kirsty comes out of her bedroom, doing up the zip of her skinny jeans. She looks me up and down. 'Bit glam for shopping, isn't it?'

I shrug. 'Nothing wrong with making an effort every now and then.'

Kirsty raises an eyebrow at me. She raps on Mark's door — even though I'm sure he's still asleep. 'Mark! We're off. Take care of Mum.' She slings her handbag over her shoulder and pads down the stairs. 'Come on, then, Posh Spice. Let's get this show on the road.'

We're sitting on the National Express coach and it's been about a million hours already and we're still aaaaaaaaages away from the Queen and it's soooooo hot because the air con's on the blink. Kirsty seems perfectly content, though. She's flipping through the pages of a glossy magazine, and for the past half-hour she's been banging on about this new tattoo she wants.

'Ooh, I could do with going to Selfridges,' she says, and she shows me a picture of a new perfume. 'It's on sale.'

I smile like I think that's a good idea, because shopping in London is, after all, what I promised her, but I'm also racking my brains to think of a way to broach the whole going-to-Buckingham-Palace thing. 'Our coach back isn't till half four,' I say. 'We could do a bit of sightseeing.'

Kirsty shrugs. 'I'm not fussed.'

'Yeah, but we may as well. Seeing as we're there, and all.'

Kirsty doesn't say anything – just flicks through her magazine.

'Madame Tussauds,' I plough on. 'The Houses of Parliament. Uh, you know, uh ... Buckingham Palace?'

Then, all of a sudden, the coach pulls into Victoria coach station and comes to a stop. Kirsty grabs her handbag from under the seat and shoves her magazine inside.

'Kirsty?' I say. 'What about Buckingham Palace?'

I'm swept along the aisle in the hustle and bustle of all the other passengers getting off the coach. Kirsty's a couple of metres in front of me, but I can hear her voice, loud and clear. 'Can't be bothered with that,' she says matter-of-factly.

This is going to be tougher than I thought.

Pretty soon we're traipsing along Regent Street. Kirsty wants to look at the posh shops, and she's peering in all the windows with a big grin on her face. It's absolutely rammed with tourists and students and shoppers, some probably shopping for their Loved Ones. I frown. Loved Ones who'd definitely turn up for a summer carnival, I bet.

'Ooh, wanna go in here?' Kirsty says. I follow her gaze. It's Hamleys. The world's oldest, biggest, most jam-packed toy store. And it's just typical that there are a million kids with their parents all banging about inside, all looking incredibly happy − which is totally not fair: some kids have two parents to live with, and I don't have any.

I frown again. 'Not really,' I say. 'I want to go to Buckingham Palace.'

Kirsty drags me inside anyway. 'It's miles away,' she says. 'What do you wanna go there for?'

Before I can reply, this girl barges past me and treads on my foot, racing to the back of the store as if her life depends on it. 'Oi!' I shout. 'Watch it!'

Then I notice that she's dragging her dad along by the hand and saying, 'Come on, Daddy, I want a new Bratz doll!' She is, in all honesty, being super annoying, and I, in all honesty, am jealous. And not just of the Bratz doll.

74

My eye catches a shelf full of stuffed teddies, all wearing funny costumes. There are bears in police uniform and bears dressed as Beefeaters. And there's a bear dressed as a king, with a red velvet robe and a golden crown. Just like the one Dad's worn for the last four years when he's been crowned at the Merchant Stanton Carnival.

Just like he's going to wear this year.

'I want to go to Buckingham Palace,' I say to Kirsty. 'And I'm not taking no for an answer.'

Kirsty clenches her jaw at my outburst. 'Billie . . .' she warns through gritted teeth.

'I mean it. Let's go.'

'We'll go home if you can't behave,' she retorts, and she takes me by the arm and starts to drag me out of the shop.

Now I realize that drastic measures are needed. I look around, and spot a security guard hovering by the escalators. Nothing else for it. 'YOU'RE NOT MY MUM!' I yell in my loudest, most terrified voice. Technically, it's not a lie.

Kirsty opens her mouth in shock. 'What?' she hisses.

A few people turn round, but the security guard is obviously rubbish, because he hasn't even heard. I'm going to have to really go for it. 'STRANGER!' I yell. 'STRANGER!'

This time the guard moves quicker than I've ever seen anyone move in my life.

'She's joking,' Kirsty says to the small crowd gathered round us. Even with her fake tan, you can see her face is all flushed. 'Tell them, Billie.'

The guard is now attempting to prise Kirsty's hand off my arm. 'What's going on, miss?' he asks. I have to stop myself laughing: normally every time Kirsty's referred to as 'miss', she has a right go, saying, *What, do I look single?* but I can't give the game away.

'She's making it up,' Kirsty pleads with the guard. Then she turns to me. 'You wait till I get you home.'

The security guard looks me up and down, and then studies Kirsty's face. We do look a bit alike, you know, what with being related. Same green eyes as Dad. 'Do you know this woman?' he asks me.

I swallow hard. I know I've got Kirsty right where I want her, but I don't know if she'll ever forgive me.

'That depends on Buckingham Palace,' I hiss at her.

She narrows her eyes and stares at me for the longest time. 'Fine,' she says eventually. 'But you're grounded, do you hear me?'

I beam at her. I don't care if I'm grounded until I'm seventy-two, as long as Dad's home. 'Misunderstanding,' I say to the guard. 'She's my auntie.'

He frowns and starts banging on about the boy who cried wolf, but just then the security alarm goes off and three kids run out of the shop in panic. The guard doesn't give us another thought, and pegs it out of the shop after them.

'What the hell was that all about?' Kirsty fumes. She's absolutely seething.

I shrug my shoulders. 'I just really want to go to Buckingham Palace,' I say.

'You're your mother's daughter all right,' she mutters under her breath, but I catch what she's saying. 'Right little madam.'

'What?' I ask. 'What about Mum?' It's the first time Kirsty's ever mentioned her.

Kirsty just rolls her eyes and storms off out of the

shop. 'Well, come on, then,' she shouts back over her shoulder, and I run to catch up.

This is it! We're walking down Constitution Hill, and I've had Kirsty banging on about how blinking mad she is at me, but all I'm thinking is *This is it!* If I stand on tiptoe I can just about see the roof of Buckingham Palace in the distance. But it's quite tricky to stand on tiptoe when you're walking along, so I have to stop that after a while.

We turn the corner, and there it is. Buckingham Palace. Home of the good lady the Queen, Dad's saviour and soon to be my most favourite person in the world. My stomach sort of flips over as we get closer and my palms are sweating.

There are about a million tourists milling around in front of the palace, taking photos of the guards by the little wooden boxes, and of themselves by the railings, and of the horse poo that litters the pavement outside.

'Satisfied?' Kirsty huffs.

The main gates are closed, but that's to be expected. They can't be letting all and sundry in. I run forward and try to catch the attention of one of the guards outside. 'Hello!' I call. 'Can I have a word?'

They completely ignore me, which is totally rude. But after a moment a muscly policeman loitering inside comes over to me. 'All right, love?' he asks through the railings. He looks past me to Kirsty, and gives her this little smile. I turn round to see Kirsty smile back at him, and I roll my eyes, because she obviously thinks he's fit. But then I realize that if she's pleased about seeing a fit guy, maybe she'll go easy on me later.

'How do I get in?' I ask.

The policeman tears his gaze away from Kirsty and looks at me. 'What?'

'To the palace. How do we get in?'

He shakes his head. 'You can't, sweetheart. It's closed at this time of year.'

'What do you mean?'

The policeman nods his head at a sign on the railings. 'Summer opening's end of July to October.' He checks his watch. 'You're a month early.'

I shake my head and give a little sigh, because this guy's obviously a bit thick. 'I don't mean just *anyone,*' I say. 'I mean me. How do *I* get in?'

The policeman throws back his head and laughs. 'Oh, I'm sorry,' he chortles. 'Didn't realize we had the Queen of Sheba here.' He turns to Kirsty. 'She's a one, isn't she?'

Kirsty frowns. 'Tell me about it.'

I'm starting to get annoyed now. 'Look,' I say, trying to keep calm, 'we've come all the way from Merchant Stanton for this. I just want to see her,' and I stamp my foot a bit because he's just wasting time. 'It'll only take a minute.'

He looks at me and sees that I'm totally serious. 'Have you got an invitation?' he asks.

'Well, no, not exactly.'

'Well, then, can't let you in. Appointment only.'

I let out a puff of air. 'If you just tell her I'm here,' I reply. 'Billie Templar. She'll have got my letter.'

'What letter?' Kirsty pipes up.

'School project,' I say over my shoulder, thinking quickly. And then, because no one's doing anything, I start rattling the gate, trying to get it open.

'Whoa, whoa, whoa!' the policeman cries. He grabs my hand and tries to prise it off the gate.

'Get off!' I yell, and before I know it, I'm sticking my leg through the gates and kicking him on the shin.

The policeman recoils in shock. 'Owwww!' he yelps. 'You little—'

'Billie!' Kirsty cries, horrified.

I retreat, and I know that my cheeks are all red because I'm angry. Some woman tourist starts clicking away at me with her camera. 'I just want to see the Queen!' I shout, and my voice is all shaky because I'm trying not to cry.

'I'm so sorry,' Kirsty says to the policeman, and she gives me this look like she's absolutely going to throttle me. 'It's been a difficult time at home.'

The policeman's fuming – he's opening his mouth to speak, but then he sees that I'm blinking really hard, trying to stop the tears from falling down my cheeks. After a moment his face softens. 'All right,' he says quietly. 'I'll let it slide.'

Kirsty beams at him dead gratefully, and then takes me by the arm and leads me away from the gate.

'She's not here, anyway,' the policeman says.

I spin round to face him. 'What?'

He shakes his head like he can't believe he's helping me. 'She's never here when they open the palace to the public,' he explains. 'The Queen always goes to Balmoral for her holidays.'

My mind starts racing and I'm wondering how many Take That posters I'd have to sell to buy *those* coach tickets.

'But right now she's off opening a school somewhere,' he continues.

'On a Saturday?' I ask.

The policeman rolls his eyes. 'Part of her Jubilee celebrations.'

Kirsty takes me by the shoulder. 'Time for home, I think,' she says.

I don't say anything as she gently leads me away, because I'm thinking what a complete and utter waste of time this has all been, and how I've blown my super-secret savings for nothing. Now I'll never go on my trip and I'll never get Dad to come home and I'll never win the three-legged race with him ever, ever, ever again. It's all the stupid Queen's fault. And I don't even care if that's treason.

CHAPTER SEVEN

I'm in an utterly miserable mood as we head back to Victoria coach station. Kirsty's not spoken to me all the way here, and I just know I'm probably going to be grounded for the rest of my life and forced to play with Jade as punishment.

We walk past one of those tacky souvenir stalls that seem to be everywhere. Union Jack tea towels are hung up all around it. There's a stand of postcards with different views of London. Blinking Buckingham Palace is at the forefront.

Kirsty peers at a row of pint glasses laid out on a little table, all with LONDON written on them. 'S'pose I'd better get Mark something,' she says. She picks up the nearest pint glass and reaches into her bag for her purse. She lets out a sigh. 'Do you want anything?'

I'm too distracted to realize she's being nice to me, despite everything that's happened, because all I can see is the Queen, right in front of me. She's everywhere – on plates, on mugs, on coasters. Her face is even on a key ring. And for a moment I want to pick up all the plates and mugs and coasters and key rings, and smash them on the ground because I'm so annoyed with Her Majesty; but instead, my mind starts whirring, because one of the plates has a picture of a little girl waving a flag and handing the Queen a bouquet of flowers. I remember what the policeman said outside Buckingham Palace, and not just the bit when I kicked his shin. *She's off opening a school somewhere*, he'd said.

That's how I'm going to do it!

The idea hits me like a bolt of lightning, though it's definitely less painful. If I can't go to the Queen, because she's off in Balmoral or doing something for the Jubilee, I'll get the Queen to come to me. Simples!

'Billie?' Kirsty says. 'Do you want a souvenir? To cheer you up?'

Right in front of me is a little shelf full of notebooks, so I grab one of those. And next to them is a tray of pens. Not normal biros, but pens in the shape of a man playing the bagpipes. It's all they've got, so it'll have to do. Well, actually, it's not all they've got – next to them are some rude pens. The kind where if you tilt the pen upside down, a naked lady appears. But I reckon I'm in enough trouble already.

I beam up at Kirsty and she hands the stallholder a tenner, and before she even gets her change I'm scribbling away in my notepad.

HOW TO GET THE QUEEN, I write in big capital letters at the top of the very first page. I'm thinking so hard, Kirsty has to nudge me on. I don't even look up as I walk down the street, and I accidentally tread on four people's feet.

1   Open a school. This isn't a bad idea, but it's really just copying the other kids, and I reckon the Queen might be bored of schools by now.

2. Open a hospital. I remember seeing a plaque outside the hospital Mark went to when he fell off a ladder at work, and it said: 'Opened by the Princess Royal, Princess Anne', which isn't quite the Queen, but perhaps she was busy that day.

3. Get everyone to break World Records. There was this little village in Jersey that I saw on the news, and they saved their homes and made themselves famous by hula-hooping and eating doughnuts. Which isn't a bad way to pass the time of day.

'Ow, Billie, watch out!' Kirsty cries, because I walk smack into her. I didn't realize she'd stopped. I look up from my notepad and see that *everyone* around us has stopped.

'What's going on?' I ask.

'Changing of the Guard,' a guy standing next to me says.

I spot a little sign on the wall that says HORSE

GUARDS PARADE. 'I thought that was Buckingham Palace,' I say, but the man doesn't hear me.

And then everyone starts getting their cameras out and going, 'Oooooooh' and, 'Aaaaaaaah' like it's the blinking fireworks, and I have to elbow my way to the front to see what all the fuss is about. And right there, as clear as day and as bold as brass, are four soldiers, all dressed in blue blazers with gold buttons on and white trousers with thigh-high black riding boots. They've got big gold helmets with a red Mohican haircut, and from one hip hangs a big shiny sword. With a 'Quick, March!' the soldiers start marching out of the archway they're standing under and off down the path.

'Wait!' I shout, and I run forward to catch them, but there are too many people in the way trying to get photos. 'Do you know my dad? He's in the Yorkshire Regiment!'

Before I can start shoving people out of the way – or, if I have to, kicking them – Kirsty grabs my elbow. 'We're gonna miss the coach,' she says, and manoeuvres me out of there.

★

Back on the coach, I'm a bit annoyed that the soldiers didn't answer me, but I'm even more annoyed because Kirsty's trying to talk to me, when all I want to do is make notes in my notepad. She's got this sad sort of look on her face, like she knows I'm a 'problem child' – which is what Mrs Hussein called me after the Matilda Midgely Two Grazed Knees incident.

'What happened today, Billie?' Kirsty asks.

I shrug. I'm busy.

'All that stuff in Hamleys . . .' she ploughs on. 'Kicking the policeman at Buckingham Palace.'

'I was only joking,' I say, not looking up.

'Joking?' Kirsty says this so loudly, a woman sitting across the aisle tuts. She leans in to me and lowers her voice. 'Look, I've got enough on my plate with Mum without you mucking around. If you don't start behaving, the Social are going to come along and say I'm not fit to look after you. Is that what you want?'

I'm not going to tell her what I've got up my sleeve, but I know she's doing her best for me. I shake my head.

'Well, then,' she whispers. 'How about a truce?'

I look up at her. 'All right,' I say. 'I'll try and be good from now on.' And it's true – I've got enough to think about with getting the Queen to visit Merchant Stanton; I don't need Kirsty or Mr Law or the Social on my back.

Kirsty smiles down at me, and then shuffles back into her seat. She fishes her glossy magazine out of her handbag and starts flicking through the pages. 'Ooh, look,' she says after a moment. 'That's exactly what I want.' She shows me a picture of a WAG and her husband.

'A footballer?' I ask.

'A butterfly,' she replies, and shoves the magazine right in my face. 'On her back.'

I stare at Kirsty blankly – it's like she's talking a different language.

'For my next tattoo,' she explains.

I look at the picture again. 'Yeah, it's nice,' I say, and pick up my pen and notebook.

Hang on a second . . .

A butterfly tattoo.

My mind starts going like the clappers, because

I've just thought of the most brilliant thing ever. And I'm almost jumping up and down in my seat, I'm that excited. I start remembering everything I've seen today.

Changing of the Guard.

Soldiers all dressed up, marching.

My bagpiper pen.

A tattoo! That's it! That's how I'm going to get Her Majesty to come to me! I'm going to stage a military tattoo. Just like they have in Edinburgh every year, where lots of different army regiments get together and march and play drums and bagpipes and stuff. It's a massive, spectacular spectacle.

And it should get the Queen to Merchant Stanton, no probs.

CHAPTER EIGHT

My plan can't really start until Monday because if I'm to stage a military tattoo, the first thing I need is recruits. Not that I know very much about them, but I reckon the Queen might get a bit bored if it's just me playing the bagpipes. Mr Law keeps saying I need to be a Team Player, and if I don't want to tell Kirsty about it — she'll just think it's another silly scheme of mine, one that will Probably Cost Money, and Mark won't want to know, because he never does — the only other people I know are the kids in my class. They can be in my team.

I can hardly sleep that night — there's so much to do in such a short space of time, so I stay up for hours designing my recruitment poster. It says:

OUR TOWN NEEDS YOU!

and it's got a picture of a finger pointing out of the page, like in a poster they used to recruit soldiers in the First World War. And underneath that, I've put:

DO YOU WANT TO GET INVOLVED IN
THE MOST EXCITING THING TO HAPPEN
IN MERCHANT STANTON
IN THE HISTORY OF THE WORLD?
IF SO, MEET ME IN 6H AT 3.30 P.M.
MONDAY.

And then I've put *Billie Templar* because I don't want people to think it's a hoax.

The next morning I take Nana May a cup of tea and the Sunday papers. She doesn't really understand what's going on in the world, but she likes looking at the pictures. I knock on her bedroom door. The sound of the telly blares out from inside.

'Morning, Nana,' I say, pushing open the door

and popping the tea on her bedside table. I throw the papers down on the bed and smile as Nana May looks at me, joy on her face. She's still in her blue nightie and slippers and she's shuffling around, dancing to the musical she's watching. She does this every Sunday. Always the same film – this old movie called *Singin' in the Rain*.

'Morning, sweetheart,' she replies. She's dead tiny, is Nana, even smaller than me, so when she grabs my face to give me a kiss, she has to stretch a little bit. 'We're siiiiiiiinging in the rain,' she trills and links my arm in hers. 'I wish we *were* singing in the rain, it's so muggy today. Come on, love, you know the words.'

I laugh and look at the telly. Of all the films Nana May watches, this is my favourite, because the main guy's called Don, like Dad. It's the good bit, where Don's dancing in the street because he's just kissed the lady. It's pouring with rain but he doesn't care – he's dancing away, twirling his umbrella, jumping up and down the pavement, sploshing in puddles. He's having a whale of a time. So is Nana May. She's doing high kicks now, which is no mean feat; the doctor once said she might need a new hip if she's not careful. I high-kick next to her. 'Just siiiiiiinging in the rain,' I join in and beam at Nana. 'What a glorious feeeeeeeling, I'm haaaaaappy again!'

Then I break off and start free-styling because it makes Nana May laugh. 'Look,' I say, and I body-pop my way around the room. 'I'm Justin Bieber!'

Just then, Mark pops his head round the door. 'What are you doing?' he asks and rolls his eyes at us.

Nana May just laughs and carries on high-kicking.

'Come on, Mark,' I say, body-popping over to him. I wave my arms in his face. 'I'm haaaaappy again!'

Mark grabs my arms and scowls at me. 'You'll tire her out. You know how she gets.' He marches over to the telly and switches it off.

Nana May stops high-kicking. 'What are you doing?'

'You should be packing, Nan,' Mark says to her gently. 'For Hope Springs.'

And just like that, as if we're balloons that somebody's stuck a pin in, Nana May and I sit down on the bed, dejected.

'These clothes aren't going to pack themselves,' Mark says, heading over to Nana May's wardrobe. 'Come on, Billie. Think on.'

He's telling me off! As if he's my dad or something!

'Fine,' I say, and I get up to help because I figure at least it will pass the time until tomorrow, when I can go to school and pin up my poster. Because one thing's for sure: Mark's *not* my dad. And only I can bring him home.

The clock ticks 3.26 . . . 3.27 . . . I can't wait for everyone to turn up — then I can get this whole tattoo rolling. In class this morning, Mrs Hussein was going on about how we should do more to help each other — she'd read an article in the paper about a woman who got her community together to clean up old beer bottles and plastic bags from their estate, so that should help.

Hmm . . . 3.32. Clearly good timekeeping will have to be the first rule I lay down.

3.34. I check my watch again, and look up at the clock on the wall to check it's the same. Where is everyone? I walk over to the door and peer out into the corridor. It's quiet, except for the strains of 'When the Saints Go Marching In', which the school band insist on playing over and over again. I check the plaque on the door, just in case I've been sitting in the wrong room, but I know without looking that it's my classroom, 6H.

My shoulders slump a bit, and I head back inside. 3.42 . . . And then I think, *What if I've got the wrong day? What if it's really Tuesday?* but I know in my heart that I haven't done some sort of time travel to the future, and it's blinking Monday all right.

There's a lump in my throat as I reach down to pick up my bag. My idea of staging a military tattoo and getting the Queen to come to Merchant Stanton was the most fantastic one ever, and nobody's even going to know about it. Perhaps it's because I put my name on the poster. Perhaps that's put people off – like they think I'm going to bang on about the carnival or something.

Just as I'm about to head off, there's a creak as the door opens. My heart leaps into my mouth as someone comes into the room.

'Hi,' says Sarah, and sits down at the yellow

table, which is where she normally sits. 'Is this it?'

I frown. 'So far,' I reply. 'There must be some sort of hold-up.'

Sarah nods, and we both sit there in silence for a bit. *Blinking Nora*, I think, because if I'm honest, I'd probably prefer *anyone* else to have showed up. Not because Sarah's not nice or anything, but because I can't spend the whole meeting with a tissue under my nose to block out the smell. I'm not being funny but I'd probably prefer *Andy Nelson* to walk through the door.

'What's this all about, then?' Sarah asks. I look at my watch again: 3.47. I sigh, because I don't reckon anyone else is coming.

And just then, the door creaks again. 'Am I late?' Jake Whittaker asks as he comes bounding into the classroom. He scratches at his hands because he's got a nut allergy and is lactose intolerant, and his mum makes him wear little white gloves all day to stop him getting killed by accidentally touching a brazil nut or a glass of full-fat milk.

'Seventeen minutes.' I frown, but secretly I'm pleased someone else has bothered to turn up. Even if that someone *is* wearing gloves in the middle of a heat wave.

'What's this all about, then?' Jake asks, his podgy face all pink.

'I just asked that,' Sarah said, 'but she didn't reply.'

I reach into my bag and take out my notepad and bagpiper pen. 'Right,' I say in as commanding a tone as I can muster. 'We're going to stage a military tattoo.'

Both Sarah and Jake look at me with their mouths open. Which is annoying, but at least they're not laughing at me like I thought they would. 'What?' they cry in unison.

I take a deep breath. 'A military tattoo,' I repeat, 'like they have in Edinburgh.' And I launch into how brilliant it's all going to be and how we'll need lots of people to march.

'What?' they both cry again when I've finished.

Sarah coughs politely. 'My actual question, really, is *why*?'

I hesitate. I don't want to tell them about the Queen, because they're bound to laugh at that and not take it seriously — and just getting them to turn up and not run out of the classroom as soon as I introduced the words 'military tattoo' into the conversation was difficult enough.

'I just think it'll be fun,' I say. 'Our school's never done anything like it before. Mrs Hussein will be well pleased.'

The clock on the wall ticks loudly as Sarah and Jake both think about that.

'OK,' Jake says after a moment.

Sarah shrugs. 'If you like.'

I beam at them and rush over to the whiteboard — this is going to need more than my mere notepad.

THINGS WE'LL NEED FOR A TATTOO, I
write at the top.

'Right,' I say to the team. Well, pair. 'Fire away.'

I'm hardly overwhelmed by the responses. Largely because there aren't any.

'Well?' I say after a moment. 'What things are we going to need to stage a military tattoo? You know — that you might have seen on the telly.'

Still nothing. So I start them off. SOLDIERS

TO MARCH, I write underneath. BAGPIPES.

And it clearly has an effect, because Sarah and Jake both shove their hands in the air, like I'm Mrs Hussein or something, and before I can pick one, they're shouting things out at me.

'Fireworks!' Sarah cries. 'Drums!'

'Horses!' Jakes yells. 'Flags! Ballet dancers!'

I'm not quite sure about the last one, but I go with it because I'm pleased they're so enthusiastic.

'Horses!' Jake cries again.

'We've already got that,' I say.

'I know, but we should have a lot of them,' he replies. *Fair enough.* I smile to myself. *The kid's thinking big.* 'And a cannon!' he yells.

Blimey. Now we're talking.

And before I can say, *The Queen's going to LOVE this*, we've got a whole list of things to include in our tattoo. Now it's just the small matter of getting hold of them.

I divide the list between the three of us. I've got soldiers, drums and the cannon, Jake's got horses and fireworks, and Sarah's got flags, bagpipes and ballet dancers.

'There's no time to lose,' I say to the team as I wipe the board clean and shove my notebook in my bag. 'We'll reconvene at three thirty tomorrow with our findings.'

Jake and Sarah head out of the classroom, but I wait a minute because I'm feeling all shaky. Not in a bad way. *Excited* shaky. I have to take a deep breath, because I know, I just *know* that this is going to be blinking brilliant.

CHAPTER NINE

*I*t's not blinking brilliant. Not by a long shot. Things aren't going well. At all.

It's 3.30, and Sarah, Jake and me are back in the classroom and we're no further along than yesterday.

Jake sits at the blue table shoving his special nut-free dairy-free wheat-free crackers into his mouth. For the last five minutes he's been telling me how he asked his sister all about horses, because she goes riding at Merchant Stanton Stables, but she was busy watching *Gossip Girl* and wouldn't talk to him — except bits of cracker keep flying everywhere and I'm finding it hard to concentrate.

'Bottom line is,' I say, crossing my arms, 'we haven't got a horse.'

'Phhhtt,' Jake replies. He swallows his mouthful. 'Yet.'

I roll my eyes and turn to Sarah. 'How did you get on?'

Sarah looks down at the table. 'Umm, I was going to go to the library to research flags, but I had to do something else.'

I let out a big sigh. 'Why couldn't you just look stuff up on the Internet?'

Sarah bites her lip. 'We, uh, we don't have the Internet,' she mutters.

'Broken, is it?' Jake says through another mouthful of crackers. 'Ours went down for three hours the other week and my brother was well annoyed because he was chatting up this girl on Facebook and by the time it came back on she'd gone off with someone else.'

'It's not broken,' Sarah says, but I don't really have time for this.

'If you want something doing, do it yourself.' I pull my notes out of my school bag. Last night I spent about four hours on the Internet, trying to find out about fireworks and bands and drums and cannons and all the things we wrote down. And these two came up with nothing.

'There's good news and there's bad news,' I say. 'The good news is, we can *definitely* get fireworks and bands and drums and cannons and all the things on the list.'

'Yahoo!' Jake cries, brandishing his now-empty cracker packet in the air. He clearly doesn't get out much.

'You haven't heard the bad news.' I frown. 'We can get all these things, but it's gonna cost.'

Sarah looks up from the table. 'How much?'

I peer down at my notes. 'About fifty pounds,' I say.

Jake looks at me brightly. 'That's not too bad,' he replies. 'My dad gave me that for my birthday.'

I take a deep breath. 'And then five thousand, nine hundred and fifty more pounds,' I mumble.

Neither of them says anything for a moment.

Then Jake lets out a low whistle. 'Not being funny, but I don't think my dad can stretch to that.'

Sarah looks crestfallen. 'Where are we gonna get six thousand pounds from?'

I've been thinking about this – ever since I realized that staging a tattoo was going to cost the same as buying a car or a posh holiday to the Bahamas or 6,000 ice lollies from the corner shop. No amount of Take That posters or Barbie dolls with missing legs is going to get us there.

'We're gonna ask Mr Law,' I reply.

A few minutes later, after I'd made Jake close his mouth because he was so shocked, we're outside Mr Law's office. I've been here a million times before, but this time I'm actually nervous. Funny, really. The strains of 'When the Saints Go Marching In' reach us from the hall, where the school band have their rehearsals. Though seeing as it's the only song they ever play, and they've been playing it for as long as I've been in the junior school, I don't know how many more rehearsals they think they need.

All of a sudden the door flies open and Mr Law comes hurrying out with a pile of folders under his arm. He almost bowls me over.

'Billie?' he asks with a frown. He's a bit confused when he sees Jake and Sarah with me, and then a look of disappointment spreads across his face. 'What have you got these two involved in?' he asks.

Well, that's just tickety-boo, isn't it? 'Nothing,' I say, and fold my arms. Why do I always get the blame for everything?

'I find that hard to believe,' Mr Law sighs.

I stick out my chin to show him that I'm dead annoyed, but I can't be too cross as we need his help. 'We need to ask a favour.'

He checks his watch. 'I've not got time for this, Billie,' he says. 'Book an appointment to see me.'

'But you're right here,' I reply. Is he mad?

He brushes past me and starts to pace off up the corridor.

'Mr Law?' I shout, and I motion to Jake and Sarah, and together we chase after him.

He crosses the reception and opens the main door. 'Not now, Billie,' he says. He jogs down the front steps and takes his car keys out of his pocket.

Just as he clicks open the lock on the car, I go for it. It's now or never. 'We need money,' I say.

Mr Law has one hand on the car door handle, but he turns to look at me. 'What for?'

'For the best event this school has ever seen.'

He frowns again. 'Do you mean a bake sale or something?'

I shake my head. 'Better than that.'

He opens the door and shoves the pile of folders onto the passenger seat.

'We need six thousand pounds.'

Mr Law backs out of the car so quickly he forgets to duck and smacks his head on the door frame. 'Owwww!' he cries, and has to bite his tongue because he's clearly about to say a rude word.

He rubs his head and stares at us. 'What could you three possibly need six thousand pounds for?'

I don't like to tell him about the whole Queen plan, so I shrug my shoulders. 'It's something to do with helping each other and being an "asset to the community",' I say, echoing what I heard in class earlier.

'You've clearly been paying attention to Mrs Hussein,' he says, rolling his eyes. 'But our funds are already tied up, I'm afraid.' He actually looks a bit sorry for me. 'There's nothing left in the budget.' He climbs into his car and clicks his seatbelt on.

'But it's a brilliant idea,' I say, and before I know it, I'm holding onto the handle of the car door so that he can't shut it. 'It's going to be good for the school and the whole of Merchant Stanton.'

Mr Law grabs the handle from inside the car. 'I'm sure it is,' he says through gritted teeth, yanking at it, 'but there's no money.'

And with one final tug, he slams the door shut. He starts the car and zooms away.

Jake, Sarah and me stand there in silence. Well, as much silence as there can be with 'When the Saints Go Marching In' blaring out in the background. I put my hands on my hips. 'Thanks for nothing,' I say to Jake and Sarah.

'What?' Jake asks.

'You could have backed me up,' I reply. 'Why am I having to do everything?'

'I – I'm not very good with confrontation,' Jake stammers. 'And I don't like talking in public.'

'Mr Law isn't talking in public,' I reply.

Jake just shrugs unhelpfully.

'Sorry,' Sarah mutters.

Hmm – everyone says sorry. Fat lot of good 'sorry'

is. Especially when no one ever really means it.

'You got any bright ideas, then?' I say, because I'm not giving up. Not when it's this important. But I actually have to shout it because the band is so loud now. Trumpets are trumpeting and bugles are blaring and flutes are trilling and French horns are honking and cymbals are crashing and oboes are oboe-ing and—

And it's everything you need for a marching band. A marching band for a military tattoo!

'I've got it!' I cry – so loudly that Jake steps back a bit in shock. 'The band! The band can be in our tattoo! And it won't cost us anything!'

It takes a moment for what I'm saying to sink in, but then Jake and Sarah turn in the direction the music's coming from.

'If we get the band to be in our tattoo,' Sarah says, 'we can see who else we can get too.'

'Uh-huh.' I nod. 'We can get things for free ourselves.'

'Like a horse?' Jake says in surprise. 'And a cannon?'

I nod, because it's the best idea we've had yet.

'Sure,' I say, even though I've no idea how to go about getting all these things.

Sarah and Jake beam at me. 'This could really work, you know,' Sarah says.

I hope so, I think. *It has to.* I jerk my thumb towards the hall. 'Let's get cracking,' I say, and we all bound back up the school steps.

CHAPTER TEN

I waltz into the hall and try to get Mrs MacLean's attention. She's in front of her music stand looking a bit flustered because Michael Owugu from 6T has shoved one of his socks in the end of Chris Anderton's bugle and it won't come out, so 'When the Saints Go Marching In' is sounding a bit off.

'Mrs MacLean, can I ask a favour?' I say as she hurries to Chris's side.

'Not now, Billie,' she says, looking frazzled.

'But it's important. It's a chance for the band to shine. Give them something to really practise for.'

But Mrs MacLean isn't listening because Chris,

in an effort to dislodge the sock from the bugle, tugged so hard that he smacked his elbow in Natalie Keener's eye, and now she's crying and Mrs MacLean is practically pulling her hair out.

Mrs MacLean may not be listening, but the rest of the band are.

'A chance to shine?' Darren Curtis asks, looking at me intently.

Mrs MacLean grabs Natalie and her streaming eye under one arm and Chris and his muffled bugle under the other and marches them out of the hall. 'From the beginning while I'm gone,' she barks to the band, but she doesn't notice that everyone's turned towards me.

'Something to practise for?' Aria Braden asks, flicking her blonde fringe out of her eyes. 'Like what?'

I take a deep breath. 'Well,' I say, 'we' – and I point to Sarah and Jake, who's gone all shy again and is lurking behind a row of stacked chairs – 'are staging a military tattoo, and we need a marching band to be in it.'

Nobody says anything for a little while.

'What?' Aria cries. 'Why?'

I shrug my shoulders. 'Just because,' I reply. 'It's fun, isn't it?'

'When you say "be in it",' Darren says slowly, narrowing his eyes at me, 'do you really mean, "be the *main* thing in it"?'

I shake my head. 'No — we've got lots of other things going on.'

'Well, then, we don't wanna know.'

'Hang on a sec,' Aria says, and steps in front of him. 'Let's not be so hasty.'

'Mrs MacLean thinks we're the worst band this school has ever had,' Darren says softly, sidestepping Aria. 'If we're the star attraction, we could really show her.'

I think about this for a second. 'I don't know . . .' I reply. 'We've got fireworks and a cannon and soldiers and everything.'

The rest of the band pipes up. 'Please,' they shout. 'Oh yeah, let's be in it.' And, 'Go on, give us a chance.'

Darren stands his ground. 'Main attraction or nothing,' he says.

'Who made you boss?' Aria cries, folding her arms.

Darren brandishes his tuba in the air, which is no mean feat considering it's almost the same size as him. 'I'm the only tuba in this band, and you can't play half our songs without me,' he says defiantly. I don't know why he says 'songs' because they've only got the one, but he's got a point, I'll be honest.

Jake just shrugs at me, but Sarah nods her head. 'Fine,' I say to Darren. 'You can be the main attraction. But I bet the soldiers won't be happy about it.'

The whole band cheers loudly. So loudly they don't hear Sarah whisper to me, 'But we haven't got any soldiers yet,' which is just as well.

'Keep practising,' I say loudly to make myself heard over the din, 'and we'll be in touch about the marching.'

Just then Mrs MacLean comes back, minus Natalie; Chris is holding his bugle in one hand and Michael's sock in the other.

'What's going on?' she asks as she realizes that not only is no one playing 'When the Saints Go Marching In' but that little Amir Aban from 3F is so excited he's running around smacking his flute on the bums of all the girls.

'Nothing,' I say quickly, before Darren gets a chance to tell her about the tattoo, and I grab Jake and Sarah and wheel them towards the door. 'We're off.'

As we leave, I shake my head at Darren and raise a finger to my lips. He understands what I'm saying and nods back at me. Mrs MacLean taps her conductor's baton on the music stand and instructs the band to start. 'When the Saints Go Marching In' blares out louder than ever before, and Mrs MacLean is so startled she accidentally knocks the music stand and it topples onto the end of Chris Anderton's bugle and he bangs his teeth on the mouthpiece. It's really not his day.

That afternoon I walk home, pleased that things are finally starting to happen. We've got at least one thing in the tattoo sorted, but the more I think about it, the more I realize that there's so much more work, and that finding a cannon and fireworks and drums and ballet dancers *for free* is going to take an awful lot of persuading – and time, which is the one thing I don't have. It must take the Edinburgh Tattoo organizers all year to put a show together, and we've only got a few weeks, because soon it'll be the end of term and the race to decide the carnival king.

Before I know it, I'm walking past Hope Springs. I've not been back since my rant at Derek and Mr Featherstone and that poor man with the IV drip pole. I try and shove my chin down into the collar of my school shirt because I don't want anyone to see me.

'Billie!' No such luck. A voice shouts at me from the common-room window.

I shove my hands in my skirt pockets and pick up the pace. 'Yahoo! Billie!' the voice cries again. I don't even need to look to know it's Derek.

Just don't make eye contact, I think as I scurry past. *Don't look up at the window. Just don't look—*

I can't help it. Thinking about not looking makes me want to do it, and before I know what I'm doing, suddenly I'm staring right at Derek as he taps on the window at me.

Bits of party streamer dangle from the tufts of black hair above Derek's ears, and a little paper party hat slides down over his glasses. I'm not being funny,

I think as I look into his harassed eyes, but perhaps he's in the wrong job.

Derek motions for me to come inside and, even though I don't want to, I'm still feeling pretty bad about all the shouting I did last time; maybe I'd better say sorry after all.

With a sigh, I head up the steps.

The common-room table is strewn with half-eaten sandwiches, sausage rolls, Scotch eggs and used paper plates. On one wall hangs a home-made banner with HAPPY BIRTHDAY OLIVE! on it.

'Come in, come in,' Derek cries as I traipse in. 'Couldn't give us a hand with this lot, could you?'

I blinking said it was child labour. The residents are sitting in armchairs staring into space, their party hats perched wonkily on their heads, though there's a group of five old men huddled in one corner; one is wearing the remains of a bashed piñata on his head; another is stumbling around wearing a blindfold, clearly under the impression they're still playing Pin the Tail on the Donkey. I don't know why he's bothering with the blindfold, though – it's the blind man I sold the deformed Barbie to.

There's an empty chair at the back of the room. The lady with auburn hair catches me gazing at it. She's wearing a BIRTHDAY GIRL badge, so I guess she's Olive. 'You know him,' she sighs. 'Never joins in with this sort of thing. I mean, honestly. Who in their right mind wouldn't want a slice of birthday cake?'

I check my watch. I've not got time for this. I came here because I felt bad, but nobody seems to have minded my shouting, after all. 'Mr Law said I only had to help out once,' I say to Derek.

There's a banging sound and the old man with the IV drip comes shuffling in. He looks just as sad as when I last saw him, but he's making a bit of an effort – he's tied a balloon round the IV pole with HAPPY BIRTHDAY on it.

Derek sighs. 'I know,' he says to me, 'but you could make them tea, or tell them a story or something.' He looks around the room and gestures to the residents in the armchairs. 'Look at them. They're bored. They're sad and depressed. No one ever comes in here and they can't make their own fun.'

Before I can even say anything, it all kicks off.

Two of the men in the corner launch into a duel, using rolls of wrapping paper as their swords. Derek runs over and tries to separate them, but they're having too much fun. They start swatting at him, sheer joy on their faces. 'Stop it at once!' Derek commands, but no one pays attention to him.

'We're making our own fun!' one of the men cries. 'You can't write us off just yet!'

And while Derek's got his arms up in front of his face to shield himself from the blows, the rest of the group start kicking a balloon about. 'Nice one, Cyril!' one man shouts as it rolls over to the guy with the IV drip. It comes to a stop by his foot. He looks down at it for a moment, and then, his face breaking into a grin, shuffles forward and kicks the balloon back.

'Wey-hey!' the men cry. 'On me 'ead!'

I burst out laughing because honestly it's the funniest thing I've seen all day. I had no idea old people could be this much fun. Or *have* this much fun.

One old man bends down to pick up the balloon, and even from the other side of the room I can hear his bones crack. 'Oooh, me back!' he cries, hunched over in pain. 'Nurse!'

With the two rolls of wrapping paper tucked neatly under his arm, and the two duellers shoved into armchairs, Derek tries to straighten him up. 'You've made your point,' he cries as the young nurse and two other care workers come running in. 'You've had your fun. Now it's time to calm down.' He turns to me. 'Billie, Ovaltine, please. You know where the kitchen is.'

And just like that, order is restored. By the time I come back with a tray of hot drinks, all the residents are back in their armchairs in front of the telly, though everyone's just staring into space again. The joy and chaos of the last few minutes has completely evaporated, and a distinctly sombre atmosphere fills the common room.

And just as I'm thinking what a shame it is, because I was enjoying them running – well, *shuffling* – around just as much as they were, I get another brilliant thought in my head.

Soldiers.

We need soldiers to be in the tattoo. And if this

lot are bored and depressed but enjoy a laugh, maybe they'd like to be in it.

Derek's out in the corridor, gossiping with the young nurse, so I take my chance. 'Can you all just stand up and march from one side of the room to the other, please?' I ask.

Nobody moves. 'Please?'

The old man with the piñata on his head stands up. Carefully placing one foot in front the other, he slowly, slowly walks across the room. The man with the blindfold follows a few paces behind, his arms still outstretched like a zombie.

It's not great. We're going to need help. Expert help.

I glance at Olive and pick up a paper plate. 'Mind if I have some of that cake?'

I take a deep breath. I can't believe I'm up here after all the things I said, but desperate times and all that . . .

I knock on the door of Mr Featherstone's little attic room and don't even wait for a response.

He's sitting on his bed, his shoulders slumped, and

in his lap is the same blue AIRMAIL letter. Screwed-up pieces of paper are littered over the floor and at least three pencils have been broken in half.

I plonk the cake down on the chest of drawers. 'It's raspberry jam,' I say. 'No one should miss out on raspberry jam.'

Mr Featherstone frowns at me, but doesn't quite meet my eye.

I point to the mess on the floor. 'This looks like my room when I'm trying to do my spellings.' I smile, then turn to him, dead serious. 'I need your help.'

Mr Featherstone lets out a grunt. 'I might have guessed.'

'You were in the war, right?' I plough on, ignoring his foul mood. 'I bet you did loads of marching.' I swallow hard. 'I need you to help the others to march properly. For our tattoo. I need soldiers to be in it.'

'What makes you think I'd want to help you?' he says irritably.

I stare down at the ground. 'I'm sorry for all those things I said. It's a . . . stressful time. With my dad and everything.'

Mr Featherstone looks me over for a moment, his grey eyes giving nothing away. 'You shouldn't play at war.'

'I'm not!' I protest. 'It's for a good cause.'

'War's not a laughing matter,' he says quietly, almost under his breath. 'You should know that as well as anyone.'

I look down at my shoes. He's right. War's *not* a laughing matter. But I'm not doing this for a laugh.

I nod. 'I must be mad, asking,' I mutter. 'But I wouldn't unless I was desperate. Nothing ventured, and all that. Sorry to bother you.'

I let out a sigh and head back downstairs.

'I'll be back tomorrow,' I say to the common room, and ignore the look of surprise on Derek's face. 'And I've got a brilliant game for everyone.'

The residents perk up a bit at that and start chatting amongst themselves, and even though I'm annoyed that Mr Featherstone won't help, I allow myself to smile. Maybe this could just work, after all.

CHAPTER ELEVEN

After school I get the biggest shock of my life. Well, two big shocks, actually.

Firstly, I kick off our meeting because Sarah and Jake and me are all correct and present, and that's all the organizers we've got, when Tamwar Siddiqi from 6T bursts into the room. 'Sorry I'm late,' he exclaims breathlessly, and then, bold as brass, waltzes across the classroom and sits down at the blue table.

'Uh, what do you think you're doing?' I say, folding my arms. 'This is a private meeting.'

Sarah coughs politely, and raises her hand. 'I'm not Mrs Hussein,' I say crossly. I feel a bit bad then because she looks really shocked.

'I invited him,' she says softly. 'He's going to help us with the tattoo.'

'Sssssh!' I snap, and look around frantically in case anyone's heard.

'What? It's not a secret, is it?' Jake pipes up.

'Well, no, not exactly,' I reply. 'Not when we have to ask people to be in it. They can't be in what they don't know, can they?' I slump down into a chair. 'But the fewer people we have to tell, the better.'

'I've already squared it with my uncle,' Tamwar says. 'He's happy to help.'

'Doing what?' I ask in surprise.

'His uncle runs one of those temporary fireworks shops,' Sarah says. 'I figured that'd be one more thing to cross off the list.'

I look from Sarah to Tamwar. 'That's brilliant!' I cry, leaping to my feet. I lean over the desk and shake Tamwar's hand. 'Welcome to the team.'

Sarah gives me this shy sort of smile, and then she reaches into her tatty old rucksack. 'And I got this . . .' She finds a battered white megaphone and holds it out to me across the table. 'To command the troops.'

'Omigosh!' I say, because I can't believe I hadn't thought of it. 'That's *blinking* brilliant!'

Jake peers at the megaphone closely. 'It's a bit grubby,' he says, pulling at his latex gloves. 'Where did you get it?'

'Charity shop,' Sarah mumbles. And then she coughs. 'I mean, I was just passing. It's not like I'm in there all the time, or anything.'

Jake frowns. 'My mum says you've got to be careful with charity shops,' he says, and gestures to the megaphone. 'You never know where that stuff's been.'

Sarah goes bright red then, and I can see she's dead embarrassed, so I give the mouthpiece a bit of a wipe with my school shirt and put it to my lips. 'IT'LL BE FINE!' I say, and the noise echoes around the room.

Tamwar and Sarah jump back in shock, but then burst out laughing. After a moment even Jake joins in, and for once, I'm pleased I've got this little crack team on my side.

'Now I've got a surprise for *you*,' I say, shoving the megaphone in my rucksack and slinging it over my shoulder. 'Follow me.'

★

Jake and Sarah and Tamwar turn to me with raised eyebrows as we stand outside the care home. Even though I went '*Ta-da!*' and gestured to Hope Springs, they still look confused.

'Soldiers?' Jake asks, a hint of scorn in his voice. 'Are you sure?'

'Got any better ideas?' I ask, and I lead the way up the steps.

The three of them shuffle behind me as we walk down the empty and bare corridor. 'It smells of wee,' Jake whispers, and then he realizes what he's said because he adds, 'I mean the old people, obviously – no one else,' and he looks over at Sarah, and she's gone bright red again, so Jake shuts up.

'In here.' I open the common-room door.

It's just as joyless as it was when I left yesterday. The residents are still sitting in their armchairs, the telly on in the background. I'm beginning to wonder if any of them ever move at all.

'I'm back,' I say loudly. 'I've got that surprise I mentioned. Remember?'

It's spooky how quiet it is. Derek's at the back of the room, sweeping up with a dustpan and brush. 'Billie?' he says, looking over in surprise. 'What's all this?'

'I've brought some friends,' I say, gesturing to Tamwar and Jake and Sarah.

'To help with the tea?' Derek asks. 'How thoughtful. Off you pop, then.'

I clear my throat. 'Uh, no, actually, Derek, not tea,' I say, and he looks even more surprised. 'I wanted the residents' help with something.'

A few of them perk up at that. Derek waits with bated breath. 'Well?'

'How would you all,' I ask them, 'like to be in our tattoo?'

No one says anything. The sound of *Deal or No Deal* blares out on the telly.

'You what?' Derek says after a moment.

'We,' I say, gesturing to Tamwar and Jake and Sarah, 'are staging a military tattoo, and we thought everyone might like to get involved.'

'*You* thought,' Jake mumbles.

Derek folds his arms. 'Absolutely not.'

One old man – the one who had the piñata firmly wedged over his head yesterday – struggles up out of his armchair. He takes a minute to get his breath back. 'I – wouldn't – mind,' he pants.

'We haven't got the room.' Derek frowns.

'Not in here, obviously,' I say, laughing. 'We'll practise outside. In the front garden.' I'm not going to give up; we *need* these old folk.

'Oh, please let us,' the old man gasps. 'I don't want to just sit around watching telly all day.'

'Me neither,' Olive pipes up.

'Think of it this way,' I say to Derek, ploughing on with my charm offensive. 'We'll be in the garden, but you can keep an eye on everything while you put your feet up with a nice cup of tea and a garibaldi.'

Derek's face softens and he looks at his watch. 'All right. You can have half an hour with them.'

Jake and Tamwar and Sarah and me all smile at each other, and a few of the old men and women look pleased at the prospect of doing something different.

'But it'll take you nearly that long to get their

shoes and coats on!' Derek sinks into an armchair by the window with a smirk on his face.

He wasn't wrong. About ten minutes later, after we've helped those who are interested into their wellies and jackets and hats, even though it's still blazing hot, a scraggly, motley crew of old folk stand in a line in front of us.

One old man – the one who was so keen to join in – slowly raises his hand and salutes me. 'Basil Worthington, ma'am,' he says to me. 'I was in the Second World War.'

'Blimey!' Sarah exclaims next to me. 'Did you fight in the D-Day landings?'

Basil shuffles on the spot and looks shifty. Next to him, Olive rolls her eyes. 'He was born in nineteen thirty-nine,' she explains. 'He never saw action.'

'I saw it on the news,' Basil retorts.

'Right,' I shout at them through the megaphone, keen to crack on. The megaphone's got a loop of string attached to the end so I can put it round my neck. 'Let's see what you've got. Quick march!'

They all shuffle forward at various paces, no one bothering to listen to the 'Left, right, left, right!'

instructions Tamwar's calling out. And if this is their 'quick march', I'd hate to see what they'd do if I yelled out 'As slow as you can' – they may as well not be moving at all. And Cyril has to wheel his IV drip pole along wherever he goes; it's making him even slower than the others. Add in the fact that six of them have got walking sticks and Zimmer frames, and the blind man has wandered off in the wrong direction . . . Things aren't exactly going to plan.

'Stop!' I shout to everyone. 'Let's go again. Back to your starting positions.'

That takes another four minutes.

'This is tremendous fun, isn't it?' Cyril says to Basil. The word 'fun' hadn't entered my head, to be honest.

'Wait a second,' Tamwar says, pointing to the old folk with walking sticks. 'They could put them against their shoulders like guns. That's what they do in military tattoos.'

The four residents who need walking sticks sling them over their shoulders and start to march, but obviously we've not thought this through, because for someone who needs a walking stick, walking without one takes a very . . . long . . . time indeed. One man falls over, he's that used to a walking aid. He lies on the ground and his face crumples like he's about to cry. 'This is worse than Dunkirk,' he whispers, his eyes drifting off into the distance.

'Is it time for breakfast yet?' Cyril asks.

I look up to the heavens, exasperated. I thought these old people would be dead enthusiastic, but they're hopeless. The Queen'll think they're a right shambles. *We're* a right shambles.

Just as I'm rolling my eyes in despair, I catch sight of Mr Featherstone looking out of his little attic window. He's frowning down on all of us. He catches my eye and shakes his head in disbelief. After a moment he opens the window. I hold my breath.

'It's all a bit *Dad's Army*,' he cries, but I'm too stressed to ask him what he means.

He starts to explain, but Olive calls out, 'Shut up, you old crank!' Basil and a few of the women snigger next to me. Mr Featherstone glares at them and slams the window shut.

'Wait!' I cry, but it's too late. He's gone. And I'm letting out a big puff of air, thinking how terribly this is going and wondering what on earth I've got myself into, when someone on the other side of the street whistles at us.

'What the hell are you lot doing?'

I spin round as I recognize the voice. Andy Nelson and two of his mates are on their bikes, circling round the front lawn of the care home.

'It's none of your business,' I snap at him, and turn back to the troops. 'ONCE MORE, FROM THE TOP,' I shout at them through my megaphone.

Andy's up on the pavement with his bike, showing off and doing wheelies in front of his mates. 'Why are you hanging out with coffin dodgers?' he yells, and his mates both laugh with him. 'Are they the only friends you can get?'

I ignore him and try not to notice the blind man talking to the apple tree because he thinks it's a person. Out of the corner of my eye I see Mr Feather-stone still glaring at me from his bedroom window.

'You're such a loser, Billie,' Andy yells, circling right up in front of me.

Now he's doing my head in and he won't leave us alone. 'SHUT UP!' I yell at him through the megaphone.

Andy recoils in shock, but then bursts out laughing. 'Ooooooh,' he taunts, 'I'm really scared.' He leans forward and laughs right in my face. 'Geek!'

For God's sake, he's so annoying.

'Just ignore him,' Sarah says beside me.

Easier said than done. 'Once more, from the top,' I say to the troops.

But no one's listening. Cyril's leaning on his drip pole, trying to do a wheelie with it, like Andy. Olive and two other women are loitering on the lawn having a good old gossip. Basil's pretending to shoot everyone with an imaginary machine gun. Things couldn't be worse.

'What a ragtag band of brothers you are,' a gruff voice rings out.

Everyone turns to see Mr Featherstone walking down the front steps.

Olive and the other ladies open their mouths in shock. Cyril taps his IV bag to check his medication. 'Stone the crows!' he cries.

Mr Featherstone rolls his eyes. 'Let's not make a song and dance about it. You heard her: *once more, from the top.*'

I gaze at him in amazement, and he nods his head at me.

'Right!' I cry, and everyone shuffles back into place in front of me.

'Thumbs in line with seams,' Mr Featherstone calls after a moment, and the residents swing their arms right, left, right, left, sheer delight on their faces.

I look over at Jake and Tamwar and Sarah, and they're all beaming at me, positively beaming. Turns out I'm a bit of a genius, getting these old folk to be our soldiers. We're really starting to get somewhere.

Then Mr Stephens storms down the steps, a panicked Derek trailing after him. 'What's going on?' he demands, towering over me.

'We're just learning a few moves, that's all,' I reply, trying to look as innocent as possible.

But Mr Stephens starts to round up the old folks. 'You can't just swan in and out whenever you like.'

He frowns. 'I don't want another visit from *Panorama*, thank you.'

He and Derek herd the troops up the steps. They look a bit sad, but they start shuffling back towards the entrance.

Next to me, Andy snorts with laughter. 'Even your new friends are fed up with you,' he hisses. He spots Sarah and flaps his hand under his nose. 'Feel at home here, do you?' Then he thinks for a moment and says, '*Urine* good company,' and bursts out laughing like it's the funniest thing ever.

Sarah goes red and looks like she's going to cry. That's it! We've had next to no rehearsal, Andy blinking Nelson is being totally annoying, and Mr Stephens has just told me off like he's Mr flaming Law. We haven't got enough time before the carnival for all this faffing about.

I turn to Andy again. 'FOR GOD'S SAKE!' I say to him through gritted teeth. 'IT'S FOR THE QUEEN!'

Everyone stops what they're doing at that. I'd forgotten I was still holding the megaphone. I drop it so that it dangles around my neck as silence descends. The old folk stop in their tracks. Mr Stephens and Derek turn to face me in surprise. Mr Featherstone's eyebrows shoot skywards. Andy stops spinning round on his bike. Even Jake and Tamwar and Sarah look at me in shock.

'*What?*' everyone cries in unison.

'Uh, nothing . . .' I say, and I step back because now everyone's coming at me. The old people are marching towards me quicker than they ever did in rehearsal, and if I wasn't desperately trying to think of a way to explain myself out of it, I'd have told them what a marked improvement they were making.

'The Queen?' Jake looks at me, his eyes wide.

'The Queen's coming *here*?' Sarah whispers.

'Is anyone taping *Deal or No Deal*?' Cyril asks.

I take a big breath. Actually, now's as good a time as any to let them know exactly *why* I'm planning this tattoo.

Out of the corner of my eye, I see Andy and his mates looking at me as if I'm mental. 'Do me a favour,' he says, but I ignore him.

'What are you talking about?' Mr Stephens frowns.

'The, uh, the tattoo's for the Queen,' I say slowly as everyone moves in closer, forming a semicircle in front of me.

'When?'

I bite my lip. 'Uh, before the carnival,' I mumble eventually.

'Yeah, right,' Andy cries. 'As if she'd come here. You're such a liar.'

'I'm not lying,' I say, and I stick my chin out to show that I'm serious – even though, strictly speaking, I *am* lying. Sort of. 'I'm doing this for the Queen.'

Mr Stephens looks at me sceptically. 'Really?' he asks. I force a smile and try not to look shifty.

'You got her then?' Mr Featherstone whispers, peering at me curiously. I nod at him, but I can't quite meet his eye.

Sarah studies my face. 'Are you serious?' she asks softly. 'You don't have to make it up, you know. We'd do this for fun anyway.'

I shake my head. 'I know,' I reply, 'so why *would* I make it up?' I'll not mention the sending-my-dad-home bit just yet.

Everybody turns to each other in amazement.

Jaws hang open in shock. Tamwar looks like he's going to pass out.

And then everyone starts talking at once: 'The Queen's coming to Merchant Stanton!'

'We're going to be famous!'

'What on earth am I going to wear?'

I hold up my hands in protest. 'Well, not just yet . . .' I try to say, but everyone's too busy whooping and cheering and chatting to listen. Even Andy and his mates are huddled together, whispering. 'I mean, she's not definitely confirmed – we're practising in case she *does* come . . .'

Two of the old ladies start brushing their hair and smartening themselves up, as if the Queen's coming this very moment. The blind man's hugging the apple tree like it's a long-lost friend. Cyril wheels his IV drip pole around Basil in a celebratory circle. 'Now I've got something to live for!' he cries in joy.

'Hang on a sec . . .' I say, but nobody's listening. There's nothing for it: I pick up the megaphone and bark into it, 'WAIT A MINUTE!' and everyone quietens down immediately. I'm about to tell them that the Queen's not a definite yet, and that actually,

I've not heard anything back from her, but the looks on their faces make me hesitate. Especially the old folk. Their faces are full of such hope and joy and . . . *liveliness* . . . that I can't bear to tell them the whole truth. Not yet, anyway.

I let the megaphone drop. 'Uh, that's why the tattoo's got to be brilliant,' I say instead. 'Fit for a Queen. Literally. So keep practising till we're next back.'

Mr Stephens beams at me. 'Perhaps now the council will do something about this place,' he says, and he leads the old folk back inside again. This time, I swear they practically skip up the steps. There's definitely a new lease of life to them.

Olive grasps my hands in hers, her eyes shining. 'Just wait till my daughter hears about this,' she whispers, and her voice cracks as if she's about to cry. 'Thank you, Billie.' She leans forward and plants a kiss on my cheek.

With a parting glare, Andy and his mates ride off home, and Jake and Sarah and Tamwar pick up their bags. They each give me a dazzling smile.

'This is brilliant news, Billie,' Jake says. I've never

seen him looking so happy. Honestly, he needs to get out more. Shame his mum won't let him, what with his allergies.

I nod. 'I know,' I mumble – but as we all say our goodbyes, I can't quite look them in the eye.

That's the thing about lying. Before you know it, things get out of control and you've got old folk telling you you're the only reason they've got to live, and friends you've never really had before thinking you're the best thing since Dairylea triangles.

I pick up my school bag, stuff the megaphone inside and head home, not entirely sure what I'm going to do about this 'trying to get the Queen to come and see our tattoo when I've already promised everyone she's a definite' business.

CHAPTER TWELVE

I head home with a heavy heart because I'm just realizing what I've got myself into.

And it gets worse, because Kirsty's waiting for me when I get there. 'We need to talk,' she says. My first thought is that something's happened to Dad, but there aren't any cars on the drive, so it can't be that bad. 'I've just been speaking to Mr Law,' she says.

It *is* that bad.

Kirsty motions for me to sit down on the sofa and folds her arms. 'What's all this about six thousand pounds?' she demands.

I'd forgotten about that. 'Uh, nothing,' I reply.

'Nothing? Mr Law said how "insistent" you were. What are you up to, Billie?'

I shrug my shoulders. 'It was just a joke. Can't anyone have a joke these days?'

'He's already made you do community service at Hope Springs,' Kirsty replies. 'You're skating on thin ice, young lady.'

She bites her lip and then flops down on the sofa next to me. 'Remember our conversation about the Social?' she asks. 'On the coach back from London?'

I nod reluctantly.

'Mr Law says you've been spending a lot of time hanging around after school,' Kirsty says, looking at me curiously. 'Are you sure there's nothing you want to tell me?'

I shrug my shoulders again. She lets out a sigh. 'Fine,' she says after a moment. 'Have it your way. You're grounded.'

'What?' I leap off the sofa. 'That's outrageous!'

This time it's Kirsty who shrugs. 'You're not being straight with me, Billie. I know you're up to something, so I've no choice. And I've been so busy at work I've still not given you a proper punishment for all that Buckingham Palace business.'

I was kind of hoping she'd forgotten about that. 'But you can't—'

Kirsty holds up her hand to silence me. 'I've had a word with Mandy and, despite everything, she's happy to help out.'

I don't say anything, but I've got a terrible feeling I know where this is going.

'I'm working till ten all next week,' Kirsty continues, 'so Mandy says you can go round to hers every day for tea. Thinks it'll do Jade good to have some company.'

I let out a groan and sink back onto the sofa. 'Why do you hate me so much?' I whisper.

Kirsty lets out a snort and taps me on the knee. 'Don't be dramatic,' she replies. 'But you have to go straight there. No hanging around after school. No more mucking about, Billie. None of your silly little games. No more funny business. You wouldn't want me to have to tell your dad, would you?'

She's got me there. We all know Dad's got more important things to worry about than his daughter being all random and wayward at home. But if I have to go straight round to Jade's and I can't organize the tattoo, how am I going to get him sent home?

'Understood?' Kirsty asks.

I frown at her. 'Loud and clear,' I mumble.

Kirsty gets up off the sofa and wanders into the kitchen, leaving me sitting there, thinking just how rotten everything is turning out.

CHAPTER THIRTEEN

A knock on my bedroom wall wakes me up the next morning. One sharp knock, followed by three quieter ones. I prop myself up on my elbows and knock back so that Linda knows I'm awake. Though why she doesn't just get me an alarm clock, I don't know.

I sleepily rub my eyes as sunlight streams in through the curtains, and for one glorious moment all is well with the world.

Then I remember everything that happened yesterday. The grounding. The care home. The blinking megaphone. I let out a groan. 'Oh, please let it all have been a dream,' I say to myself. And then my eye falls on my notebook and bagpiper pen beside my bed. The notepad's open at the page with the heading UPDATE ON CONTACTING THE QUEEN, and underneath I've written:

Email: Have been fobbed off with a standard automated response.

Phone: Can only get through to the general number and the receptionist won't help because she thinks I'm just having a laugh.

In person: Not allowed into Buckingham Palace. Kicking the policeman did not help.

Letter: No response yet.

Last night I tried desperately to email and phone again because I'd told that lie. If the Queen doesn't come, not only can she not send my dad home but everyone will know I'm a liar, and the old folk will probably all top themselves to give them something else to do.

Maybe everyone will have forgotten about it, I think,

and that makes me feel a little better. That's it. I'm sure they will have. Perhaps Jake and Sarah and Tamwar thought I was kidding. Perhaps the old people will just question their medication.

Suddenly things don't seem so bad any more.

The doorbell rings.

'I'll get it!' I yell, and I practically leap out of bed I'm in such a good mood.

Across the landing, Kirsty's got her door open and she's lying in bed with a flannel over her forehead, like she always does the morning after Wednesday bingo club. 'Quietly!' she calls out, and winces in pain.

I'm humming as I skip down the stairs and fling the front door open.

I stop humming. My good mood evaporates. My mouth opens in shock. 'What the—?'

Standing in front of me is the local gymnastics team. All seventeen of them. They're wearing their blue leotards and prancing around our front garden. Six girls are on their hands and knees in a pyramid formation. Two bigger girls are throwing a smaller girl back and forth between them. One little girl is doing roly-polys by the gate. 'What the—?' I say again, because I can't believe what I'm seeing.

A tall girl with brown hair scraped into a bun pushes her way to the front of the troupe. 'Holly Turner,' she says, sticking out her hand. I ignore it and carry on staring at the gymnastics routines. 'We want in,' she says matter-of-factly.

'With what?'

Before she can reply, four ladies with flowing skirts and no-nonsense looks on their faces waltz up the garden path. 'Yoo-hoo!' one of them calls. 'Are you Billie Templar?'

I nod. One of the ladies, with a short bob of silver hair, hands me a bunch of flowers. 'We're the Women's Institute,' she says proudly, like she expects me to give them a medal or something.

'So?' I say.

The woman frowns, but then forces a smile. 'We thought we could make more of these' – she indicates the bouquet – 'or, at a push, knit.'

'What?' I say. This is all getting too weird.

'For the Queen,' the woman says. 'I'm sure she'd love to see it.'

Blinking heck.

I open my mouth to tell them 'No way, José,' when a bunch of lads from the secondary school down the road traipse through the front gate. They're wearing football kit and start doing keepie uppies on the front lawn, though every now and then they get smacked on the shins by the girl doing the roly-polys.

'I don't know what you think's going on,' I say, thrusting the flowers back at the WI lady, 'but you've all got it wrong.' And before things can get any crazier, I slam the door on all of them.

'What's all the noise?'

I spin round to see Kirsty at the foot of the stairs. She looks tired and there are dark circles under her eyes. 'Uh, nothing,' I say, and I shuffle to one side to block the front door. All these random people from Merchant Stanton carrying flowers and doing roly-polys would most definitely count as 'funny business' in Kirsty's book.

She tries to peer over my shoulder, but I have a genius idea. 'You look like you could use a coffee,' I say.

She narrows her eyes at me like she thinks I'm up to something, but then yawns and nods her head. 'That I could,' she replies, stumbling sleepily into the front room.

I let out a sigh of relief, but at that moment someone opens the letter box and starts blasting a kazoo through it.

'What was that?' Kirsty calls.

'Just putting the kettle on,' I say, dashing into the kitchen.

As the kettle boils, I hold onto the kitchen counter to steady myself, taking long, deep breaths. I have no idea how everyone's heard about the tattoo and the Queen, but this is sheer madness.

I'm pouring water into the mug when there's a thud at the kitchen window. Mike, the local window cleaner, and two of his mates have positioned his ladder against the back door and are strumming banjos. I dash over and fling open a window. 'What do you think you're doing?' I hiss at them.

'We're the George Formby Appreciation Society,' Mike replies – and before I can even ask who on earth George Formby is, they launch into a song about cleaning windows, grinning maniacally as they strum.

'Stop playing your banjos at me!' I cry.

Mike looks put out. 'They're ukuleles,' he says sulkily.

Then a tall guy with acne on his forehead leans in through the window. He opens his mouth and starts burping 'God Save the Queen'.

I recoil in horror because the smell is disgusting. 'Reckon she'll like that,' the man says when he's done.

'It's a military tattoo,' I shout, 'not blinking *Britain's Got Talent!*' and I pull the window towards me.

But Mike's got his hand wedged in there, and he's not moving. 'Oh, let us be in it,' he pleads. 'The Queen'll love George Formby, I know she will.'

I stare past him because more and more people are pouring into our back garden. There's a group of little girls in tutus doing pirouettes. Four men wearing T-shirts saying EXTREME SCRABBLE CHAMPIONS 2008 head towards me. Craig starts bellowing out an opera song. He's the owner of the pub Dad and Mark drink in and he reckons he's a celebrity because he once went to an *X Factor* audition – though he didn't realize it *was* an audition and only went into the building because he needed the loo.

'Billie?' Kirsty calls out from the front room. 'Is everything all right?'

No, I think. *It's blinking not.*

I look at the madness in front of me and let out a long sigh. 'Fine,' I say through gritted teeth. 'You can all be in it.'

There's a chorus of whoops and cheers, and I have to shush everyone before Kirsty gets suspicious. 'First rehearsal ten o'clock Sunday morning, Butterfield Park,' I say. 'Now leave me alone.'

I slam the window shut and sink to the ground, not sure what's just happened. I'm not being funny but what's the Queen going to make of this shambles of a tattoo we're organizing? Another thought pops into my head and my mood darkens. If I can get the Queen to come *at all*, of course.

CHAPTER FOURTEEN

Two days later, I'm in Butterfield Park. I had to lie to Kirsty and tell her I was popping round to Linda's for a while. The park's at the edge of Eddington fields, just opposite the entrance to Merchant Stanton Hospital. I dash in before any patients can try to join in the tattoo — dancing on their crutches or something.

Gathered around the old oak tree is the most random mix of people I've ever seen in my life. I've got my megaphone on the cord round my neck, and Sarah's thrust an old battered clipboard into my hand. I stare down at the list on it and start ticking groups off, one by one.

MILITARY TATTOO, JULY 2012

Director: BILLIE TEMPLAR
Assistants: SARAH KNOWLES, JAKE WHITTAKER,
TAMWAR SIDDIQI

PARTICIPANTS	(No.)	SKILL
Merchant Stanton Ballet Class	(7)	Ballet
Under 18s Football Club	(11)	Keepie uppies and ball skills
WI	(4)	Flower arranging and knitting
Merchant Stanton Gymnastics Club	(17)	Gymnastics – emphasis on roly-polys
Merchant Stanton Junior Marching Band	(16)	'When the Saints School Go Marching In'
Craig from the pub	(1)	Opera, X Factor style
Tamwar and his uncle	(2)	Fireworks display
Extreme Scrabble Club	(4)	Extreme Scrabble playing
Mike the window cleaner	(3)	George Formby songs while on ladders

So there we have it. Sixty-five people stand in front of me, all staring at me with crazy grins on their faces. Honestly, you'd think nothing like this had ever happened in Merchant Stanton before.

'Are you going to do anything?' Sarah asks me.

'Like what?' I say.

Sarah shrugs. 'I don't know, but I reckon you should. This is your idea, after all.'

What on earth could *I do*? I could probably tell you who's married to who in Albert Square, but that's about it. I'm rubbish at a lot of things, which is why I have to make stuff up to tell Dad in the letters I send him. And I only win the three-legged race 'cos Dad's dead fast.

I thrust the clipboard at Jake and put my megaphone to my mouth. 'Right, then,' I say. 'Who's first?'

Everyone starts pushing forward. Some of the gymnasts get jostled out of the way by the footballers. A ladder smacks a Scrabble player round the head. Darren Curtis elbows his way to the front of the crowd, brandishing his tuba. 'You said we were the main attraction,' he grumbles at me.

'I don't think so, lad,' Craig bellows. 'I've been on *The X Factor*, you know.'

Everyone rolls their eyes at that. A lady from the

WI makes a rude gesture with her knitting needle.

Sarah peers at the clipboard in Jake's hand. 'We've not put the people from Hope Springs down,' she says.

'Oh yeah,' Jake replies. He makes a note.

'You can't just put *old folk marching*,' Sarah says.

Jake thinks for a second and makes another note.

'*Well-old folk marching?*' Sarah asks. 'That's even more disrespectful.' She looks at me, but I just shrug.

'They *are* well old, I guess,' I say. I haven't got time for this. Everyone's still pushing past each other, trying to be first on the tattoo bill.

One of the ballet dancers sticks up her hand. 'When *is* this tattoo, by the way?' she calls.

A hush descends on the crowd and they all turn to look at me. *That's a blinking good question*, I think, because I hadn't actually come to that. My mind races. I know it has to be before Saturday 21 July, because that's when my dad needs to be back to do the race with me, and win, and play the king at the carnival the day after. And the war's a bit of a way away, so he'll need to be back at least the day before. He'll need time to rest and recover and do a little bit of practice with me on the old three-legged race, like. Which means the Queen will need to sign the form to send him home the day before that.

I check my watch. It's 8 July. Taking into account the fact that this lot will need a bit of practice, and that I've not officially heard anything from the Queen about coming yet, I reckon we'll need a bit of time.

'In eleven days,' I say, spur of the moment, just because I'm eleven and I like the number. 'The nineteenth of July.' There, that sounds reasonable. Plenty of time.

'Oh no,' the eldest Scrabble player groans, shaking his head. 'I'm in Egypt then.' The other members of his team stare at him in disbelief. 'What?' he asks. 'I've booked a cruise.'

Mike strokes his beard. 'Actually,' he says slowly, 'that won't work for me, either. I've got the in-laws coming for dinner.'

And before I know it, everyone starts up again, arguing about what date the tattoo should be, depending on what's best for them. 'I'm pretty sure I've got a stag do in Magaluf,' one of the footballers calls out. 'I can't miss it, I'm best man.'

'Shall we have a vote?' Amir Aban pipes up.

It's all a bit overwhelming, to be honest. Sixty-five people staring at me, shouting to make themselves heard. Sarah shuffles over and picks up the megaphone from around my neck. She puts it to her mouth and barks into it. Except she pulls a bit too tight on the cord and yanks me with her.

'QUIET!' she yells, and everyone's so surprised they immediately shut up.

Sarah goes red as everyone looks at her. 'It's all sorted, isn't it?' she says. 'It's the nineteenth of July because that's when the Queen's coming.' And then she turns to me. 'Isn't that right, Billie?'

I'm so surprised at Sarah's forthrightness that before I know it, I find myself nodding.

'So we can't move the date – the Queen will have put it in her diary,' Sarah finishes. She's got a point, I'll give her that. Even if the Queen doesn't know anything about it yet.

'Uh . . . right,' I stutter. 'It's the nineteenth, and that's all there is to it.'

The Extreme Scrabble player tuts at me. He turns

and leaves the park, clearly disappointed. 'Bleeding Egypt,' he mutters to himself.

'So where were we?' Sarah says, and Darren starts tooting on his tuba.

All through school the next day I'd been hoping Kirsty would have forgotten what she'd said about me being grounded, but when the bell rings for home time and I trudge across the playground, Mandy waves to me.

Jade, swinging her school bag around her ankles, lumbers after me. 'Mum's making burgers,' she says, her eyes shining as she thinks about tea.

'Lovely,' I reply, but Jade doesn't notice how unenthusiastic I am.

'Oi, Billie!' a voice shouts across the playground.

I spin round to see Tamwar standing by the door of 6H, Sarah and Jake beside him. All three of them give me this quizzical look. Before I can explain, Mandy grabs me by the shoulders and gives me a squeeze.

'All right, Billie, love?' she asks, and she hugs me really tight for ages. When she finally lets go, her eyes look a bit teary. I smile back at her because I don't want to be rude. Eventually Mandy fishes in her pocket and pulls out a chocolate bar. Jade's eyes light up.

'Ready, girls?' Mandy asks, picking up Jade's school bag.

I just manage to mouth, '*You're in charge*' to Sarah and Tamwar and Jake before she grabs me by the hand and walks me to her car.

Except they don't understand. 'What?' Tamwar yells back.

I roll my eyes. With my spare hand I point to Mandy, and shrug my shoulders, but they still look confused. Then, in a – quite frankly – genius flash of inspiration, I remember Andy's comment outside the care home the other day and waft my hand under my nose, mouthing '*Urine*'. But before I can make little horns with my fingers and scrape my foot on the ground to be a bull for the '*charge*' bit, Sarah bursts into tears and runs off, with Tamwar and Jake following behind. Blinking tickety-boo.

I'm not prepared for how sad and depressing Mandy's house is. The front curtains are closed, even though it's four in the afternoon, and it's not as tidy as usual. There are empty crisp packets and dirty clothes lying on the floor.

'Excuse the mess,' Mandy says as we go into the front room. 'I've been a bit . . . preoccupied,' and she glances at a framed photo of Steve above the fireplace.

She looks a bit teary again, so I say, 'I hadn't noticed,' which is a big fat lie, but there you go.

Mandy gives me a big smile and hurries into the kitchen, blowing her nose.

Which leaves me and Jade. I head over to the sofa and, after moving a pile of newspapers, sit down. Jade stands by the fireplace, munching on her second chocolate bar. Neither of us says anything for a while, so I ask, 'Shall we put the telly on?'

Jade just shrugs. 'Not fussed,' she replies. Which is about as entertaining as a conversation with Jade gets.

I let out a big sigh. I can't believe I'm being forced to come here. Just as I'm making a mental note to phone Amnesty International, because I reckon I'm practically being held hostage, my eyes fall on the pile of newspapers beside me. The headline of the top one reads: 400TH SOLDIER WOUNDED ON FRONT LINE, and underneath it there's a photo of a man I don't recognize.

I look at the date and a lump forms in my throat: JULY 8, the paper says. Yesterday. 'Do you know this man?' I ask Jade, holding up the paper to show her.

She crunches the last of her chocolate bar as she mulls it over. 'Nope,' she splutters with her mouth full.

I scan the article. The man was shot and severely injured the day before yesterday. There's no easy way to say what I'm thinking, so I just come out with it. 'He was injured *after* your dad, wasn't he?' I ask.

Jade shrugs. 'I guess so.'

That's it! I can't be faffing around at Jade's while Dad's still out fighting and more and more soldiers are getting injured by the day.

'Can I use your phone?' I ask.

Jade just shrugs again, and wanders over to her computer in the corner of the room. She looks as happy as Larry – whoever Larry is – as she taps away at her virtual home on *The Sims*.

I dash out into the hall. I don't know why I'm so convinced I'm going to get an answer this time; all I've ever got from calling the number for Buckingham Palace is a snooty receptionist who keeps telling me I need to put my request in writing and won't put me through to the Queen, or to the Queen's lady-in-waiting or whoever's responsible for sorting out her diary. Or even someone who knows where her diary is.

And sure enough, I'm greeted by the familiar 'Good afternoon, Buckingham Palace.'

I take a deep breath – and for some reason put on a Scottish accent. 'Och, aye, I'd like t' speak to the Queen please.'

The receptionist doesn't say anything.

'She'll be expecting me *calllll*,' I plough on. I have *no* idea where this accent's coming from.

After a moment the receptionist sighs and says, 'Is this the little girl who keeps on phoning?'

Oh God. She knows. She's going to think I'm a prank caller and have me locked up in the Tower of London. I panic, unsure what to do. Through the sitting-room door I can see Steve's picture on the mantelpiece, and it's like he knows I've let my dad down.

'Arrrrrrrrrgggggh!' I yell in frustration, and I punch the phone because I don't know what else to do. There are a couple of clicks and the line goes silent, and just as I'm looking at the red scratch on my knuckle where it hit the handset, another voice comes on the line.

'This is the office for the Queen's Diamond Jubilee Programme. May I help you?' a posh-sounding woman says.

I'm so stunned I practically drop the phone. 'Oh, h–hello,' I stutter after I regain some sort of control. 'I'd like to speak to the Queen, please.' At least I used my real voice this time.

The woman lets out a long sigh. 'If I had a pound for every person who asks me that . . .' she mutters.

'It's for an event I've organized, so I just need to check her diary,' I say.

The woman tuts. They're not half rude down in London. 'The nineteenth of July would be great if you've got it,' I plough on.

I hear a flicking of pages and then the woman asks, 'What company are you with?'

'What?'

'The name of the company you're phoning on behalf of.'

And just as my mind's racing to try and think of something to say, because the only companies I can think of are Primark and Walkers Crisps and they don't sound particularly tattoo-like, the woman adds, 'This is for the Jubilee schedule of events, yes? That's the number you've come through on.'

I clear my throat. 'Uh-huh,' I reply, and hope I sound convincing. I remember the Buckingham Palace policeman's words about the Queen opening a school for her Jubilee. We even had a bank holiday last month because of it, and there was a lot of flag-waving in the streets. I had to spend it on my own because Kirsty was out with her mates and Mark was just sunbathing in the garden.

'So what company are you phoning on behalf of?' the woman repeats. Her voice is more demanding this time.

I look at Steve's photo on the mantelpiece again.

'The, uh, the British Armed Forces,' I stutter. 'We're doing a military tattoo.' Technically the tattoo *is* for them – they just don't know it yet.

I can hear more rustling on the other end of the phone. 'Why are *you* phoning?' she asks after a while. 'You're a little young, aren't you?'

'Oh yes,' I say; it never occurred to me that I'd need an adult to do things officially. Why do grown-ups insist on dealing with adults when half the time they don't know what the heck they're doing anyway? 'Well, the man who's in charge isn't here right now,' I say, trying to stay calm, 'but he asked me to confirm the date.'

Then she asks me the question I've been dreading since 'the man in charge' just popped out of my mouth.

'What's his name?'

Blinking good point. What *is* his name, whoever *he* is? The only person I can see is Steve, and it's no good saying him because if this woman checks her records, she'd see he's too busy being injured. I can't say my dad either, because he's too busy trying not to get shot. So I say the first male name I can think of. 'Mr Featherstone.' I have no idea why *that* came out.

The woman perks up a bit at that. 'Len?' she asks in surprise.

Len? I rack my brains trying to remember if I've ever heard him called that – by Derek perhaps. 'Yes, Len,' I say, and even though it doesn't ring a bell, I go with it because the sound of Len's name has stopped this woman from huffing so much. 'Do you know him?'

'Not personally,' she replies. 'I'm just going to put you on hold.'

The sounds of violins and pianos tinkle down the phone at me. I can feel Steve's eyes staring at me. It's as if he knows it's all a lie.

'What's your name?' the woman asks after a while.

I tell her, and she replies, 'I'm sending Mr Featherstone a letter. Is he still at the same address?'

'Hope Springs?' I ask in surprise. 'The retirement home?'

There's more rustling at the other end of the phone. 'No, I haven't got that one,' the woman says. 'I've got the Windsor address.'

Well, I may be rubbish at geography, but even

I know that Windsor is nowhere near Merchant Stanton, so clearly she's got her wires crossed, and her Len Featherstones muddled. So, in my second flash of genius that day, I give her *my* address. It's all very well her addressing the letter to this other Mr Featherstone, but when he gets it, he's going to wonder what the heck Buckingham Palace is doing contacting him about a military tattoo.

'We'll pop our response in the post as soon as possible,' the woman says. 'Thank you for your call, young lady.' And she rings off, just like that.

I'm too pleased to even care *exactly* how random that phone call was. I do a little jig on the spot because I'm so excited. I got through to Buckingham Palace, and this woman seems to think the tattoo could be part of the Jubilee schedule of events, which means she's sending the Queen, which means my dad's coming home. Huzzah!

'What's going on?'

I spin round to see Jade in the doorway, munching on a cookie. I narrow my eyes at her. 'How much did you hear?'

'Everything.'

I frown. That's what Kat said once on *EastEnders* when she thought Alfie was having an affair, but she hadn't *really* overheard everything, she was just calling Alfie's bluff. 'Yeah, right,' I say.

'What's a military tattoo?'

Oh God. She *did* hear everything. 'Don't worry about it,' I say, and thinking fast, I add, 'What time's tea?'

'You were trying to get the Queen,' she says. 'And you said it was for the British Armed Forces.'

I give a big sigh. 'Don't tell anyone,' I say, lowering my voice. 'Please. It's a secret.'

Jade mulls it over for a second. She brushes crumbs off her shirt and says, 'All right.'

I beam at her, and just as I'm thinking she might not be as bad as I'd thought, she adds, 'As long as I can be in it.'

I roll my eyes. What on earth could Jade do in the tattoo? I've never seen her do anything apart from play on the computer and eat, and even with the random mix of acts we already have — and I'm thinking the Extreme Scrabble players and the

George Formby Appreciation Society here – I don't think she'd fit in. 'I'm not sure it's your cup of tea,' I say. 'Why don't you go back to your computer?'

Then Jade says the strangest thing. She swallows hard and her voice sounds like it's catching in her throat. 'If it's for the army,' she says softly, 'I'd like to help. I think my dad would want me to.'

I look at her. She's never really said anything about her dad and the army before. Granted, I've never asked, but there you go. I have a horrible feeling I'm going to regret this, but I nod. I guess I know how she feels. 'OK. You're in.'

Jade looks pleased as punch, and practically skips her way to sit down at the kitchen table for burgers and chips, while I'm still hovering by the phone, wondering what the blinking heck I've got myself into.

CHAPTER FIFTEEN

Eight Days until the Tattoo

It turns out that Jade's not a bad person to have on your team, especially when you're grounded, because she's good at making up things to say to her mum. I told Jade that we needed to meet everyone for our next rehearsal after school, but that Kirsty was insistent on Mandy taking me home straight away.

'Leave it with me,' Jade had said, and before I know it, here we both are in Butterfield Park at five o'clock, along with Jake, Sarah, the marching band, the ballet dancers, the WI, Craig from the pub, the Scrabble players, the footballers, and Mike the window cleaner.

Best of all, we've recruited someone else. Someone *official*.

Craig from the pub is laughing and joking with a man in a suit he introduced as being from the council. 'Top-notch idea,' the council man says to me as he shakes my hand vigorously. 'Just what this town needs.'

'Is it?' Jade asks, having overheard.

'Absolutely,' the official replies. 'All we ever get is doom and gloom. With Merchant Stanton being a military town, the only time we're in the papers is if one of our boys is killed or maimed in action.'

I gulp at that, and glance over at Jade, who goes really quiet and stares down at the ground.

'Right then, everyone,' I yell as quick as I can, and motion for all the participants to get into position. They stand in a line in front of me.

'OMG!' Jade exclaims when she sees the troops – and I'm pleased to see that she's brightened up a bit after the official's tactless comment. 'This is amazing!'

Seeing it all from an outsider's point of view makes me realize that this tattoo might – just *might* – be blinking brilliant after all. The Queen's *bound* to love George Formby and flowers and Extreme

Scrabble. It'll be unique, if nothing else. And so I start the rehearsal with joy in my heart: this is going to be the best thing since blackcurrant Fruit Shoots.

Then everything starts to go wrong.

Sarah calls for the rehearsal to start but everyone begins doing their own thing at once. The marching band start blaring out 'When the Saints Go Marching In' as loud as they can – it's sounding quite good actually – but right next to them, Mike and his mates play their banjos and bleat on about leaning under lampposts and waiting for ladies to come by. Then the footballers start moaning: their ball skills aren't that good after all – footballs go flying everywhere. One of the ladies from the WI is trying to do her flower arranging, but the pollen keeps setting off Jake's allergies so he's sneezing away, and Craig from the pub is strutting back and forth, pretending he's this old rocker Mick Jagger, which I've seen Dad do once when he was drunk and doing karaoke in our front room. To top it all, Jade's mobile starts going, and she just lets it ring and ring because she doesn't want to speak to whoever it is – so we've got the strains of Shakira on top of everything else. The official from the council frowns and shakes his head. I don't blame him. It is, quite frankly, an utter shambles.

I look over at Sarah and Jake. 'What did you do with them yesterday?' I demand, folding my arms. 'They're terrible.'

Jake doesn't reply because his eyes are streaming, and Sarah is still being mad at me because of my *urine charge* comment; she won't accept my apology, even though it's not my fault she's rubbish at charades.

I turn to face the troops. 'Whoa, whoa, whoa – *Stop!*' I cry into the megaphone. 'Everyone! *Stop!*'

The noise slowly dies down as everyone stops what they're doing and looks at me.

I let out a low whistle. 'I'm not going to lie,' I say. 'It's awful.'

No one says anything for a moment. Then Craig steps forward. 'How dare you!' he cries, shaking his fist at me. 'I've been on *The X Factor*, you know.'

I don't bother replying to that. 'The Queen's coming in eight days,' I stress, speaking very slowly to make myself heard. 'What do you think she's going to make of all this? It's a complete and utter mess.'

It's not the most tactful thing to say, I admit, and everyone takes it badly; before I know it, there's shouting and swearing and jostling and prodding. It's mayhem.

'Get that thing out of my face,' one of the ballet dancers screams at Darren, shoving his tuba.

'There's no need to be so rude,' one of the WI ladies yells as Mike shoves his banjo in the ribs of a footballer who's smacked a ball at his head. 'Watch where you're putting your banjo!'

'It's a ukulele,' Mike seethes through gritted teeth.

'Please,' I cry, trying to break them up. 'This isn't getting us anywhere.'

Craig's practising his strutting, though I've no idea what Mick Jagger's got to do with opera, but he's kicking his legs out so violently he clips one of the Extreme Scrabble players in the back.

'Watch it!' the Scrabble player cries, and he launches himself at Craig. Fists are flying. The ballet dancers start pulling the hair of the girls in the marching band. One of the WI ladies brandishes her bouquet of flowers like a sword.

'Please stop!' I cry, but nobody's paying the slightest attention to me.

'What's going on?' a voice cries over the madness.

I turn to see Tamwar and a jolly, smiley man. Behind them is a group of men dressed in their finest clothes, with turbans on their heads, and ladies wearing long beaded tunics over trousers. Salwar kameez, I think they're called. One of the men is carrying a stereo.

Everybody stops fighting when they see this army before us. 'Tamwar?' I ask, confused.

Tamwar looks at me sheepishly. 'This is my Uncle Hassan,' he says, and I notice that the jolly man is carrying a cardboard box with the words FIREWORKS written on the side. So far, so good.

'And everyone else?' I ask.

'I couldn't not tell everyone,' says the uncle, beaming. He looks like he's about to burst, he's that excited. 'This is our family. We all want to join in this wonderful tattoo to meet the Queen.'

I look at Tamwar's family. There must be about fifteen of them. 'Doing what?'

The man carrying the stereo places it on the ground and presses a button; music blares out of the speakers. Without hesitation, all fifteen members of Tamwar's family launch into a perfect Bollywood-style dance routine. The ladies shake their hips and wobble their bellies while the men dance around them. I can't help it – I clap along to the beat.

'Wow!' I say when they've finished and stand before us, panting. 'You. Are. In!'

Tamwar and his family cheer and hug each other in celebration. '*Thanks,*' Tamwar mouths at me.

'Hang on a second,' Craig booms out, loud and clear. 'There's not enough room for the likes of you.'

Tamwar's family quieten down to hear him. 'What?' Tamwar's uncle asks.

Craig clears his throat. 'I mean,' he says slowly, as if he's trying to find the right words, 'we've already got enough acts. We don't need any more.'

Before I can say anything, everyone else in the crowd pipes up. 'He's right,' one WI lady says. 'We can barely agree on an order as it is.'

'We don't need anyone else,' Mike chips in.

'Especially not more dancers,' says a ballerina, narrowing her eyes at one of Tamwar's young cousins.

'But they're brilliant,' I say, unable to believe the others don't agree. 'The Queen'll love it.'

'I don't think so,' the WI lady says. 'It's hardly . . . *British*.'

A hush descends on the crowd. Tamwar's uncle speaks very quietly. 'I was born in this country,' he says, and he gestures to his family. 'Most of us were.' Then he holds out the cardboard box. 'And look, I've got the fireworks.'

Craig snorts. 'We can get our own fireworks.'

'Most tattoos have an international element, you know,' Jade pipes up beside me. 'The first overseas regiment to participate in the Edinburgh Tattoo was the Band of the Royal Netherlands Grenadiers in nineteen fifty-two.'

Wow. Someone's clearly been on Google.

'We don't need it,' Craig replies, folding his arms.

'But they're the best thing we've got so far,' I blurt out in anger. Why can't anyone see that?

It's probably the second least tactful thing I've said all afternoon. Everyone starts shouting again, but this time they're shouting at me.

'How can you say that?' One of the footballers glares. 'I've been playing since I was three!'

'We've won awards for our flower arranging,' a WI lady mutters. 'Rude little girl.'

'Who put you in charge?' Craig demands.

And everyone starts pointing their fingers and jabbing the air in front of me.

'We didn't vote for you!'

'You're just a kid!'

'How can you possibly know what you're doing?'

'But it was my idea,' I start to protest, but nobody's paying any attention to what I've got to say for myself.

'We'll form our own tattoo!' Craig yells, and a few of the WI ladies and footballers cheer.

'Yeah!' they say. '*Our* tattoo. It'll be better than yours.'

'But you – you can't—' I stutter. This is getting out of hand. 'The Queen's coming to *mine*.'

'Not if we put on a better show,' Craig replies with a smirk. Lots more people start cheering at that. 'Who's with me?'

And before I know it, the WI, the footballers, Mike and the window cleaners and the ballet dancers are all standing behind Craig. '*We are!*' they all yell, jeering at me.

Craig looks at me triumphantly. 'This is war!' he cries, which is a bit off – the only reason I'm doing all this is *because* of the war. 'Who do I speak to, officially, like?'

'Wh-what?'

Craig rolls his eyes at me. 'I can't just go directly to the Queen, can I? Who did you speak to to get her here?'

'I . . . uh—' Oh God. I don't know what to say. My mind can't think fast enough. Everyone's still coming at me, wanting an explanation. And it's frightening, because half the group are adults, and should know better, and not only am I just a kid, if it wasn't for me they wouldn't be doing this stupid tattoo, and it's not my fault they're all rubbish, apart from Tamwar's family. And as they're pointing their fingers and jeering, I'm backing away, and before I know it, I'm through the park gates and in the street. And I'm looking wildly around to see if there's anyone to help me, but the street's empty, Jake's still sneezing, Sarah's still mad at me, and Jade's playing with her phone.

And I'm just about to yell out, because I can't take it any more and my cheeks are all hot and my bottom lip is quivering, and I know I'm going to burst into tears, because this is Just Hor-ri-ble. I'm only doing this to get my dad home and everyone's ruining it, absolutely ruining it and I want to stamp my feet and shout and—

And then someone gasps.

Thank you, I think. *Someone's going to help. Finally.*

But the gasp wasn't for me.

Everyone stops shouting and pointing at me and stands stock still.

I spin round to face the road, and it takes me a moment, but eventually I see what everyone's looking at.

And I see why they're so quiet.

An ambulance is parked just inside the entrance

of Merchant Stanton Hospital. Its back doors are open and a paramedic stands to one side, waiting for the platform lift to descend. And on the lift, being lowered to the ground, is someone in a wheelchair. He's wearing his beige army uniform, and his beret is perched on top of his head.

'Dad!' Jade cries, and she runs forward.

As she gets nearer, she stops and frowns. The paramedic walks round behind the wheelchair and manoeuvres it off the platform. Now Steve's a bit closer, we can see him better. See his injuries.

One side of his face is covered in bandages, from the crown of his head, over his right eye, and down to his mouth. The left side is all red, and the skin looks like it's been pulled tight. He's been badly burned.

His right arm's hoisted up in a sling, but that's not what everyone's staring at. It's his legs. Or lack of them. His legs stop at the top of his knees, and where they should be dangling down from the chair, it's just nothing. Empty space. No legs.

I look over at Jade. She's standing in the middle of the road, perfectly still, her mouth open in shock.

It must have been her mum phoning her so many times, to let her know. To warn her that the next time she sees her dad he'll be in a wheelchair because he can't walk any more.

I gulp because my throat feels all dry. You could hear a pin drop, it's so quiet. The silence is horrible. It's the sort of silence you get at funerals, when you're all standing around the grave with your head bowed while the vicar says a prayer and they lower the coffin into the ground.

No one knows what to do.

It's too quiet – and that's not right, because we're *not* at a funeral. Steve didn't die. He's right here before us, in his wheelchair, with his badly burned face and his stumpy thighs stopping at his knees.

A memory pops into my head. Something I saw on the news when they showed clips of Armistice Day. I clap my hands. Just once.

A couple of people nearby look over at me, but nobody else joins in.

So I do it again. I clap slowly, but a couple of times now as Steve is wheeled towards us.

And just as I'm thinking, *Oh God, clapping's probably*

the worst thing you can do when you see a man with no legs, someone next to me starts clapping too. It's Sarah. She gives me a little half-smile, like she knows it's the right thing to do. So I clap again, and she joins in, and after a moment Tamwar and Tamwar's uncle do too. Then one of the ballet dancers starts clapping. And then Mike. Then Craig. Then the WI. And before I know it, the whole street's clapping, and the clapping's getting louder now, and faster, and it's more like applause – the sort of applause you get at the end of a play when someone's done a really good bit of acting. And it's like we're all saying, *We're not clapping because you're injured. We're clapping because you were really brave and you lost your legs fighting to save other people, which is more than most people ever do, and you did really well before you got blown up.*

The clapping goes on and on, and my hands are getting sore. A few of the ladies in Tamwar's family are sniffling, and the Extreme Scrabble players are wiping tears from their eyes, and the footballers are giving Steve the thumbs-up, and Steve looks at us with his one good eye, and even though it's sort of smiling, it's really sad too.

And as Jade finally runs forward and gives her dad a big hug, I know that, more than anything, I want my dad back in one piece, and there's no way that's going to be in a wheelchair. Because there's no way he'd ever be crowned Merchant Stanton Carnival King again if he couldn't run. You can't take part in a three-legged race if you've only got two legs between the pair of you. I frown and make a little vow to myself, right there and then. *He's* not *coming home like that. He's just* not.

CHAPTER SIXTEEN

Seven days until the Tattoo

Everyone seemed to calm down a bit after they'd seen Steve. Jade went home with him in floods of tears, and I think they all realized they'd taken things a bit too far.

Except for Craig, who decided that we *were* going to have two tattoos after all and he'd be the other leader, thank you very much. He went off with the footballers, Mike and the window cleaners, the ballet dancers and the WI, promising them free drinks and pork scratchings in his pub. Sarah, Jake and I got Tamwar and his family, the fireworks, the marching band, the Extreme Scrabble players and, because they weren't there, we're claiming the old people and the gymnasts.

Nobody else but me seemed to think it was bad to argue over something like a tattoo when we'd just seen a soldier who'd been blown up. As I walked home, I couldn't help thinking how rubbish everything was turning out. Again.

It gets worse as I turn into Fairfield Lane: I see Andy Nelson at the end of my road. He's mucking about on Mr Clewson's tank, jumping up and down on the turret and pretending to fire the machine gun. Mr Clewson comes out of his house shouting blue murder, so Andy jumps off and scrambles onto his bike. Then he spots me and comes riding over. I'm not in the mood for this. As if having a million people pointing and coming at you, then having to watch your dad's best friend wheel by wasn't bad enough.

'What do you want, Andy?'

Andy circles round me, then pretends he's going to run me down, swerving away at the last minute. He thinks it's dead funny. 'No friends today?' he asks.

I frown. 'I could say the same of you,' I reply,

because for once he hasn't got his mates with him.

Andy narrows his eyes at me. 'I meant your coffin dodgers,' he hisses.

After the day I've had, that's just the last straw. Before I know what I'm doing, I'm right up in his face – so close I could bite his nose.

'What are you doing?' he screams at me, and falls off his bike in surprise.

'Don't talk about coffins!' I shout.

He's obviously taken aback, because he scrambles back on his bike and turns round. 'Just want to know why you hang out with them, that's all,' he mumbles.

I let out a sigh. 'They're helping me get my dad sent home,' I say.

Andy pulls a face like he thinks I'm joking. 'From the war? How?'

I shrug my shoulders. 'You wouldn't understand. Just leave me alone.' And I push past him and run up the driveway to my house. As I burst through the front door, I turn back to see if he's gone, but he's still there on his bike, looking at me with a funny expression.

★

The house is in darkness when I get in. I switch on the light in the front room and see a stack of cardboard boxes against the wall. Nana May's things. 'Nana May?' I call, but I check my watch and realize she's probably asleep in her room. She normally has her tea and then falls asleep straight after *The One Show*. Mark must be out with his pals, and Kirsty's working lates. She's left a note on the kitchen table.

Billie,

Mandy says you're at the cinema with Jade and her friend and her mum. Hope you had a nice time. Mark put Mum to bed before the football, so don't disturb her. Leftovers in the fridge if you're still hungry. Use a plate and cutlery - we're not animals. Bed by nine and wash behind your ears.

See you in the morning.

Love,

Kirsty

So that's what Jade said to Mandy. The more I think about it, the more I realize Jade's not that bad after all. It can't have been easy seeing her dad like that. I give a little shudder, and try to blank out the thought that it could be *my* dad in the wheelchair.

No. I won't let that happen.

I wander over to the fridge and pick out two containers of leftover Chinese. As I'm sitting at the kitchen table with my knife and fork, munching on cold chicken in black bean sauce, the front door slams.

'Kirsty?' I call.

Footsteps pad down the hall and Mark comes into the kitchen. He's got grass stains and grazes on his legs from the football.

'All right, Bill?' He slings his rucksack down on the floor. He goes to the fridge and starts glugging from the carton of orange juice. I frown as I think of Kirsty's 'We're not animals' comment.

'Did you win?' I ask.

Mark wipes his mouth with the back of his hand and rolls his eyes. 'The ref was a complete idiot,' he sighs. 'Didn't know the first thing about the game.'

He shuts the fridge and rummages around in the

cupboard, then finds a couple of slices of bread and shoves them in the toaster.

'Steve's back,' I say after a moment.

Mark nods. 'Yeah, I heard.'

Neither of us says anything for a while, and in the silence I remember the newspaper I saw at Jade's house. 'More soldiers have been wounded,' I say. 'The four hundredth soldier.'

The toaster pops up. 'Do you think Dad knows him?' I ask.

'I doubt it, Bill. The army's a big old place.' He takes a bite of toast and picks up his rucksack. He winces because the toast is hot and he's burned the roof of his mouth.

'Go away, Susie Smoke,' I say, pointing to the steam coming from the toast, but Mark just ignores me.

'I've got flat-hunting to do,' he says as he heads out of the kitchen. 'Shouldn't you be doing homework?'

I look down at my Chinese food, but I'm not really hungry any more. I push my plate away and let out a big sigh. Mark stops at the kitchen door and studies my face. 'Dad'll be all right, you know,' he says after a moment. Then he gives me a little smile and goes up to his room.

I hope so. Though there's only one way to make sure, and that's to get him sent home. And only one person can do that, and I've not heard anything from her yet.

I pick up the takeaway containers and throw them away. Just as I'm scraping the remains off my plate into the bin, a cream letter catches my eye. It's torn at the bottom, but there's an official-looking picture at the top. I use my knife to prod away bits of food – and there, as clear as day and as bold as brass, is a letter from the Queen! Well, from the woman I spoke to on the phone, at any rate.

My heart skips a beat. I don't even care that my fingers are getting covered in noodles and eggshells and bits of old tissue as I delve inside and dig out the letter. I hold it up to the light.

Dear Mr Featherstone,

Thank you for your recent enquiry about the inclusion of your event in the Schedule of Events for Her Majesty's Jubilee Year. As I'm sure you can appreciate, we receive a high volume of requests and therefore cannot reply to everyone.

We do already have an event — albeit of a very different nature to a military tattoo — planned for Her Majesty in a neighbouring area on that date. However, given your connection to Her Majesty, I am delighted to be able to assist. We will send an official from the Jubilee Schedule to assess your proposal. If it is up to scratch, Her Majesty may well visit both areas and combine the two events on the same day.

The official, Tony Hills, will be arriving at 2 p.m. on the 1 th of July, at the nominated venue, Butterfield Park. Please have your event ready to show him on this date.

Yours sincerely,

And it ends there because it's torn at the bottom, so I can't see exactly who it's from.

A million thoughts are racing through my mind. They're sending an official! There's every chance we're going to be included in the Jubilee Schedule! The Queen's going to come and send my dad home!

My heart feels as if it's about to burst. I'm the happiest I've been since this whole tattoo business started – the sort of happy when you just want to reach out and hug someone, but the kitchen's empty and Mark will be too busy in his room.

But as I scan the letter once more, my heart sinks. I can't see the date. There's a splodge of food that, no matter how hard I try, just won't come off. And it's covering the date when this Tony Hills will be coming to check up on us. It just says *1 th*. It's the 11th today, which means he'll be coming any time soon. And we haven't even started yet. Not on *our* tattoo anyway. Oh crumbs. With the bottom being torn, I can't see the phone number to call to check, and I can't remember what I did when I punched Jade's phone and got through to the woman in the first place. I hope Kirsty didn't read it before she binned it, else I'm doubly doubly grounded.

And then three words leap out at me: *Up to scratch*.

This is going to be harder than I thought.

The next day, after school and after more lies to Kirsty, we meet in Butterfield Park. Craig and his lot are there too so we do our best to ignore them. '*Battlefield* Park, more like,' one of the Extreme Scrabble players mutters to me. Everyone's in a funny mood: this isn't turning out to be half as fun as they thought it would be.

So I decide to cheer them up. I wave the letter at them. 'Good news,' I say, and everyone peers at me curiously. Their eyes get wider and wider as I explain about Tony Hills coming to check us out. I just happen to miss out the fact that I don't know the *exact* date he's coming.

I beam at everyone and wait for them all to start hugging me and patting me on the back and telling me how spectacular I am.

'Why?' one of the gymnasts asks.

'Why what?'

'Why would they be sending an official if the Queen's already confirmed? What's the point?'

Oh heck. I hadn't thought of that. Now you come to mention it, that's a blinking good question.

My mind whirrs a mile a minute while I try to think of a decent response. 'It's just a formality,' I say. That's exactly the sort of thing they say on the news. 'They have to work out the timings and everything. So the Queen can go to the other event and not be late and all that.'

People slowly start nodding, and I let out a sigh of relief because I think I've got away with it. Then I remember that today's the 12th, and that's one of the '1 th' days when Tony Hills could be coming, so I look sharply around me as Sarah orders everyone to start rehearsing.

We seem to be safe. For now.

CHAPTER SEVENTEEN

Six days until the Tattoo

I'm in class, and Mrs Hussein's banging on about the Battle of Waterloo, but she's not going into any details about the weapons they used – which I know all about because I looked it up on the Internet a few weeks ago for fun. And just as she's asking the class to do a drawing of the moment Napoleon was defeated, and I'm getting out my red colouring pencil because clearly there was a lot of blood gushing about, there's a knock on the door and little Amir Aban from 3F pokes his head round.

'Billie Templar has to go to the office,' he says.

'But I haven't even done anything!' I yell.

Mrs Hussein just rolls her eyes and orders me to

leave, which is totally rude and unfair, so I pick up my school bag and traipse out.

'Phone call for you,' Mrs Rutherford says as I get to the office. She points to a phone in the corner.

My stomach flips over a bit, because if people get phone calls in the middle of the day at school, it's never good news. I try not to think of the newspaper headline that might say 401ST SOLDIER WOUNDED.

I sit down, pick up the phone and inhale deeply. 'Hello?'

'Billie?' a familiar-sounding voice asks. It takes me a moment to recognize it, and I'm so surprised he's calling me, I practically fall off the chair.

'Derek?' I say. 'What do you want?'

'There's someone here to see Mr Featherstone,' he says, and he sounds really stressed. 'But Mr Featherstone is at the hospital.'

I gulp. 'Is he OK?' Why's he telling me this?

'It's just a check-up,' Derek replies. 'But this chap says he's the official from the Jubilee Schedule of Events.' My heart skips a beat. 'And he's given your name as a back-up.'

Oh, crumbs. What's he doing at Hope Springs?

My mind thinks back to the conversation I had with the woman on the phone. Did I tell her about it? How does Tony Hills know Mr Featherstone's there? I can feel the colour draining from my face.

I reach down into my bag and pull out the letter. I peer at the '1 th' bit closely and, now that I know it's meant to say 'the 13th', which is today's date, I can just about make it out. *Friday the 13th*. Just my luck.

'Keep him there, Derek,' I say. 'Just stall him. I'll be there as soon as I can.'

I put down the phone and grab a piece of paper from the nearest desk. I scribble a few words:

> Sarah,
> Please gather all tattoo participants and bring them to Hope Springs Retirement Home AS SOON AS POSSIBLE. The official will be waiting there. Mix-up with dates. WE CAN'T MUCK THIS UP!
> Billie

I fold it in two, sling my rucksack over my

shoulder and head out of the office. Mrs Rutherford studies my face. 'Everything all right?'

I start rubbing my jaw. 'Dentist appointment. Completely forgot about it.'

I head towards the front entrance. Mrs Rutherford frowns. 'Is someone collecting you?'

'Uh, yep. My brother,' I reply quickly. 'That was him on his mobile. He's in the car park waiting.' I hope I sound convincing – I doubt whether Mark even knows where I go to school.

Just then, a little girl from 4H stumbles into the office with sick all down her shirt. She puts her hand over her mouth and starts retching again.

'He'll need to sign you out. Wait there,' Mrs Rutherford calls to me, pointing to the chairs by the reception doors and grabbing a wastepaper bin. A nervous-looking Year Three boy is sitting on one of the chairs, holding his finger in the air. There's a bit of blood trickling down it.

I haven't got time for this. 'My brother's waiting,' I call to Mrs Rutherford, but she's holding the bin to the little girl's mouth.

She gets up, flustered, and looks out of the office window to the car park. 'Where?' she asks.

Oh blinking heck. Now I'm for it. 'There!' I cry, pointing to a car.

'That's Mr Law's.' She frowns. Oh why, oh *why* did today have to be Friday the 13th?

'I meant the one behind,' I say, and give her my best smile.

The little girl starts to retch again, and Mrs Rutherford holds the bin out. I hop from one foot to the other, desperately trying to get out of this, when all of a sudden, a group of ladies walk through the car park and head towards the reception doors. This is it!

I shove the note at the Year Three boy. 'Give this to Sarah Knowles in 6H,' I say, and I do my best to look threatening. 'Else that won't be the only finger you'll need a plaster for.' The boy squeaks in horror and I feel a bit mean. I squat down so our faces our level. 'Well, not really,' I whisper, 'but can you just do it please because it's really important?'

The boy nods at me, dazed, and I prepare to make

a run for it. As the ladies reach the reception doors, they knock on the office window. Mrs Rutherford smoothes down her shirt and tries to waft away the smell of vomit. She presses the buzzer – and *voilà!* – the doors open.

As the ladies walk into reception, I dart past them and out through the door. Freedom!

I'll worry about the consequences later.

I run all the way to the care home, and I'm red in the face and puffing and panting when I get there. As I burst into the common room, a stocky man in a suit gives me the dirtiest look I've ever seen. He's slumped in an armchair, clutching his leather holdall to his chest. I can't really blame him, to be honest, because he's surrounded by sheer and utter madness.

Cyril is on one side of the common room, showing off wheelies on his IV drip pole. Basil and a few other old men and women are walking very slowly from one side of the room to the other, with walking sticks and window openers and snooker cues slung over their shoulders for rifles. And Olive, wearing just tights and a buttoned-up blazer, is tap dancing in front of him. Though it's more like she's tap dancing *at* him, really.

I gulp. 'Mr Hills?'

The man nods and from the way he's looking at me, I know it's all over before he even opens his mouth.

He inches his way out of the armchair and manages to push past Olive. 'Turns out I've been on a bit of a wild-goose chase.' He takes a pad out of his jacket pocket and peers at his notes. 'There was nobody at Butterfield Park, which was the registered venue for the event. There was nobody at the address we sent the letter to. So I came here, which was the final place mentioned in your telephone conversation with my colleague.'

He raises his eyebrows as he looks at all the residents. 'I think I've seen enough.'

I force out a laugh. 'This . . . this isn't it,' I say, gesturing to the old folk. 'No, this is just a bit of fun I have with them sometimes. Something to take their minds off dying, and all that.'

I feel terrible for saying that, because Cyril gives

me a really sad look. I hate to think how many times I've mentioned that the poor man is near to death.

'There are others, then?' Tony Hills asks.

I nod. 'We've got gymnasts and everything.' Best not to mention the Scrabble players.

Tony Hills shoves the pad back in his pocket. 'Hardly sounds like a military tattoo,' he says, heading for the door. 'Not one fit for the Queen, anyway.'

'Please,' I say. I look down at his leg, and part of me wants to kick his shin for old times' sake, but instead, I grab his hand and tug at his sleeve. 'We've all worked really hard. You don't know how much this means to everyone.'

By now I've got tears in my eyes but I don't want to let go of his arm to wipe them away: I know, I just *know* that as soon as I do, he's going to leave and report back to the Queen that we're the most ragtag band of chancers he's ever seen. 'You don't know how much this means to *me*.'

Olive's still tap dancing in front of him, blocking his way as he tries to leave. He lets out a sigh and turns back to me. 'Do you know how many requests we get from people wanting to meet the

Queen?' he asks. 'What makes you so special?'

'But we are,' I blurt out. 'Just wait and see.'

Tony Hills looks at his watch and frowns. 'It hardly helps that the organizer didn't bother to show up.' He nudges his way past Olive and out of the door.

I'm chasing him down the corridor now, and through the front door and down the steps to his car. I think about grabbing hold of the handle, like I did with Mr Law, but somehow I don't reckon that'll help.

'Please,' I say again, and I have to bite my lip to stop crying. 'Please help me.'

Tony Hills gets into his car and winds down the window. 'I'm sure you've all tried very hard, but I can tell you now. The Queen won't be coming.' He gives me this tight little smile that doesn't reach his eyes. 'Sorry.'

There's that word again. *Sorry*. Fat lot of good 'sorry' is if the Queen won't come to your tattoo and sign the piece of paper that lets your dad off having no legs.

As he zooms out of the car park, I slump down on the front steps. I try to block out the sound of tap dancing coming from the corridor as I wonder how on earth I'm going to get round this.

Dear Dad,
I am leaving town to join the circus because I've discovered I'm brilliant at juggling and one of Kirsty's boyfriends thinks I should go professional. I reckon we'd make a ton of money and you could retire from the army and just play golf and go to the pub all day. Hope you're OK. Stay safe, please.
Love, Billie

I re-read the letter, then screw it up and shove it in my bag. I wish I *was* a professional juggler. Or a professional anything. Then Dad could come home. Heck, I'd even settle for being an *average* something. Instead, I have to keep making stuff up. Oh crumbs. I'm turning into Mr Featherstone. Next thing I know, I'll be babbling on about the Prime Minister's dirty jokes or something. And then I remember that I have to forge Mark's signature on my absence note for the pretend dentist appointment I needed to get me here just so Tony Hills could tell me the Queen's not coming.

I must have been sitting thinking on the steps for ages. Suddenly I see a group of people coming towards me.

Sarah's biting her nails nervously, Jake's playing with his gloves, and Tamwar and Jade's eyes are shining with excitement.

I look behind them and see everyone else. The gymnasts are in their leotards, all limbering up. Darren's got the marching band tuning their instruments.

Just then, there's a ringing of bells, and eight Morris dancers jangle their way onto the front lawn. 'Are we too late to sign up?' one of them calls, adjusting his knee-high socks.

The Scrabble players are wearing suits, though I'm not sure if this is to impress the official or because they're actually accountants by day, Extreme Scrabble players by night. One is shaking the little green drawstring bag the letters come in. Another turns to him in panic. 'Have you got all the letters?'

'Yes,' his friend replies.

'*All* of them? And the vowels?'

The first player straightens his tie. 'I counted them all out and I counted them all back again,' he replies.

'*What?*'

'Yes,' the man sighs, 'they're all there.'

Everyone gathers in a circle around me. 'Well?' Sarah asks hesitantly. 'Where is he?'

I honestly don't know what to say to that. Everyone's looking at me with such expectant faces – I don't want to let them down. But how can I get out of it? The Queen's not coming to see them in the tattoo and there's no way round that.

'He was taken ill,' I blurt out before I know what I'm saying. More lies. I bite my lip because I'm worried I'm going to turn into one of those people who lie so easily they actually forget what's true and what's not. 'He had to leave suddenly,' I add.

'What did he say before he left?' Sarah asks, and when she looks at me, it's as if she's looking right into my soul. She knows, I think. She knows it's not good.

'Uh, well . . .' I stammer. 'It's not the best news . . .'

And before I can say any more, there's uproar.

'She's not coming?' Holly the gymnast cries, her eyes flashing with rage.

'We've all practised so hard!' Aria Braden yells.

'I cancelled my holiday to Egypt!' one Scrabble player cries. 'I can't get a refund!'

I hold up my hands to protest because as everyone is closing in on me, I get a horrible feeling this is going the way of the Butterfield Park incident the other day. *Battlefield* Park has never seemed more appropriate. 'Wait!' I say. 'I mean, it's not *definite* bad news—'

Everyone quietens to hear me out. And just as I'm racking my brains to think of something to say, Andy Nelson pops up. He's got a knack of turning up at the most inopportune moments, that boy. But this time, he's not alone. He's got two little boys with him, both with the same messy black hair that Andy's got, so they must be related.

'Not now,' I hiss at him as he pushes his way to the front of the crowd. 'I'm busy.'

Andy doesn't say anything – he just looks from

me to Sarah to Jake and Tamwar, and takes in all the
Extreme Scrabble players and Morris dancers. Then
he clears his throat. 'Can you help me too?' he asks
quietly.

'What?' I'm so surprised, I practically fall off the
steps in shock.

He scuffs at the ground with his trainers and then
jerks his thumb towards the two little boys. 'They're
my cousins,' he says, looking everywhere but directly
at me. 'My uncle's on the front line too.'

'What?' I say again, but louder this time. This is
unbelievable. 'You've never said anything about that
before.' All the times he's made fun of me and called
me names – and all the while, we're in exactly the
same boat.

Andy shrugs. 'Didn't want to,' he mutters. Then
he looks around at everyone again. 'But if you're
using this lot to get your dad sent home, can you get
my uncle sent home too?'

Sarah raises her eyebrows at me. 'How are we
getting your dad sent home?' she says. Suddenly
everyone starts whispering to each other. I figure
now's as good a time as any to come clean. About

this bit, at least. 'I was going to ask the Queen to send him home when she came for the tattoo,' I say softly.

A few of the adults tut to each other, like they think I'm deluded, but they don't say anything to me.

'That makes sense,' Jake says. 'But why are you using the past tense?'

Wow. Someone's been paying attention to Mrs Hussein's grammar lessons.

'She *is* coming, isn't she?' Holly the gymnast asks. 'The Queen?'

I look down at Andy's two little cousins, who can't be much older than five or six. It's rotten not having your dad around. I'm eleven, so I can only imagine what it's like when you're that young. Except I don't have to imagine too hard – I know exactly what it's like to not have your *mum* around when you're that young.

'Please can you ask the Queen to send our dad home too?' Andy's little cousin asks, and it just about breaks my heart.

I look into everyone's faces. Such blinking hope.

I mean, what can I say? 'Yep,' I mumble after a while. 'I'll ask the Queen when she comes.'

'So she *is* coming, then?' Sarah asks. 'Just to clarify . . . ?'

I nod – firmly this time. 'That's what the official says. Nineteenth of July. Just like we agreed.'

And everyone starts breaking out into cheers and whoops of joy, and Andy's two little cousins look super, super happy, and even Andy's beaming at me, which I've never seen him do before, and the Extreme Scrabble player rattles his bag of letters, and the gymnasts all do cartwheels in celebration, except the one little girl who can only do roly-polys.

'The Queen's definitely coming!' they all cry, happy and excited and jubilant.

And I'm smiling at them all, and trying not to get too jostled around by all the pats on the back, but inside I'm thinking, *Oh God. Oh God. Oh God. How am I going to get out of this?*

CHAPTER EIGHTEEN

Five days until the Tattoo

Things seem to happen at warp speed after the whole 'lying to everyone that the Queen's definitely coming, and giving Andy and his little cousins false hope that she'll send their dad home, while having to come to terms with the fact that she won't be sending *my* dad home' incident.

Firstly, Jake, who it turns out is a bit of a whizz with computers, decides to tell the whole world that the Queen's coming to our little town, and he puts loads of stuff on Twitter and Facebook and Yoursphere. Which brings a whole new army of problems: I've got more and more people asking me to get the Queen to send *their* relatives home from the war too. Jake showed me all his emails from kids whose dads and mums and uncles and aunties and cousins and neighbours and friends are all in the Armed Forces, and they don't want them getting shot or blown up either. Which I can totally understand, and if the Queen *was* coming, I *would* get her to sign a note for all of them.

Secondly, a photographer comes from the *Merchant Stanton Recorder* to take a photo of us when we're rehearsing. I tried to hide, but there I am amongst the gymnasts and Scrabble players, all beaming to camera. It'll be in next week's edition. Everyone is super excited about being local celebrities – *our* tattoo has definitely got one up on Craig's. However, it means that I'll have to get up early and dispose of as many copies as I can before Kirsty sees it and grounds me again for 'funny business'.

Thirdly, in a bid to make his tattoo the best, Craig's only gone and *bought* everything they need. He was so annoyed that the *Merchant Stanton Recorder* didn't take *his* photo that he held a raffle in the pub to raise funds. So now, instead of a marching band, Craig's hired the Yorkshire Colliery Brass Band. And one of the Morris dancers says he saw a massive wooden box delivered to the pub – the kind magicians use to saw their assistants in half – so they're pretty keen to outdo us.

And last of all – and this is definitely the worst – Dad calls.

It's Saturday night, and Kirsty's watching some American drama. I'm upstairs in the bathroom brushing my teeth. The phone rings, and after a moment Kirsty yells out that it's Dad. At first I'm thinking, *How totally ace is it to hear from Dad – it means he's alive and not been blown up*, and I'm trying to ask him about all this carnival king business again, when he interrupts me with: 'Now, Billie, what's all this about the Queen?'

I gulp and almost fall over in the hall in shock. 'How did you hear about that?' I whisper.

'One of the lads in my regiment,' Dad says. 'His little boy read about it on the Internet.'

I make a mental note to throttle Jake. 'Uh . . . yeah,' I manage to stutter. 'It's no big deal.'

'No big deal?' Dad booms. 'The Queen's going to meet my little girl? It's the best news I've had all year!'

I grin, and my heart beats a little faster, and I totally ignore the thoughts whirling around my head going, *Oooh, but it's not true.*

'But there's no need to slacken,' Dad says, and he puts on a serious voice. 'I've really been missing them.'

'What?' I ask.

'Your letters.' He laughs his brilliant booming laugh. 'They really cheer me up. I've not had one in ages.'

My words seem to stick in my throat at that. 'I've been busy,' I say. 'You know, with the Queen and everything.'

'Right,' Dad replies. 'Still, glad you're not too busy to speak to your old dad.'

'Course not,' I say, and for a split second I think maybe I should launch into just *why* I'm trying to get the Queen. He'd understand, I'm sure he would.

And just as I'm about to 'fess up, Dad says, 'Good. Now, put Kirsty on, would you, love?' and I have to traipse down the hall to get her.

And while Kirsty and Dad are deep in conversation, all I can think is, *Heck, if Dad thinks I'm meeting the*

Queen, things have got way, way out of control.

But then I get a sudden surge in my stomach, because I've just thought of something. Something tickety-boo fantastic that could just about save my bacon.

CHAPTER NINETEEN

Four days until the Tattoo

FOUR DAYS! This *has* to work. I've not been round to Linda's for ages, and I feel a bit bad because I know she gets lonely.

She beams at me as she opens the door. 'Hello, love,' she says, and then she peers at my T-shirt and jeans. 'Hmmm,' she grumbles. 'I'll iron those for you. Get Kirsty to drop round anything else she wants done too.' She's dead good like that, Linda.

I know the drill by now, so I head into her front room and plonk myself down on the sofa while Linda goes through all her rituals. She's got this thing where she has to walk through doors again and again, so she takes ages to follow me into the house. Kirsty says it's because she thinks something bad will happen if she doesn't do it every time, and I guess if you believe that, you don't want to *not* do it and chance it.

Linda's front room is really tidy and everything is pretty much pink. Pink wallpaper, pink cushions, pink picture frames. And she's got a million little china dolls lined up on the windowsill, all wearing old-fashioned pink dresses. Kirsty says Linda needs to get out more, but I guess it must be difficult if you have to keep walking to and fro through doors all the time.

After about five minutes Linda comes into the front room, looking a bit flustered. 'Are you hungry?' she says. She knows she doesn't need to ask – before I can reply, she's whipped out a plate of chocolate biscuits. 'It's too hot for a Sunday roast. Pizza all right?' she asks, and I nod as I stuff biscuits in my face. Fur Ball bounds in from upstairs and starts rubbing herself against my legs, purring loudly.

Linda heads into the kitchen and then stops. She comes back through the door and turns round and goes back again. She wipes her palms on her apron. 'Sorry about this,' she says. 'It's worse than normal.

It's just . . .' She trails off as she concentrates on going back and forth through the door.

'A stressful time?' I offer, thinking back to what Kirsty said the day Steve got blown up.

Linda nods. 'You heard from your dad?'

'Yep. He phoned yesterday.'

'Good,' Linda replies. 'That's nice. He's doing OK, I gather?'

I nod.

'Good,' she says, though more to herself. Then she finally goes into the kitchen and starts rattling about with pots and pans. 'Put the telly on if you like,' she calls.

Normally I'd jump at the chance to watch anything on her fifty-two-inch plasma-screen TV. She's got all the mod cons, Linda, on account of not getting out much. 'Like to have my little world around me,' she says, 'so I can still be in touch with the world, even if I'm not out in it.' She gets all her food delivered and works from home – something to do with valuing old coins – so she doesn't have to leave the house at all unless it's *really* important, like a doctor's appointment, or a fire.

But not today. Instead, I follow her into the kitchen. Last night after Dad phoned I realized that, with the world and his wife thinking that the Queen was coming, I didn't have anyone to ask what to do about the fact that she's not. I can't talk to Kirsty or Mark — they will see straight through me and know that I've made everything up, and then Kirsty will ground me *for ever*. But then I thought of the one person who doesn't get out much and probably wouldn't have heard the local gossip.

'Can I ask you a question?' I say as Linda bobs down to the oven and slides in a big ham and pineapple pizza. 'If you had to get the Queen, how would you go about it?'

Linda doesn't look up, but says, 'Is this about your tattoo?'

I stare at her open-mouthed as my brain tries to take in the fact that the one person I thought could help now can't. I'm right back to square one. 'How do you know about that?' I cry. 'You don't get out!'

Linda laughs and says, 'Your dad mentioned it.'

'What? When?'

'On the phone last night.'

For a moment I wonder if Linda is a spy – she's clearly been listening in on my phone conversations with Dad. Then I realize what she means.

'You've spoken to Dad on the phone?' That's a bit odd. Why would Dad be phoning Linda? He can't be that fussed to know what's going on in *Coronation Street.* 'Dad's never said.'

It's as if Linda's read my mind, because she says, 'He likes to know how you're doing. We speak about you a lot. Amongst other things.'

'What other things?'

'Oh, this and that,' Linda says with a shrug. 'Do you want garlic bread?'

I nod and then trudge back to the sofa. If even Linda's heard that I'm trying to get the Queen, what hope do I have? I thought she was the one person whose advice I could ask, but now *everybody* knows and I'm stuck with lies, lies and more lies.

I switch on the TV and flick absent-mindedly through the channels. Typical. A fifty-two-inch plasma-screen telly, and there's nothing on. And just as I'm about to settle for something rubbish on CBBC, I come across an American chat show. The host is chatting to Tom Cruise. And sitting next to him on the sofa is someone who looks just like him.

And Tom Cruise is laughing, going, 'Oh my God, we could be twins,' and the audience are all cheering and whooping away like they always do, and the chat show woman's saying to this other Tom Cruise guy, 'You're the best lookalike I've ever seen – were you really not separated at birth?' and the audience start cheering again.

That's when it hits me.

The best lookalike I've ever seen. That's what she said.

I leap off the sofa like someone's lit a rocket under me. 'Linda, can I use your computer?' I shout through to the kitchen. I don't bother to wait for a reply – I bound up the stairs and burst into Linda's study, which is really the box room at the back, which in our house is my bedroom. And as I'm searching on lots of different websites, my mind's whirring: I've just found a way to get out of everything!

If I can't get the real Queen to come and watch the tattoo – *both* tattoos – that the whole town has invested so much in, and if I can't get the real Queen to sign the note that's going to send my dad

– and everyone else's mums and dads and cousins and friends – home, I'll get the next best thing.

Her spitting image.

Actually, it's not as easy as you'd think to get a lookalike. Every company I find on the web seems really keen to give you Michael Jackson or Simon Cowell, or Elton John – but no Queens.

It takes me aaaaaaaages to track down one that does the Queen, and I'll be honest, I'm not impressed. It's basically an old woman who looks like every other old woman I've ever seen. She's wearing a white gown, a blue sash that's all frayed round the edges, and a tiara that looks like it's made out of tin foil. She's also a bit squinty-eyed. Still, she's the only one I've found.

I click on the link that shows me the price, and I nearly fall off my chair in shock: £150 for the whole day, plus travel, plus expenses. I'm looking at nearly two hundred quid; actually, I'm looking at the floor, because by now I *have* fallen off the chair in shock.

Linda must have heard the thud. 'You all right up there, Billie?'

'Uh-huh,' I manage to reply, though I'm still feeling a little dizzy with it all.

'Dinner's ready,' Linda shouts. She's at the foot of the stairs, walking back and forth between the hall and the front room. Honestly, you'd think with her rituals she'd get rid of all the doors and make one big open-plan space.

I head downstairs with a sigh, because the genius idea that was going to solve all my problems is not going to work. There's no way I can afford two hundred quid – not even if I used the very, very last of my super-secret savings *and* sold all my books and toys and posters. I can't believe she's worth two hundred quid – she doesn't look any more like the Queen than my nan does. In fact, Nana May could probably do a better job than this woman, and she's going a bit senile and sleeps a lot.

That's it!

Not my senile, sleeping nan, obviously. But where else can I find an old woman?

I sit at the table and practically wolf down the pizza in one mouthful because I'm so eager to get to Hope Springs before they all go to bed. Or, worse, die.

CHAPTER TWENTY

Three days until the Tattoo

It's not until after school the next day that I can visit Hope Springs. Kirsty caught me as I was coming out of Linda's and wanted me home before she went out for the night, even though I made up a totally brilliant excuse about going round to Jade's.

There's a funny vibe at Hope Springs. It's, well . . . full of hope. The common room's empty, though the telly's blaring out as usual. I can't really say too much, though, because I watch an awful lot of telly when Kirsty and Mark are out and I've got no one to talk to. At least, I did before all this tattoo business started. I've been far too busy to keep up with what's going on in Albert Square.

I check my watch. Four-thirty.

I head into the dining room and practically have a heart attack – because there, in the seat at the far corner of the table, eating his beef stew and slurping his tea with the rest of them, is Mr Featherstone.

And he's talking to Olive, who's sitting next to him. No, more than that. He's laughing. Actually laughing with her.

'Well, this is a turn-up for the books,' I say.

Mr Featherstone beams at me. 'No,' he replies. 'That's me cutting off your trouser leg and putting it in the library.'

Oh God, I think. *He's finally cracked.* 'What?'

'A turn-up for the books,' he replies, and he and Olive descend into a fit of giggles. Even though I'm stressed, I can't help smiling. I'm so pleased that he's got a friend. Everyone should have a friend. Even if they do wear gloves, or only have one school uniform.

I peer into the faces of the old women seated around the table. There are three of them and, surprisingly, none of them have white hair. Olive's hair is auburn, so she's no good. One lady's hair is brunette, though there's a fine brown line running across her forehead, and it's pretty obvious the hair dye's run. The other lady's completely bald, so I guess she's my best hope.

'You ever thought of wearing a wig?' I ask.

The woman looks up at me in horror. 'How rude!' she cries.

'No, no, I didn't mean— I meant, could you, if you needed to?'

She thinks for a moment, then shakes her head. 'Too hot and itchy,' she says, and goes back to her tea.

So I try the old lady with the hair dye that's run, because at least she's used to putting unusual things in or on or near her head. But it turns out she's completely deaf and just smiles at me and waits because she thinks I'm going to put on some sort of show or something.

I let out a long sigh. Another brilliant idea foiled. I wander back round the table to Mr Featherstone. Olive's nudging him in the ribs, going, 'Don't be so daft, you're never too old.'

Mr Featherstone just shakes his head.

'It's only a plane ride away,' Olive's bleating on. 'Twenty-four hours, and you're in Oz.'

Mr Featherstone frowns. 'I said no,' he says. 'Just leave it. Please.'

'But they're your family,' Olive protests.

Mr Featherstone holds his breath. If I didn't know better, I'd say he was biting his tongue.

'I'll help you book the tickets,' Olive ploughs on. 'You could be there by—'

'I SAID LEAVE IT!'

Everyone stops what they're doing. Basil's spoon hovers in mid air. Cyril chokes on his tea. All eyes turn to Mr Featherstone.

Derek moves towards him. 'Come on, Mr F,' he soothes.

'Don't call me that!' Mr Featherstone thunders. He scrapes back his chair and struggles to his feet. Derek moves towards him again. 'I can get up on my own,' Mr Featherstone bellows. 'I don't need your help.'

Olive rolls her eyes. 'You can't even write a letter to your family with your arthritis,' she mutters under her breath, but I hear her.

Derek tucks his arms under Mr Featherstone's elbows. 'No man is an island,' he quotes, hoiking him to his feet. 'And why can't you accept that you *do* need help?'

Mr Featherstone glares over at me. 'Enjoying the show, are you?'

My face flushes and I turn to leave before he can shout at me again. But just then a thought pops into my head. 'Uh, Derek, can I just check everyone's practised their marching?'

Derek gives me this look – like he can't believe I'm asking at a time like this.

'What?' I shrug. 'We're on a tight deadline.' Derek's holds Mr Featherstone's arm and the pair of them head for the door. 'Derek?' I repeat.

'Stop bothering us, lass,' Mr Featherstone mumbles as he shuffles past me.

I clench my fists because he's making me angry again. 'You shouldn't be nasty to people who bother to come and visit,' I say.

Mr Featherstone looks me up and down. 'Don't give me that. You're only here because you want something. If it's not ripping us off with your cast-offs, it's because you want something from us for this tattoo of yours.' He carries on towards the door with Derek. 'Just leave us alone.'

'That's not true,' I blurt out before I can stop myself – or tell myself that, actually, he's right.

But Mr Featherstone's gone, so I head out of Hope Springs just as Queen-less as when I arrived, but feeling a lot more rotten about everything.

I'm still thinking how mean Mr Featherstone is when I let myself into my house. The faint strains of Mark's drum and bass drift down from his room.

There are more of Nana May's boxes in the porch. She's got more stuff than we realized. As I navigate my way past them into the front room, I hear a creak on the stairs. 'Kirsty?' I call. 'Mark?'

I head back into the hallway and peer up the stairs. Nana May's sitting halfway up in her blue nightie, her head in her hands. 'Nana May!' I yell. 'Are you all right?'

She looks up at me and her eyes are glistening.

'Why are you crying?' I bound up the stairs and take her by the shoulders. 'What's wrong?'

Nana May looks at me with a blank face. 'I can't remember,' she whispers. 'I came up here to do something and I can't remember.'

Her toothbrush is in her lap. 'Well,' I say gently, squatting down so our faces are level, 'let's look at the evidence, shall we?' And I take her toothbrush and hold it up to her. 'Were you going to brush your teeth?'

Nana May thinks for a second and then her eyes light up. 'That's it!' she cries. 'Oh, you're a clever girl.' She grabs my face and kisses my cheek. 'Such a good girl.'

I laugh and plonk myself down on the stairs next to her. I squish into her and lean my head on her shoulder. 'Well, you're a good nana,' I say.

Nana May snorts at that, but I don't tell her off for being disgusting, like I might with other old people. 'I used to be,' she says.

'What's that supposed to mean?' I ask.

She doesn't answer but gazes off into the distance. I can feel her heart beat. She's thinner than she used to be. Her arms are bonier.

Nana May suddenly looks sad. 'I'm sorry I don't

remember everything,' she says, her voice barely a whisper. 'It's so . . . *frustrating*.'

I take her hand and hold it in mine. I know she doesn't quite understand what's going on. 'You've still got your health,' I reply, which is what Dot says sometimes on *EastEnders*. Then she says a quote from the Bible, but I don't know any of those.

I help Nana May up and escort her downstairs to her washbasin. 'And you're still the best nana anyone could wish for,' I add. The best grandparent full stop, considering the alternatives.

CHAPTER TWENTY-ONE

Two days until the Tattoo

The Queen's coming the day after tomorrow, apparently. I can't think of any way to get out of it. To make things a million times worse, it's the final day of the summer term today, and all Sabrina Mitchell and everyone can talk about is who's going to win the three-legged race and play the Merchant Stanton Carnival King this year. It's doing my head in.

Andy Nelson's really quiet in class, though, and he doesn't join in with Sabrina and the others when she starts taunting me. He even tells her to shut up, but then just pretends it's because he's got a headache.

We finish school early, so Jake and Sarah and

Tamwar, and the marching band and some of the gymnasts, try to get some practice in before the rest of the group turn up. As it's only just gone one, we head for Battlefield Park, figuring we'll have it to ourselves.

We're wrong.

Craig and the Yorkshire Colliery Brass Band are marching up and down, and they look super smart in their red coats with brass buttons. They've got the most magnificent instruments. 'Cornets and soprano cornets,' Darren cries when he sees them. 'Flugelhorns *and* tenor horns.' He looks at his tuba forlornly. 'Euphoniums,' he squeaks.

They look brilliant, I'll give them that, and I get so carried away with how good they are, I think, *The Queen is going to love them*, before I remember that we haven't even got the Queen.

After a little while, as we're all staring at Craig's team with our mouths open in shock, the Yorkshire Colliery Brass Band march off to one side and take a break.

That's when the pirates come on.

Eight of them, all dressed like Jack Sparrow, all

ducking under each other's arms and clashing swords, putting on the most brilliant swashbuckling display we've ever seen. It's like a dance routine, it's so well rehearsed.

And just as they're finishing and the rest of my team look like they're going to have nervous breakdowns, we hear the roar.

'What the——?' Jake cries, and we all turn to see two nervous-looking men pushing a wooden box towards us, their faces red and strained. The box has an iron chain poking out of an air hole and CAUTION and THIS WAY UP written on it. Below that is BEWARE OF THE TIGER! Definitely *not* a magician's assistant, then.

'*Tiger?*' I cry.

Craig smirks as he walks over to the two men and shakes their hands. Beside me, I hear Jake gulp. 'Is anyone else scared?' he whispers.

'Of the tiger or Craig?' I ask. I march over because this is unbelievable. 'How did you get all this?' I demand, and then I step back a bit because I'm not being funny, but the wooden box doesn't look *that* strong.

Craig shrugs his shoulders. 'This has to be fit for the Queen,' he says, as if he's talking about booking some tin-pot band for one of his pub nights. 'Anything it takes . . .'

Another man approaches, and as Craig slaps him on the back, I recognize him as the official from the council. Typical. Don't people have principles? Then I remember that I can't really talk, seeing as I've lied to everyone about the Queen, so I just frown at Craig and head back towards my team. Except now it's not just my classmates. The Extreme Scrabble players and the Morris dancers have turned up too. 'How did you get here?' I ask as I wander over.

'I called them all at work,' Sarah replies, and she gestures to Craig's team. 'Figured we'd need the extra rehearsal.'

She's right, but clearly no one's in the mood because they're slumped on the floor, heads in hands, utterly dejected. 'Where are the old people?' Sarah whispers to me.

I shake my head at her, trying to forget about Mr Featherstone yelling at me. 'We'd better take them off the list.'

That just makes everyone even more devastated. 'How can we compete with *them*?' one of the gymnasts sobs, glaring at Craig.

'Come on, everyone,' I find myself saying, like I'm the blinking Prime Minister or something, trying to rally the troops for war. 'Don't feel so down. Ours is just as good.'

'They've got tigers,' Darren replies. 'And *flugelhorns*!'

'So?' I try and think of positive things to say and flap my hands in front of my face because I'm getting all bothered in this heat. Hot, bothered and stressed. 'We have ... a *junior* marching band, which the Queen will love, because she's got grandchildren!'

I lean forward, and I'm sure I can detect the trace of a smile on Darren's face. 'What else?' he says.

'Uh, well ... we've got Tamwar's *brilliant* family,' I say, and Tamwar beams at me. 'Seriously, all that "changing a light bulb, patting the dog" stuff – the Queen'll really dig it. She used to be in charge of India, right?' A few of the gymnasts nod at me, as if they're starting to believe what I'm saying.

But the funny thing is, *I'm* starting to believe

what I'm saying. As I stare at this motley crew before me, I realize how much trouble everyone's gone to, putting this whole show together, and my stomach flips over – I can't believe everyone's bought it so far. 'And the tradition of Morris dancing is dead old and historical, isn't it?' I say. 'So she'll love you.'

One of the Morris dancers starts blinking really hard, like he's got something stuck in his eye. 'Do you think . . . ?' he whispers.

'I *know*,' I reply.

Sarah smiles over at me like she thinks I'm doing a really good job rallying the troops. I smile right back at her, and brandish my megaphone. 'And we have the best organizer in the history of everything that's ever been organized,' I say, and Sarah looks confused. 'It's true,' I say, gesturing around at everyone. 'You've always got us all together.'

'I helped too,' Jake mumbles quietly.

'Yes, you did,' I reply. 'Jake helped too,' I repeat, a little louder so that everyone can hear. 'With, um . . .' I think for a second. What *exactly* has Jake done?

Jake pulls at his latex gloves nervously, and goes bright red when everyone turns to look at him. He lets out a little squeak and sort of shrinks into his clothes to avoid the stares. 'Flags,' he mumbles, and starts rooting round in his rucksack. 'I forgot to say.'

He pulls out a multi-pack of flags. 'Look . . .' he exclaims breathlessly. 'I've even got Chile . . .' He walks over to where Craig's lot are rehearsing, and places the Chilean flag firmly in the ground. After another couple of paces he takes out another flag – Belgium – and sticks that in the ground too.

Nobody says anything for a moment, and he blushes again. 'It's a s-silly idea,' he stutters, and he starts shoving the flags back into his rucksack.

Then one of the Morris dancers lets out a whoop. 'Give us Japan, if you've got it. My sister lives there.'

And with that, the whole team jump to their feet and follow his lead.

We race round the part of the track that Craig hasn't marked out for his tattoo, and plant all the flags Jake's brought with him. Germany, Scotland, Australia . . . There's even a flag for somewhere called Burundi, but I reckon that's made up.

'What are you doing?' Craig asks as we run around like madmen.

'Tattoos are traditionally multi-cultural affairs,' I say, echoing Jade's words from days earlier.

'Not round here, they're not,' Craig replies. He sticks his nose in the air like he thinks he's better than us, and goes back to the man from the council.

I'm so angry with him I want to shout at him and kick him on the shins. He looks so smug and really he's just being nasty about Tamwar's family.

But just as I'm about to march over and wave a flag right in his face, with the most brilliant timing, we hear the sound of a trumpet. Not Darren on his tuba, or one of the Yorkshire Colliery Brass Band playing his bugle. It's a trumpeting sound coming from outside the park. It sounds like an animal. Like an—

'ELEPHANT!' Jake cries. 'ELEPHANT!'

Everyone turns to see Tamwar's uncle leading an elephant into the park, accompanied by twelve members of his family.

'What on earth . . . ?' I say, and Tamwar grins at me.

'Anything they can do . . .' he says, and jerks a thumb over to Craig. The members of the other tattoo are staring open-mouthed at us. There's a snarl from the wooden box.

'It's brilliant!' I say. 'But where did you get it from? And what are we going to do with it?'

'I have a friend who works at the zoo,' Tamwar's uncle replies, and I notice that Craig and the man from the council look really cross, as if no one else is allowed to be friends with this zoo man, who obviously has no problem renting out tigers and elephants to all and sundry. 'I thought I might ride in on it, before the dancing.'

Everyone in our tattoo rallies round and starts patting the elephant, and chatting away excitedly. The Extreme Scrabble players are stroking the elephant's trunk and jabbering away about triple word scores. Two gymnasts are trying to give another girl a leg-up onto its back, and three flautists from the marching band are staring up the elephant's bum.

'A-maz-ing!' one of the Morris dancers cries. 'This is superb!' Everyone beams at me, like I'm responsible for the elephant, or something.

And I beam right back at them. Though actually it makes me sad: all this will to go to waste, and when they find out that the Queen's not really coming, they're going to hate me, and Tamwar and his family will probably get the elephant to trample on my head.

'Is everything all right?' Sarah whispers, catching the worried look on my face.

I take a deep breath. 'Uh-huh,' I reply. 'Everything's . . . great.'

More lies. I quickly put my hand to my nose to check it hasn't grown.

And just as I'm saying 'Everything's great,' there's another squeal from the end of the park. I'm not sure I can cope with any more elephants or tigers or flugelhorns, but it's none of those anyway.

It's Kirsty.

She's walking across the park with a look of shock on her face as she takes in all the pirates and instruments and animals and window cleaners. Then she spots me in the middle of it all.

'Billie?'

I try to melt into the crowd of people admiring the elephant, but it's too late – she's clearly seen me. 'What's going on?'

I gulp. 'Well—' I start, but Kirsty just holds up her hand to silence me. Honestly, what's the point of asking someone something if you don't listen to what they have to say?

'I know all about it,' she says, and I stare at her, because I thought I'd hidden everything from her. 'The letter to a Mr Featherstone about the military tattoo was the give-away,' she carries on. 'At first I had no clue what it was on about, so I threw it in the bin. But then I started noticing that you were being all shifty . . .' She narrows her eyes at me. 'Shiftier than usual, that is – and I knew you were up to something. So I made a few enquiries, phoned a few people, followed a few leads – and here you are.' She gestures around the place. 'Sherlock Holmes has got nothing on me.'

I raise my eyebrow. 'Dad told you on the phone the other night, didn't he?'

Kirsty looks put out for a minute, but then nods. 'Yep, your dad told me.' She laughs. 'You know me, Bill. I was never going to make the police force.'

She looks like she's genuinely not angry, but I still hesitate. 'You're not mad at me?' I ask. 'You know . . .'cos I'm meant to be grounded.'

She frowns at me for a second, but then breaks into a massive grin. 'Look at all this, Bill,' she says, staring around at everything. 'This is amazing. And you did it! *You!*' She takes me by the shoulders and gives me a big hug. 'My brilliant little niece.'

Kirsty leans in to whisper to me, 'And who's he?'

I follow her gaze to one of the Morris dancers and roll my eyes. 'You've got to be kidding!' I laugh.

And Kirsty laughs with me, and it's all brilliant, all happy families, and I forget for a minute that it's all bound to end in disaster and/or being trampled by an elephant. Which is a *complete* disaster if you're the one being trampled.

'I happen to have brilliant news of my own, though,' Kirsty says, grinning wildly. 'It's about your dad.'

My heart starts pounding then. Not in a bad way. I know he's not dead, because that's obviously not brilliant news. 'Is he coming home?' I ask, and my voice sounds all small. I can hardly bear to think that it might be true, let alone say it. It would be brilliant if Dad was safe and well and not blown up and able to win the carnival race; and it would mean that I could get out of all this Queen business.

'No,' Kirsty replies. Oh. Back to square one. 'He's not coming home, but he'll be watching your tattoo!'

'What?'

'The army have allowed him and all his regiment to watch your tattoo live, via the magic of the Internet. Or, more specifically, Skype.' Kirsty beams at me. 'Isn't that brilliant? Your dad will get to see how fantastic all this is, and how hard you've worked, and just how amazing you are.'

I nod. 'Uh-huh,' I say, trying to sound pleased, but inside I'm dying.

Kirsty gives me one last hug. 'I'll see you a bit later,' she says. She practically dances her way out of the park. Just before she gets to the gates, she turns and cups her hand to her mouth. 'Your dad's going to watch you meet the Queen!' she shouts, and everyone looks at her.

It slowly starts to sink in. Dad and all his mates and the whole British Armed Forces are going to watch me and this little band of heroes I've assembled – with their bells and whistles and flags and latex gloves and megaphones and Bollywood dance routines and knee-high socks and triple-word scores and roly-polys, which is only the half of it. Because the *real* event, the thing everyone's excited about, is meeting the Queen. MEETING THE QUEEN!!!!

I look at everyone, and I think how disappointed my dad would be if he found out I'd made every-thing up.

There's nothing for it. I've got to find two hundred quid.

CHAPTER TWENTY-TWO

Finding the money has to wait a little while because this afternoon is moving day for Nana May. I head for Hope Springs with a heavy heart. I'm worried about how I'm going to get two hundred quid, and how Nana May's not going to be living with us any more, and how I've not been back here since Mr Featherstone was mean to me. Why does everything bad always happen at once? *It never rains but it pours*, Nana May always says. I wish it would – everyone's fed up with this heat wave.

Mark's already there. He's carrying loads of Nana May's cardboard boxes down the corridor. 'Where've you been?' he says, immediately bossing me about like he always does. 'We all have to muck in, you know.'

I sigh at how mardy he's being and follow him to Nana May's new room. Room G. Well, that's just tickety-boo, isn't it? Nana May's going to be neighbours with Mr Featherstone.

Kirsty and Nana May are sitting on the bed holding hands. They both look a bit teary. 'All right, Bill?' Kirsty says as I come in.

Mark stacks the cardboard boxes along one side of the wall, then wipes his forehead with his hand. 'Thirsty work, this,' he grumbles. 'Billie, go see if you can get us a brew.' He leaves to get more boxes. Honestly, what is it with this place and tea?

'Ooh yeah, a brew would be nice,' Kirsty pipes up, blowing into a tissue.

'It doesn't matter how bad life gets,' Nana May states, 'things always look a little better after a cup of tea.'

Kirsty gives me a little smile, like we both know how sad this is. She pats Nana May's hand, then gets up and starts to unpack the cardboard boxes. She holds up a green velvet dress. 'Look at this,' she laughs. 'It's practically vintage.'

Nana May smiles over at her. 'Got it in the

swinging sixties,' she says. 'Gosh, they were the days. Wild.'

'Nana!' I exclaim. It's funny thinking of Nana May having wild days. Or any days, really, where she's not sleeping or shuffling around in her nightie.

Kirsty looks at it. 'It's just my colour. What do you think, Bill?' She holds the dress against her body and starts waltzing around the room like she's at an old-fashioned tea dance. 'Come on, Mum,' she laughs.

Nana May stands up, grabs Kirsty's arms and dances with her. I start giggling, and prance around the room behind them. I'm glad that Nana May seems to be fine with moving in here. Even if I'm not.

Mark comes back with more boxes and plonks them down. 'Dance with me, Mark,' Kirsty says, but he rolls his eyes.

'I never, ever dance in public,' he insists. 'Ever.' Then he turns to me. 'Seriously, Billie,' he mutters, 'go fetch me a brew. Stop mucking about.'

So I stop prancing around the room and head out into the corridor. 'Do you want to come with me, Nana?' I ask. 'I'll take you to the common room.'

There's no one there apart from Cyril. The best armchair's by the window, so I get Nana May settled and plump up the cushions for her. 'They've got a telly in here,' I say, 'but they don't normally have black-and-white movies, I'm afraid.'

'Ooh, I like those,' Cyril perks up from the other side of the room. Nana May eyes him warily.

'This is Cyril,' I tell her, and turn to him. 'This is my Nana May.'

Cyril leans on his IV drip pole and stands up. He slowly shuffles over to us. 'May I?' he asks, pointing to the next armchair. 'May?' He laughs.

Nana May hesitates, then laughs with him. I don't want her to be lonely in here, or to turn into a grump like Mr Featherstone, so I help Cyril into the armchair.

'It's nice to make a friend, isn't it?' I say to Nana. 'I'll bring *Singin' in the Rain* with me next time, and you can watch it together.'

And before I know it, they both launch into the chorus, cackling away like they've known each other for years. I'm pleased she's happy. I think she's going to be OK.

★

Time's ticking on, and I've not even started to find the two hundred quid yet. After I've made tea for everyone, I grab my bag and wait for Kirsty and Mark on the front steps. Nana May and Cyril have come out to see us off. Nana May smiles at me. 'Come back soon.'

'Of course.' I beam back at her, then lean over and give her a great big hug. 'I'll come and visit every single day.'

It's sad Nana May won't be living with us any more, but I guess I'm here most days anyway, what with the tattoo, so it's not like I'll never see her again. I look up at the sky. It's clear blue with no clouds, but I point anyway. 'Look, a baked potato.'

Nana squints her eyes. As we're looking up, I catch Mr Featherstone staring out his window. I frown at him till he turns away.

'Must be lovely,' Cyril says in a shaky voice, 'to have grandchildren. I've not got any.' He looks at his feet. 'Actually, I've not got any family,' he whispers. Well, that blinking near breaks my heart. Imagine not having anyone come and visit you. Imagine no family nearby to see you. Except I don't have to imagine too hard – I hardly see my family as it is and we all live in the same house.

'Well, I'll come and visit *you* every day too,' I say to Cyril simply.

His face breaks into a grin. 'Are – are you sure?' he stutters, like I've just told him I'm giving him my winning lottery ticket.

'Course,' I say. 'I'm not only here 'cos I want something, you know.'

I smile pointedly up at Mr Featherstone, but before he can say anything, Mark and Kirsty head down the steps.

'We're off, Nan,' Mark says, and bends down to give her a peck on the cheek.

Kirsty's eyes are all red again. She wraps Nana May in a big hug. 'Bye, Mum,' she whispers, stroking her hair. 'I'll see you tomorrow.' She rubs her nose and sniffs. 'Right, then . . .' She looks at me and smiles. I can see it's not a real smile, but I know she's trying.

'What's for tea?' I ask Kirsty because my stomach's started to rumble.

She shrugs. 'Whatever you want. I'm off out tonight, so Mark can order a takeaway for the both of you.'

Mark looks confused. 'What? I can't.'

'It's takeaway, Mark,' Kirsty laughs. 'You just pick up the phone and give them your order and they come and deliver it. It's pretty simple.' She rolls her eyes at me and I laugh.

'No,' Mark says, frowning. 'I mean, I'm working tonight. I did say.'

Kirsty thinks for a minute. 'Can't you cancel? Someone needs to look after Billie.'

'Can't *you*?' Mark retorts.

Neither of them says anything for a moment. 'I'll be all right,' I pipe up. 'I can look after myself.'

Mark shakes his head at me. 'Don't be silly.' He looks stressed. 'I need this overtime,' he mutters to Kirsty.

'Well, I need a night out,' Kirsty tells him. 'With everything that's going on, I think I deserve it, don't you?'

Well, there's nothing like being made to feel wanted. I check my watch again. I really need to get on with finding this money. 'I can go round to Linda's,' I suggest.

Mark and Kirsty both look relieved. 'Good plan, Stan,' Kirsty says. 'Come on, then.'

I give Nana May a peck on the cheek and then, because he's looking a bit sad, I give Cyril one too. He beams at me like it's made his day. I glance up at Mr Featherstone, but this time he's staring at me with a funny look on his face.

Giving a final wave to Nana May, Mark, Kirsty and me all head out of Hope Springs and go off in our separate directions.

It's only when you're frantically running around your room looking for stuff to sell that you realize how much junk you accumulate in your life. Or eleven years, in my case.

I've got old dolls and toys and games I've not touched in about a million years, and posters of boy bands I don't even listen to any more. There are CDs and books and crayons and old shoes, and I gather them all up into a big cardboard box Nana May had left over from packing. There's not enough time to sell everything on eBay – I need the money for the lookalike immediately.

So I embark upon a little entrepreneurial venture I once saw on *Newsround*. At the bottom of our driveway I set up the wallpaper pasting table I found under Dad's bed and cover it with one of our tablecloths. I pin up a sign:

EVERYTHING MUST GO!
BARGAINS TO BE HAD!
FOR ONE DAY ONLY!

Then I sit back on a plastic garden chair, switch on my little battery-powered fan to cool my face, and wait for the hordes of excited buyers.

Half an hour goes by with not so much as a sniff of custom. A few cars have passed, but no one's bothered to stop. I look up and down the street. It's just off a main road, so there are normally people coming and going, but I can only see Mr Clewson putting out his bins, and three younger girls from my school skipping in their front garden.

After another ten minutes a woman wanders up

to me and peers at everything on my table. 'This for charity, is it?' she sniffs.

'Yes,' I reply, without hesitation. Technically it is. Not that the Armed Forces are a charity, but if I don't find the Queen, the whole town will go mad and start punching each other. Not to mention punch me. 'Anti-violence,' I say.

'Right.' The woman rummages through the pile of books I've laid out. 'How much for these?'

'One pound each, or three for a pound,' I say, trying to remember what they say on the market stalls in *EastEnders*. The woman raises her eyebrows in surprise. 'No, wait . . .' I stumble. Maths has never been my strong point. 'Three for two pounds. That's it.'

The woman rummages in her handbag and takes a two-pound coin out of her purse. 'Got any brollies?' she asks.

I shake my head. 'We're in the middle of a drought.'

She looks up at the sky. 'Happen there's a chance of rain,' she replies. 'It'll be a miracle if there is.' She smiles at me and hands me the two-pound coin, then takes the three books she's chosen. 'There you are. Good luck.'

I beam as I put the money in an empty coffee jar I found in the kitchen. 'Two pounds down,' I say to myself as the woman scurries off, still looking at the clear blue sky. 'One hundred and ninety-eight to go.'

An hour later – a whole hour later – there's *still* one hundred and ninety-eight pounds to go. I've had no more takers. Nothing. The girls skipping in their front garden weren't interested in buying another skipping rope, or shoes, and one of them threatened to tell her mum when I wouldn't stop going on at them about my Tracy Beaker books. Seventeen cars passed. I counted. One black, six green, two white, five blue, one silver and two red, and not one of them stopped.

I check my watch. Eight thirteen. I rub my arms because it's getting a bit nippy now.

A blue car turns the corner and inches along the road towards me. After a moment it pulls over and the woman in the passenger seat rolls down the window. 'Do you know where Laurel Avenue is?' she asks.

I'm about to reply, but then I have a totally genius idea. 'I do,' I say, and she smiles at me. 'But it'll cost you.'

'What?'

'Give us a fiver, and I'll point you in the right direction.' I beam back. 'Take it or leave it.'

The woman shakes her head and rolls up the window. After a moment the car reverses back down the road, obviously deciding to take the 'leave it' option. Another potential customer lost. I frown as I picture Alan Sugar shaking his head at me. 'Never give them a "leave it" option,' he's saying.

Eight forty-one. I count on my fingers the number of hours I've got until the Queen's meant to be coming to Merchant Stanton. The tattoo's starting at 10 a.m. on the nineteenth, which gives me thirty-seven hours. Thirty-seven hours to come up with the Queen; to find two hundred quid to pay the look-alike to prevent an elephant trampling me to death.

And I know in my heart that it's never going to happen.

I let out a big sigh and rub my face; my eyes feel all hot and I know, I just *know* that any second now they're going to fill with tears.

The sound of a car door slamming forces me to look up.

'Billie?' Linda clicks the alarm on her car and steps over the drive to me. 'What's all this?'

I shrug my shoulders. 'Just trying to get rid of old junk, that's all,' I say. I can't tell her what I need money for. Not now I know how chummy she and Dad are. She'd probably be straight on the phone to him. 'How come you've gone out?'

Linda motions to her handbag. 'Jill called to say my prescription was ready, but she was too busy at the chemist's to drop it round. Took me two hours there and back.' She picks up one of my stuffed teddies. 'I bought you this,' she says softly. 'For your eighth birthday.'

I look at her in surprise. 'How do you remember that?'

She gives me a little smile. 'I remember most things about you, Billie Templar,' she says. 'You're the only child I buy things for.'

She looks a bit misty at that and gazes off into the road, and I wonder if she's looking for passing trade, like me.

I realize what I've just said. 'I didn't mean old junk,' I add hastily. 'I really like this teddy, but it's good to de-clutter every now and then' – which is something they always say on those makeover shows.

Linda laughs. 'You're not wrong,' she replies. 'Go on, then. How much?'

'For the teddy?'

Linda nods. 'Sentimental, I know, but there you go.'

I bite my lip because I really want to say, *That'll be one hundred and ninety-eight pounds, please*, but I don't reckon Linda will go for it.

'I'll give you a fiver for it,' she says after a moment. 'What?' she asks, catching the look of disappointment on my face. 'Not enough?'

She fishes in her handbag for her purse. 'I've got a tenner, but that's my final offer. You'll do me out of house and home.'

I force a smile as I take the money from her.

'Thanks,' I say, and my voice seems to catch, because I'm thinking, *Twelve pounds is nowhere near enough to hire the lookalike.*

Then I get another totally genius idea in my head — I can't believe I've not thought of it before, especially when Linda's standing right in front of me.

I grab my rucksack from underneath the table and pull out the little flowery purse Dad bought me one birthday. There are seven one-p pieces inside. I take a moment to look at them and then fish one out. 'Look!' I say, holding up the penny to Linda.

She takes it from me and studies it carefully. 'What am I looking at?' she asks.

I wonder if she's having an extra-funny funny turn that makes her forget what she does for a living. 'You sell old coins,' I say.

'This is from nineteen eighty-six,' she says.

'Exactly,' I reply. 'It's the oldest one I've got. It's practically as old as Kirsty.'

Linda hands the penny back to me. 'Thanks, Billie, but it's a little different to what I normally work with.'

'It's all money, isn't it?' I reply, trying not to let the desperation creep into my voice.

Linda looks me over. 'What's this really all about?' she asks.

I'm torn. If I tell her the truth, she could help me get enough money to hire the lookalike – then I can get Dad sent home, and I'm sure she'd like that. Especially if she's as close to Dad as I'm starting to think she is. But if she *is* that close, then she's bound to tell him. Linda's always saying it's never good to keep secrets, so she'll tell Dad and he'll realize what a liar I really am.

So I put the penny back in my purse. 'Just kidding,' I say, and I force a laugh.

'It's getting late, Billie,' Linda says after a moment. 'Time to pack up, hey? Is Mark in?'

I nod even though he's not, because I want to be alone to think. I'm going to have to do some *serious* thinking about how to get out of all this.

Linda gives me a little smile and heads off up her driveway. Then, just as I'm starting to pack up all the books and toys and posters into the cardboard box, she gives a groan and unlocks her car. 'I left my phone at the chemist's. I'll have to go back,' she says, and she climbs into the driver's seat. She sits there for a little while, and through the windscreen I can see she's talking to herself. She taps herself on the head as if she can't believe she'd do such a stupid thing, but she does it over and over again.

I put the tablecloth on top of the cardboard box and fold up the wallpaper pasting table. I drag that and the plastic seat round into the garden and, with the box in my arms, head back to my front door.

Linda's car is still in the drive; she's still sitting there, tapping her head. After a minute she catches me looking at her and gives a sigh. She seems to brace herself, then switches on the engine.

I'm glad I didn't tell her the truth. Knowing she'll have to go to Jill's flat above the chemist and do her rituals with the doors all over again, which will probably take her another two hours there and back — for a moment I forget about *my* troubles.

But only for a moment.

As Linda's car pulls away, I rummage in my rucksack for my front door key.

It isn't there.

265

I take everything out – my pencil case, my purse, my library book, my notepad, my bagpiper pen, and the empty shoe box I use as a lunch box because that's what Dad's rations come in.

The key's not there.

I lift up the letter box and peer into the hall. There's my key – on the hall table, next to the phone. I left it there as I was struggling to get the wallpaper pasting table out of the door. Fat lot of good that did me.

Twelve pounds, that's all I've got. Well, twelve pounds and seven pence, if you count the stupid, worthless old pennies in my purse.

I don't know how long Kirsty will be on her night out; Mark's still doing as much overtime as he can so he can get a flat; and the only person with a spare key has just driven off and won't be back for hours because she's got OCD.

I slump down on the doorstep and pull my socks up as far as they go, but my legs are still freezing. It's proper cold now, not just nippy. I look up at the sky. Thick, dark clouds go scudding by. It's the same sky all over the world. Maybe there's the same dark clouds where Dad is. Maybe he's looking up at them this very minute too.

All of a sudden my eyes fill with tears. I try to tell myself that it's just the cold, that it's because I've been sitting out here for hours. But it's not true. It's because I've failed. I couldn't get the real Queen because she's too busy, and I can't get a lookalike because I haven't got enough money. And I'm crying now, properly crying, because we'll probably have to leave town: everyone will come at me with pitchforks and burning candles, like they do in the movies, and Dad will still be out there, trying not to get blown up.

My face is hot and red from all the crying, but just then I feel something else on it. It's cold and wet and sploshes onto my face.

A raindrop.

I look up and see more drops falling from the sky. It's fine rain at first, just a shower, and it patters all around me, forming little puddles on the pavement. I close my eyes and feel it on my face. It's cool and refreshing.

'It's raining!' a voice shouts at the end of the street.

It's Mr Clewson, examining the now-hydrated flowers in his front garden. 'Just in time for the flower competition at the carnival! It's a miracle!' He yanks a tarpaulin over the tank to stop it rusting and runs inside.

There's that word again. Miracle. I bite my lip. Miracles never happen. Not like they do in the movies. Mark once rented a DVD called *Miracles*, where Jackie Chan beats up all the bad guys and doesn't get shot once – which *is* a miracle, given how many people are shooting at him. In *Miracle on 34th Street*, which I watch every Christmas, Santa Claus exists. I frown and vow never to watch Christmas films again. They're all lies. However far away someone is, they can always get home for Christmas. Even if it's snowing or their planes and trains and automobiles don't work, or their legs have been blown off, they still make it home in time to be with their loved ones.

But miracles don't happen in real life. If they did, Dad would come home. All by himself, not because I've got the Queen to write a note to excuse him. And if Dad came home, we'd take part in the three-legged race and win, and he would take his rightful place as the Merchant Stanton Carnival King.

And while I'm thinking about it, if miracles really did happen, Kirsty would make a decent tea for once – from scratch, all by herself, with no help from Mr Yeung at the local Chinese. And Nana May wouldn't be so confused, and we'd sing and watch old black-and-white movies all day long. And Mr Law would stop yelling at me every day, and Mrs Hussein wouldn't keep calling me a 'problem child'.

And Mum would come back. *That* would be a miracle.

I think of all the rotten things that have happened in the last few weeks, and the more I think about it, the more I reckon I'm due a miracle.

'Come on, then,' I shout, looking up into the sky as the rain falls more heavily. 'Where's *my* miracle, hey?' I don't even know who I'm shouting to, or at, but I can't stop. 'It's not Christmas,' I yell, getting to my feet, and pointing at the sky. There's a heavy rumble of thunder and the clouds thicken. My school shirt is sticking to me. 'But I still want my miracle. Where's my miracle – hey?' I can feel myself getting all hot and flustered because I'm all Shouting In The Rain. It's definitely not a glorious feeling. 'Where's my blinking miracle!'

I wait for a few moments. There's nothing. Silence. The rain continues to fall thick and fast, and my teeth chatter with cold.

I slump down on the doorstep again and draw my knees up to my chin. I huddle as far under the overhang of the front door as I can, but I'm practically wet through now. I wrap my arms round my knees and give myself a hug because there's no one else here to do that. I miss Dad. I miss Mum too, and I'm fed up with not being allowed to say that for fear of upsetting everyone. And the more I think about it, the more I just want to get the heck out of Merchant Stanton. What's the point in hanging around waiting for the town to kill me? Maybe £12.07 would be enough. A one-way coach ticket to Hull, that's all I'd need. Maybe I could hitch-hike. The tears run down my cheek, and the falling raindrops mingle with them and run into my mouth. I don't want to hitch-hike.

'Where's – my – miracle?' I say in between sobs,

and I slump my head down onto my knees. Cold. Wet. Miserable.

Alone.

'Billie?'

Through my tears, I look up to see Mark towering over me. He's got flecks of paint on his forehead and hands. He looks from me to the cardboard box with all my stuff in.

'What are you doing out here?'

The rain's still falling but it's a bit lighter now. I look past Mark and watch it run off the tarpaulin on Mr Clewson's tank.

I wipe my face with the back of my hand. I'm trying to think of something to say to Mark to explain why I'm sitting in the rain with all my worldly possessions, and not at Linda's, but I'm too tired. I'm too tired to lie any more.

I don't say anything.

Mark takes his key from his pocket and opens the front door. He bends down and picks up my cardboard box and motions for me to go inside. 'Why don't I put the kettle on and you can tell me everything,' he says softly.

CHAPTER TWENTY-THREE

Mark comes into the sitting room with two steaming hot mugs of tea. As soon as we've finished this little 'chat', I think, I'm off.

I curl my legs underneath me as I sit at one end of the sofa. Mark passes me the mug with the handle towards me so I won't burn my hand. He flops down on the sofa next to me.

Neither of us says anything for a while. We stare at our mugs and watch the steam rise from them. Mark starts to blow on his to cool it down. 'Go away, Susie Smoke,' he says, and he smiles at me.

I look at him in surprise. That's what we used to say when we were younger and our food was piping hot. We'd blow on it to cool it down so we

could start shoving it in our mouths. I thought he'd
forgotten about that.

'Go away, Susie Smoke,' I repeat, and I blow on
my mug extra hard. So hard, in fact, a little bit of
spit comes out and lands in the tea. Mark throws his
head back and starts laughing, and after a moment I
join in. It feels good, just the two of us sitting there,
laughing.

Then I remember that I haven't got time to
laugh. I've got to leave Merchant Stanton before
all my lies about the Queen come out. 'Thanks for
the brew,' I say, and I stand up, 'but I've really got to
get going.'

'Where?' Mark raises his eyebrows. 'What are you
up to?'

I feel a bit sad then. I'm running off to Hull but
I don't reckon Mark will miss me that much. He's
got enough going on in his own life. 'Just places
to go, people to see, that's all.' I move away from
the sofa.

'Bill,' Mark says, putting a hand on my arm to stop
me. 'Sit down, will you? I want to talk to you.'

I hesitate. We don't really *do* talking in our family.

'Come on, Billie,' he says. 'Just give me five minutes.'

I shrug my shoulders and sit down again. All my worldly possessions are in the cardboard box already, so I've only got to shove the necessities into my rucksack and possibly change my shirt. I can spare a few minutes.

Mark stares at his tea again, and I can almost see his brain whirring, as if he's thinking of things to say to me. 'Tell me about school,' he says after a moment. 'Everything all right there?'

I nod. 'School's finished for the holidays,' I reply.

Mark nods with me, like he knew this already but just forgot. 'What about your mates? How are they?'

I shrug again. 'All right,' I say. Not that I have many friends. Not real ones, anyway. Sarah and Jake and Tamwar are only friendly with me because they think the Queen's coming. After they find out she's not, they'll probably be at the front of the lynch mob, riding in on the elephant that's going to trample me. I can make new friends, I think. In Hull.

'Do you know something?' Mark asks. 'I don't think I've ever met any of your friends.'

I bite my lip. 'You've been busy,' I reply. '*I've* been busy.'

Mark studies my face for a moment, and I start to blush because I'm worried he's going to realize what I'm up to – not just the tattoo, but the whole running-away thing. 'Busy selling all your toys?' he asks.

I nod. 'I'm trying to de-clutter.'

'Which is another way of saying you need money.' Mark frowns. 'Am I right?'

I nod again before I know what I'm doing.

'For what?' he asks.

I let out a big sigh. 'Presents.' I didn't even have to think very hard for that lie. My running away is sort of like a present to Mark and Kirsty: I know how much of a hassle I am for them to look after.

'For who? Us?' Mark asks. 'You don't have to get me or Kirsty or Nan anything. And you know Dad can't have a lot of stuff sent out to him.'

'Yeah, I know. It's not that.'

'Then what is it?'

I don't say anything for a while, and then it's Mark's turn to sigh. He lets out a big puff of air and narrows his eyes at me. 'Just tell me, Billie.' He sounds like he's really tired and starting to get annoyed with me. 'What do you need money for?'

'I just do,' I reply. 'It doesn't matter.'

'It matters when my little sister's sat in the rain trying to get rid of all the stuff we've bought her over the years.'

I shrug my shoulders. Mark sighs again. I know he's getting really cross: he looks all stern like he always does when he's telling me off. 'Billie . . .' he says through gritted teeth. 'Just. Tell. Me.'

I shake my head. 'You can't tell me what to do,' I say. 'You're not Dad.'

'Dad's not here,' Mark snaps at me.

'I know!' I shout back. 'That's why I'm going to Hull.'

I've blurted it out before I could stop myself. I clap one hand over my mouth to try and shove the words back in, but it's too late. Mark sinks back into the sofa and looks at me in confusion.

'Hull? What could you possibly want to go to Hull for?'

I roll my eyes at him. 'Don't pretend you don't

know,' I say. 'You know as well as I do that she's there.'

'Who?'

I hesitate before I say it, but I've come this far. 'Mum,' I whisper.

Now Mark's really surprised. Maybe it's because I've not said the M-word in for ever. None of us have.

'What are you talking about?' he asks.

I sink back into the sofa. I'm wondering if maybe he has some sort of brain injury that's made him forget. Fallen off his ladder again, like. 'I'm going to the station to get a coach to Hull. I should be there in no time.'

Mark looks at me intently. 'Mum's not in Hull,' he says.

It takes a few seconds for his words to sink in. 'You're just saying that so I won't go,' I say. There's no other reason for it.

Mark shakes his head. 'What makes you think she's there?'

'Dad said,' I reply, not looking at him. I stare at the mugs on the coffee table. The tea'll be cold by now. 'And you did.'

'What?' Mark's flabbergasted. 'I never said that.'

'You did,' I reply. 'I heard you. Ages ago. When I was little.' My teeth chatter and I wrap my arms around myself. 'I was sitting on the landing of our old house, and you and Dad were in the front room, shouting. Not long after Mum left. You asked Dad where she was, so you wanted to know too.'

Mark looks like he's racking his brains to remember. 'And what did Dad say, exactly?'

I gulp, because out of nowhere, I feel a lump in my throat. 'You said, *Just tell me, Dad, where is she?* and after a bit of huffing and puffing, Dad said, *She can go to Hull for all I care.*' I look Mark in the eye. 'That's what Dad said.'

Mark rubs his hands over his face. 'Oh, Billie . . .' he murmurs.

'So I'm going to Hull to find her,' I say. 'I've looked it up on the map and everything. It's fifty-one miles.'

Mark hesitates, but then reaches out his hand and places it gently on my shoulder.

I shrug it off. 'You won't notice I'm gone, after a while,' I say. 'You're moving out anyway, so you can forget all about me. You'll be glad.'

'That's not fair,' Mark protests.

'You're always telling me off.'

He bites his lip and I wait for him to get all angry again, but instead he nods. 'I know,' he replies. 'I thought I was helping.' He looks genuinely sad. 'But you can't go, Bill.'

Well, that's unexpected. The lump in my throat gets bigger. I swallow hard. It doesn't stop my eyes getting all teary, though. 'Kirsty's always off clubbing or going on dates,' I say slowly. 'She'll get married. Soon, I reckon. And Nana May's gone to Hope Springs, and you'll move out into a flat with your mates.' I bite my lip. 'And it doesn't matter if they're starting to bring the troops home – soldiers are still getting shot and Dad will probably get blown up, and even if he survives, he may not have any legs, so he won't be in the race, and he'll never be carnival king again, and I'll be left all on my own anyway.' I let out a big puff of air. 'So I may as well go and find Mum before I've got no one else.'

Mark doesn't say anything.

'And even though she doesn't want me, even

though she left us – it's probably because I did something wrong when I was a baby, like not having black hair and blue eyes,' I say – and I'm fighting back the tears now – 'I've got to try and find her before it's too late.'

Neither of us says anything. I look up at Mark; I'm surprised because he's got tears in his eyes too. I've never seen him cry. Not even when he fell off the ladder and had to have stitches in his head.

'Oh, Billie,' he says again and he wipes his eyes with the palm of his hand. 'I had no idea.'

I start to get up again. As sad as it is to see my elder brother crying, I'd best get going before the coach station closes.

But Mark holds me back. 'Mum's not in Hull,' he says softly. 'It was just an expression Dad used because he was angry. We don't know where she is.'

I frown at him.

'I've tried tracking her down,' he continues, 'but no one's got a clue where she lives now. I'm sorry, Billie. Mum's not coming back.'

My bottom lip goes all trembly.

'But it doesn't matter,' Mark ploughs on, 'because

Kirsty and me, we're not going to leave you all by yourself. And Dad'll be back before you know it.'

'In a coffin,' I mutter, 'most likely.'

Mark takes a deep breath. 'I'm just as scared as you,' he says quietly. 'About Dad being on the front line. I read the papers too.'

I look at him in shock. Mark, scared? He's never scared of anything. Not even spiders or football refs or having his head sewn up. He gives my shoulder a squeeze. 'I thought I had to be the man of the house as Dad's not here,' he says. 'That's why I keep telling you off. I was trying to be Dad. I got it wrong, and for that I'm sorry.'

Then he reaches out and folds his arms around me, and instead of struggling, I let him. It feels nice to have a hug – I've not had one in a while. And I think, *I may as well make the most of it because I don't know when I'm going to get another one* – it's not like you can go around buying them. I put my head on his chest and it moves up and down as he breathes in and out. We just sit there quietly for a few moments. Nothing else in the world but Mark and me.

'I miss Mum too,' Mark says after a while. 'I should

have known how you were feeling and been more supportive. I'm sorry, Bill.' He clasps his arm tighter round me. 'Dad's going to be fine' – his voice is steady – 'but you've got me for now.'

'Do you mean that?' I ask.

Mark nods, and kisses the top of my head. I really want to believe him. I'm tired now, and it's still raining, and I bet it would be dead cold hanging around the coach station anyway. I could stay, just for a few days, and see if he keeps his word, like.

But if I can't run off to Hull, then I have to face the music – flugelhorns and trumpeting elephants and everything.

I sit up because I've just had a thought. 'If I promise to pay you back,' I say, 'could you lend me some money?'

Mark narrows his eyes at me, trying to work out what I mean. 'I've told you, she's not in Hull,' he replies after a moment.

I shake my head. 'It's not for that. It's . . .' I hesitate because I don't want to lie any more. I'm fed up with lying, especially since Mark's been so nice to me.

But I need help – just with this one last lie. I've

got to get the lookalike to fool everyone for half an hour or so, then we can work on Dad coming home. I know Mark said Dad would be all right, but I don't want to wait another day. 'I can't say *exactly* why I need it,' I say softly, 'but it's sort of for Dad.'

Mark studies my face; I can see he realizes I'm serious. 'Wait here,' he says after a moment. He gets up off the sofa and pads upstairs. I hear him rooting around in his room, and then he comes back holding a biscuit tin. 'How much?'

'One hundred and eighty-eight pounds,' I say, staring at the tin. It's got the word DEPOSIT written on it. 'Or whatever you can do.'

Mark looks at me like I'm mad. He opens his mouth to say something but thinks better of it. He rummages in the tin and counts out a wad of notes. 'There,' he says. 'One hundred and ninety. Keep it.' He holds the money out to me.

'Are you sure?' I ask. 'Is it all your overtime money?'

He shakes his head in disbelief. 'This is your Christmas and birthday money for the next fifty years,' he laughs.

I grin as I pocket the notes. 'It's nothing illegal,' I say, 'I promise.' And then I lean over and give him a big kiss, smack on the cheek.

'Get off, you wazzock,' Mark laughs, and he playfully pushes me away. 'This isn't *Oprah*.'

I laugh with him. 'Thanks, Mark,' I say, and we both know it's not just for the money. I really mean it too. Suddenly I feel much happier. Not just because I've now got the cash to hire the lookalike, but because I've spoken to Mark about Mum. We *never* mention her. And I realize I'm not that sad about not going to Hull; even though Mark and Kirsty moan at me and tell me off, I quite like being around them. 'Do you think we'll ever see Mum again?' I ask.

Mark gives me a tight little smile. 'Maybe,' he says. 'But for now you'll just have to settle for me.' He taps me on the knee and gets off the sofa. 'Fancy another brew?' he asks, collecting the mugs from the coffee table.

'I've not got time for tea,' I say. Before he can even answer, I'm firing up our laptop, logging onto the Bargain Lookalikes website.

CHAPTER TWENTY-FOUR

One day until the Tattoo

One Queen Elizabeth II, complete with tiara and sash and corgi, booked. I got the confirmation through this morning. Her real name's Janice and she arrives at ten o'clock tomorrow, cash payable in person. I hope she's good at the signature too – once she's signed the note, Dad can start packing for home. I'm so excited I could almost cry, but I've been doing much too much of that recently. I need to give my eyes a rest.

I'm in a funny old mood today. Part of me feels really happy, like a huge weight has been lifted off my shoulders. I've had a nice chat with Mark, I've got the money, I've hired the Queen, and Dad and the whole army will see her sign the form to send him home – so 'job's a good 'un', as Dad says. But I've still got this really nervous feeling in my tummy, like something could go wrong at any time. I'm imagining a million bad things a minute: Tamwar's uncle's fireworks set fire to a Morris dancer. A pirate accidentally stabs someone. The tiger eats Craig. Though that's not necessarily a bad thing.

As each hour passes and we get nearer and nearer to the Big Day, I decide I'd better do some last-minute checks.

I spend the day wandering around the town with my clipboard, making sure that everything's tickety-boo. And everyone's in the most brilliant mood. Not just those who are taking part in the tattoo – either ours or Craig's – but *everyone*. The whole town has gone a little bit bonkers.

There are flags everywhere. Massive England flags hang from bedroom windows; Union Jack bunting is strung up on washing lines in people's gardens. There's also a tea towel pinned to the community centre gates with WILLS AND KATE, 29TH APRIL 2011 written on it – which is a *little* out of date, but the thought's there, I guess.

As I walk through the town, I count about a hundred people mowing their lawns and sweeping the pavement and cobbles outside their homes. Four ladies scrubbing their front steps. One even scrubs the cladding on the side of her house. The fluttering feeling in my tummy gets worse. All these people are going to *such* a lot of effort, and none of them know it's just for an old, squinty-eyed woman called Janice.

I walk past Craig's pub. Craig's outside, halfway up one of Mike's ladders, with a sign saying THE QUEEN'S HEAD and showing a big picture of the Queen that's really a blown-up first-class stamp. Underneath THE QUEEN'S HEAD it's got FOR ONE DAY ONLY in small letters.

Mike's standing underneath the sign saying, 'Left a bit, left a bit more,' while Craig's stretching to fix it up. The ladder looks like it's groaning under his weight and he's a bit red in the face because Mike's changed to, 'Now right a bit.' Mike's biting his lip like he's trying not to laugh, and after a moment, when the sign's finally in place, Craig bursts out laughing too. He spots a large group of men heading towards the pub door, and hurries down the ladder to serve them. 'Business has never been so good,' he says to Mike with a wink.

I smile to myself. It's fair to say everyone's excited about the Queen coming tomorrow, and I may – just may – have pulled off the most brilliant thing in the history of Merchant Stanton.

There's a queue of people outside the post office because today's the day old people get their pension. And because it's so busy, they're all taking the opportunity to get a bit of practice in. Three old men stand solemnly in the queue bobbing their heads now and then, and saying, 'How do you do? How do you do?' in funny posh voices. They turn to each other and shake each other's hands. 'Your Majesty,' they say, and then bob their heads again. One woman is trying to practise her curtsey, but she keeps losing her balance because she's got her arms full of parcels, which she drops every time she bends down.

Another woman is reciting, 'Ma'am as in *arm*, not Ma'am as in *ham*,' to herself over and over again, when the leader of the WI walks in, a blue envelope in her hand.

'It's the other way round,' she barks. 'Ma'am as in *ham*, not Ma'am as in *arm*.'

The first woman frowns at her. 'How do you know that?'

The WI woman sticks her nose in the air. 'My granddaughter met Prince Charles on one of his overseas visits. She's been practising with me over the Internet.'

I take in the WI woman's blue envelope. 'Overseas?' I ask. It's the same as the one Mr Featherstone was reading.

That's when it hits me. 'What's arthritis?' I ask.

The WI woman looks at me like I'm mad for asking such a random question. 'Pain in your joints,' she replies. 'Hands, normally. It's when you find it difficult to move. My Doug had it. Painful, awful affliction.'

Well, that explains everything. I can't believe I've not worked it all out before.

I dash up the steps to Hope Springs, our laptop

shoved under my arm. He won't be happy to see me, but I'm going to *make* him listen.

I bound through the front door and almost trip over Derek and Mr Stephens, halfway up a ladder, paintbrushes in hand. 'What's going on?' I ask.

Mr Stephens gestures to the paint pots lined up against the wall of the foyer. 'The council turned down our request for a grant,' he says, frowning. 'So we're having to spruce this place up ourselves.'

'It needs it,' I reply. 'It's a bit—'

'Soulless?' Derek interrupts. 'Depressing?' I nod. 'I know,' he sighs. 'And just think – what if the Queen pops in?'

I feel a bit guilty about that, so I give them a quick smile and head on down the corridor.

I knock on the door of Room F and don't wait for an answer. 'Listen,' I say, bursting in. Mr Featherstone's sitting on his bed, gazing out of the window. He turns to me in surprise. 'I'll set it all up for you – I just need to know their details, but it'll be easy to ask them.'

His eyebrows shoot up. 'What are you talking about?'

'So we can Skype your family,' I reply. I lay my laptop down on the bed next to him and stand so we're face to face.

He frowns at me. 'So we can what my what?'

I take a deep breath. This may be hard to explain. 'Nana May's in here because she's lost her memory,' I say, talking quickly to get it all out before he can start having a go at me. 'And I know it's really frustrating for her, but she can't help it. And Cyril's in here because he's lost his immune system. That's why he has his drip pole. And you're in here because you've lost the use of your hands, right?'

Mr Featherstone looks incredulous, but he nods at me.

'Which means you can't write letters to your family,' I battle on. 'And I'm guessing you got all angry because you've not seen them in a while as they live in Oz – the letter said AIRMAIL – and you can't get there because it's twenty-four hours on a plane and you're quite old and have arthritis. And that's probably why you're really mean all the time. It must be tough.' I gulp and look down at the floor. 'I *know* it's tough not having your family living with you.'

Mr Featherstone doesn't say anything for a long time. 'Excellent detective work,' he says eventually. 'And *I* should know. I was Commissioner of the Metropolitan Police.'

Oh, crumbs, I think. *My little rant has pushed him over the edge. He's lost his marbles as well as his hands.*

Mr Featherstone lets out a long sigh. 'My son and his family moved to Australia two years ago,' he says. 'Same time as I moved in here, after my wife died. I've not seen them since.' His eyes well up and he takes a giant sniff. 'It was Charlie's birthday last week and I couldn't even write him a card.' He stares down at his gnarled hands. 'I've worked with my hands all my life,' he says, turning them over in his lap. 'For forty years I tended the gardens of a very important person and now I can't even make a cup of tea.'

'So why don't you let Derek help you? With the letter-writing, anyway.'

Mr Featherstone shakes his head. 'I don't want everybody knowing my business,' he says. 'I can manage.'

'Clearly you can't,' I reply. And I remember one of Derek's lines: *No man is an island,* right? You can't do everything alone. I think of all the work we've done on the tattoo. I couldn't have done any of it without Sarah and her organizing, and Tamwar and his family. Even Jake and his flags. 'Believe me, I know.' I inch over to him. 'So you shouldn't be mean to people in here. You're all in the same boat, just trying to get on. Cyril hasn't got any family to visit him either.'

Mr Featherstone looks at me curiously. 'Why are you doing this?'

I shrug. I can't really explain it. I just want to help. So many people I don't really know are helping me get the Queen, even though I've made everything up. I figure this is the one thing I can do that isn't based on a lie.

'We'll spruce you up a bit before they see you, though.' I gesture to his crazy white hair, realizing now that it's only crazy because he can't hold a comb.

'Don't!' Mr Featherstone cries, and starts to bat my hand away.

I can't believe it. Here I am, trying to help, having worked everything out, and he's still being as stubborn and mean as usual. I check my watch. 'Fine,' I huff. 'I've got to go. The Queen's coming tomorrow.'

Mr Featherstone's grey eyes study me. 'You've definitely got her then?'

'Yep,' I say, and I try to look convinced.

Mr Featherstone stares at me for another moment, and then, ever so slightly, dips his head.

I nod back at him and dash out of the room.

That night, as I lie in bed, I tuck my hand under my pillow and give Dad's army jacket a squeeze for luck. Just then, right above my head, there's a sharp knock, followed by three quieter ones. I knock back to Linda, but even though I know she's there and trying to be friendly, my stomach still feels fluttery. What if someone breaks into my house in the middle of the night and steals my two hundred quid? What if Janice is late, or gets lost, or dies between now and then, because I'm not being funny, but she did look a bit old. What if Janice – as the Queen – signs the note saying my dad can come home, but it's still not enough? Someone, somewhere – maybe Dad's boss, or the enemy he's fighting – says no? But the worst thought, the one that I just can't get out of my mind, no matter how much squeezing it into the very back of my brain I try to do is: *What if Dad doesn't want to come home?*

CHAPTER TWENTY-FIVE

D-Day!

The ringing of the home phone wakes me up. My stomach's still feeling fluttery. This is it. Today's the Big Day. I throw the duvet back and leap out of bed quicker than if Kirsty had yelled up the stairs saying, 'I've made bacon sandwiches' – which she did once when she first moved in. Then she set off the fire alarm and we've not had bacon sandwiches since.

I go over to the window and pull back the curtains. It's been raining overnight, but it's not too soggy for doing our tattoo in the park.

Kirsty's been in my room: on the chair in the corner is a set of clean clothes. It's the pink dress

I wore to Buckingham Palace, along with a white cardigan. The fancy white patent shoes I wore to Dad's cousin's wedding have been spruced up and placed under my chair.

Feeling as if I've just stepped out of a box of Quality Street, I head downstairs in my outfit. I open my mouth in shock because the kitchen table's all been done up. There's a tablecloth on it and everything. Mark, dressed in a suit, walks around the table laying three place settings. Kirsty's over by the stove, cooking. Actually cooking. She looks up and smiles when I come in. 'Bacon sandwiches all right, Billie?' she says.

I nod and sit down at the table in a daze. 'Just mind you don't get ketchup down your frock,' she warns. 'Can't have you meeting the Queen of England with stains on your dress.'

Mark sits next to me, straightening his tie. 'What d'you reckon? Fit for a Queen?'

I frown. 'Why are you doing all this?'

Kirsty laughs and plonks a plate of bacon sandwiches down on the table. 'Today, Billie Templar,' she says, scraping back a chair and sitting down opposite me, 'you are meeting royalty. It's a momentous occasion.'

I'm too nervous to join in. 'There's no laughing to be had.' I think for a moment. 'Except if the Queen finds something funny – then we all laugh along with her.' I'd read something about that on the Internet. It's called 'Royal Protocol', and there's a whole heap of things you have to do – like all the bowing and curtseying and 'Ma'am as in *ham*' stuff – and things you have to *not* do, like swearing, or accidentally whacking her over the head with a ladder or roly-polying into her shins. I've made a list.

We sit munching our sandwiches, and I notice Kirsty and Mark exchanging glances over the ketchup bottle.

'Uh, Billie . . . ?' Kirsty says, clearing her throat. 'We've been talking.' Mark puts down his sandwich and gives me a little smile. 'We're so sorry that we've not been better at looking after you,' she goes on, and she sniffs loudly. 'But that's going to change. Isn't it, Mark?'

Mark nods. 'We're going to be brilliant until Dad

comes home.' He thinks for a moment. 'And possibly even after that.' He breaks into a grin and I grin back. This sitting around the table, eating something Kirsty's actually cooked, being a proper family – *this* is brilliant. Right now.

Mark motions to the clock on the wall. 'I'll go and collect Nan. Bill, you'd best get going. Can't be late for the Queen and all that.'

My stomach's still fluttery as I walk to Battlefield Park carrying my clipboard and megaphone. I can't get rid of this nagging feeling. Jake and Sarah are waiting for me outside the gates. Jake's all spruced up in a dark grey suit with a red tie, and his hair's been scraped into place with what looks like a million bottles of hair gel. He's even wearing grey latex gloves to match.

Sarah, on the other hand, is wearing her school uniform. Again. It's not been washed – again – though there are fewer food stains than normal, and parts of her jumper look bobbly, as if she's scrubbed at it with a cloth.

'Nice day for it,' Jake says as I walk up to them.

He looks up at the sky. 'The rain should hold off for a few hours.'

I nod. 'Fingers crossed. You look smart.'

Jake pulls at his tie. 'Mum bought me a new suit,' he says, his rosy cheeks flushed. 'She's dead proud of me for all this.' He motions to the park. 'You know – all the flags and stuff.'

'Right,' I reply, flashing him a smile. Then I look at Sarah. 'Is your mum coming?' I ask her.

She shrugs. 'Dad might,' she mutters. 'We'll see.'

Before I can reply, there's a roar of engines, and five men wearing leather waistcoats and trousers zoom towards us on motorbikes. They screech to a halt outside the gates. The leader takes off his helmet.

'We, uh, want to be in it,' he says in a surprisingly squeaky voice. 'Everyone should get the chance to show the Queen what they can do.'

Hmm. If they can *do* anything, they should, I think. But I just nod. 'The more the merrier.'

Craig's already in position, wearing a black tuxedo with tails. He looks like a penguin, and I have to stop myself from laughing because his bow tie's been done up so tightly, his face has gone red.

Just then, Mike and his fellow window cleaners turn up. They're dressed in their finest suits, their ukuleles slung over their shoulders, and they've got brand-new wooden ladders. I peer closer and see that all three ladders are covered in fairy lights that flash on and off.

'How do.' Mike nods to Craig. 'Everything shipshape?'

Craig flashes a toothy grin at us and strolls over to meet him. 'And Bristol fashion,' he replies.

We don't say anything, but I'm seething. Why does he have to be so smug and superior? Why can't we all just get along? 'There are more important things in life than who's got the best ukulele, you know,' I shout, but Craig just ignores me.

Just then all the gymnasts surge into the park. They're so excited, most are twirling their ribbons and dancing and prancing along. Except the girl who's famous for the roly-polys. She's still doing those.

'Morning!' Holly trills. 'We can't *wait* for this. She

motions to her troupe, all dressed up to the nines in brand-new leotards. 'We've got to look our best for the Queen, right?'

Jake nods. 'Right!' he cries enthusiastically, pulling at his gloves.

Sarah looks down at her cleaner-than-usual-but-still-quite-dirty school uniform. 'Right,' she mumbles, not very convincingly.

Jake's mum bustles over and starts smoothing his suit jacket and wiping dirt off his face with a hanky. 'Gerroff!' he groans, embarrassed. Suddenly I get a little pang of something – a sort of tightening in my chest. As annoying as it is for someone to spit on a tissue and wipe it on your face, it's what parents do, and I haven't got anyone to do that. Kirsty and Mark said they'd be nicer to me, but it's not the same. I don't think Kirsty even owns a hanky.

Everyone else crowds into the park, and I take a deep breath. The WI are wearing matching flowing skirts and waistcoats that look like they're made of carpet; they're carrying armfuls and armfuls of flowers. The Morris dancers jingle and jangle their way over, waving their hankies and knocking their wooden sticks together in excitement. The footballers are wearing brand-new blue kit with SPONSORED BY THE QUEEN'S HEAD (FORMERLY THE WHITE HART) written on the back.

'Ready, Billie?' one Extreme Scrabble player asks, marching up to me.

I nod, but I'm not really listening. I've just thought of something. 'Come on,' I say to Sarah, grabbing her hand.

'Where are we going?'

'You'll see.' I thrust my clipboard and megaphone at Jake. 'You're in charge,' I say.

Jake looks from me to his mum in panic. 'B-but . . .' he splutters. 'Talking . . . in public—'

'You'll be fine,' I interrupt, and flash him a smile. 'This is your moment, Jake Whittaker.'

His mum frowns. 'Think of your allergies,' she mutters – though I've no idea why a clipboard and megaphone would harm someone who's nut-and lactose-intolerant.

Jake hesitates for a moment and bites his lip. 'You can do it,' I say firmly.

He takes a deep breath and then nods. 'Right,'

303

he says, though his voice sounds a little shaky. He takes the megaphone and clipboard and turns to the crowd. 'Uh, excuse me, everyone,' he starts, but no one's paying attention.

'Should we leave him on his own?' Sarah whispers to me.

He's overwhelmed by the people swarming around him, wanting to know the exact running order, and what *precisely* is going on, and is there ample parking, and will there be refreshments? Jake's mum tries to shield him from the million questions while he takes a step back.

'How can we draw attention away from that lot?' Amir Aban asks, jerking his thumb over to Craig's tattoo.

'We *are* first, aren't we?' Darren Curtis asks, brandishing his tuba.

'Is Burundi actually a country?' the roly-polying girl asks.

And just as I'm rolling my eyes and thinking I should help out, Jake takes the megaphone and yells into it. 'QUIET!' he cries, and the whole park – even Craig's side – falls silent. All eyes are fixed on him.

'That's better.' Jake doesn't even blush. He looks down at the clipboard. 'Now, where were we?' His mum looks shocked by his forthrightness, but he doesn't even notice.

'He'll be fine.' I smile at Sarah and we head out of the park.

'I've never worn anything like this before!' Sarah says breathlessly as she stands in front of the mirror in my bedroom. 'I've only really got my school top and skirt.'

I had *noticed*, I think, but I don't say anything. Sarah holds out the hem of the navy blue skirt I've given her and does a little twirl. 'Won't your mum mind?'

'I don't know where she is,' I reply matter-of-factly. 'Here – try this.' I hold out a little matching cardigan. It's a bit small for me, but it fits Sarah perfectly.

She smiles at me in the mirror. 'Your dad's going to be well chuffed, you know,' she says shyly.

I shrug. 'We'll see.'

'Are you kidding?' Sarah looks at me in shock.

'You've put all this together. You've got the Queen! It's amazing. I don't know anyone who's ever done that before.'

'*You've* put it all together,' I say, largely because it's true. 'You got the megaphone, and you did all the rehearsals when I couldn't make it. You got everyone to come and practise for Tony Hills. I couldn't have done it without you.'

Sarah goes bright red at that, and I can tell she's dead embarrassed. '*Your* dad's going to be well chuffed,' I say.

Sarah frowns. 'If he remembers to turn up.'

'Why wouldn't he? He'd want to see you meet the Queen, surely.'

Sarah looks down at her shoes. 'He doesn't . . .' She falters. 'He's not always around,' she says quietly. 'He – he spends a lot of time in the pub.'

I nod. 'Right,' I say – I've seen something about that on *EastEnders*. They're all in the pub on that, mind, but some more than others.

Sarah gives me a little smile in the mirror again. 'I'll be sad when it's all over,' she says. 'I've really enjoyed helping. It's nice to have something to do after school. It's nice to have . . . friends.'

I smile back at her. 'We can still be friends after, you know.'

'You don't mind?' She looks surprised.

'Why should I?'

''Cos I . . . you know' – she nods over to her school uniform which I put in a carrier bag by the open window – 'smell a bit.'

I pretend to act surprised – it's the kindest thing to do. 'I hadn't noticed,' I say, but I'm not sure I'm that convincing, in spite of all the practice I've had at lying.

Sarah grimaces. 'Our washing machine broke,' she replies.

In 2004? I think, but I let her go on.

'Dad keeps meaning to get it fixed, but whenever he's got some money, he always . . . you know.'

'Goes to the pub?'

Sarah nods. 'Yeah.'

I think for a second. 'You done preening?' I ask, nodding to the mirror. She shrugs, so I march over to the window, scoop up the carrier bag and head downstairs. 'Come on,' I order.

I head into the kitchen, shove her school uniform in the washing machine and switch it on. 'Should be done by the time we get back.' I beam over at her.

Sarah looks like she's about to cry.

'Oh God.' I start to panic. 'Did you not want me to?'

'No, no, it's not that . . .' she stutters. 'It's just – no one's ever been this nice to me, that's all.'

I laugh kindly. 'It's a warm wash,' I reply, 'not London Fashion Week.'

Sarah joins in – then my eye catches the clock on the kitchen wall. It's 9.35.

'Oh Lordy!' I cry. I grab Sarah by the hand and we both sprint out of the door.

When we arrive back at Battlefield Park there's a huge crowd of people lining the pitch we've marked out for our two tattoos. Smart men in suits carry a flag saying MERCHANT STANTON BRITISH LEGION. Trish, Mandy and Lou are here, sniffling into tissues. Mrs Hussein stands in a huddle with some other teachers from school. Pretty much every pupil is waving a Union Jack. Even Sabrina Nelson's here –

she actually looks a bit miffed she's not joining in. Lots of little girls have brought flowers with them – which the WI aren't impressed by – and they're practising their curtseys as they wait.

'I SAID,' the WI woman shouts over the din, 'IT'S MA'AM AS IN HAM, NOT MA'AM AS IN ARM!' She looks like she's going to throttle someone.

Mark's settled Nana May in a chair beside the pitch, and Kirsty's trying to set up the Internet so that Dad and his regiment can watch everything. There's a laptop sitting on a small table – Mr Law's laptop. He and Kirsty are trying to connect to Skype. And he's laughing. Actually laughing. I've never seen Mr Law do that before. Maybe he did have that surgery to unknit his eyebrows, after all.

Kirsty spots me and heads on over. 'I understand our laptop's at Hope Springs,' she says, one eyebrow raised.

'How did you know that?'

She looks up at the sky for a moment before she answers. 'I had a very interesting phone call from your Mr Featherstone this morning.'

I open my mouth to say something, but Kirsty

holds up a hand to stop me. Honestly, she *really* needs to stop hanging round Mr Law. 'He told me. Told me off, anyway.'

I look at her, confused. Kirsty bends down and puts a hand on my shoulder. 'What I said at breakfast,' she says softly, 'about me and Mark looking after you better. We both mean it.'

'I know,' I say. 'But what's that got to do with Mr Featherstone?'

'He saw us at Hope Springs,' she explains. 'Yesterday, with Mum. How me and Mark were arguing about who was going to look after you. I'm sorry, Bill.' She squeezes my shoulder, gives me a little smile and heads back to Mr Law.

Wow. Mr Featherstone being concerned about me? What on earth is in those garibaldis?

Then Jade lumbers up to me. She's munching a chocolate bar, as usual, but she is wearing a nice dress, so she's tried to make an effort. 'My dad can't make it,' she says through mouthfuls of Twirl. 'He's being transferred to a special hospital in Birmingham to start his treatment. We're driving down there after this. The hospital's the Queen Elizabeth. Funny, huh?'

I frown. Funny what passes for 'funny', I guess.

'But he says good luck,' Jade says.

I look at my watch: 9.50. Janice will be here any minute. 'We're going to need it,' I reply. Then I smile at her. 'I never said thank you — for helping me do all this when I was grounded. So, thank you.'

Jade beams back at me. 'I guess we're in the same boat,' she says shyly. 'You know, with our dads.'

I resist the urge to say, *I hope it's a blinking big boat otherwise I'm going overboard when you stand up in it*, and just smile back at her again. She's all right, really, is Jade.

Everyone in both tattoos gets ready. The gymnasts, footballers and ballerinas are doing stretches and limbering up. So are the Extreme Scrabble players, though I've no idea why. Darren is giving a last-minute pep talk to the marching band. The WI are polishing their vases on their carpet-like waistcoats. I look around the participants. No Derek and no old folk from Hope Springs. I frown — we've barely got enough acts as it is. What will Dad make of us compared to Craig's lot?

Someone taps me lightly on the shoulder. But

before I can turn round or kick out, it's followed by three more short taps. 'Any minute now, hey, Billie?' a voice says next to me.

It's Linda.

I spin round to face her. 'What are you doing here?' I ask in surprise.

Linda's eyes dart around the crowd nervously. She gulps. 'I had to come,' she replies with a tight smile. 'It's your big day. I wouldn't miss it for the world.'

'But what about your OCD?'

Linda shrugs. 'I doubled my medication. Just for today.'

I break out into a grin at that. I'm just so happy that she's made the effort to come. I know how hard it is for her to leave the house and come to this big field, still a bit muddy after last night's rain, with pretty much the whole town jostling and pushing and crowding around her.

Linda looks down at me and pulls a tissue out of her pocket. 'Look at the state of you,' she sighs, and rubs my face with it. 'Can't have you meeting the Queen like this.'

And as she's rubbing my face with her hanky, I

can't stop grinning. That pang I felt – that tightening of my chest . . . it's gone. What with cooking my tea and ironing my clothes and buying me teddy bears and making sure I've not got toothpaste round my mouth when I meet the Queen of England, Linda's more like a mum to me than anyone. And I don't even have to save up for a coach ticket to see her.

I lean over and throw my arms around her. Linda's a bit surprised, and I feel her stiffen because it means I'm touching her, but she curls her arms right back around me. 'Thank you,' I whisper. 'For everything.'

I look up and see tears in her eyes. 'Go get 'em, Billie,' she whispers.

'It's nearly ten!' someone shouts. I untangle myself from Linda and look nervously towards the entrance of the park. No sign of Janice yet.

'We're still having a bit of trouble with the Internet,' Kirsty shouts over to me. She and Mr Law faff around with the laptop. From where I'm standing, the screen looks blank.

'Turning it on would help!' I yell.

Mr Law and Kirsty look at each other and burst out laughing. I try not to think how nauseous this makes me feel – my auntie is seriously flirting with my headmaster – and focus on the minute hand ticking round on my watch. It's 10.02.

'She's not usually late, is she?' someone asks.

By now all the participants have finished warming up, and just stand around facing the park gates, waiting. People wrap their cardies tighter around them to shield themselves from the cold. It's not raining, but it's no longer boiling, either. Small children hop from one foot to the other to keep warm.

'It *is* today, isn't it?' Jake asks me.

Everyone turns to look at me, and my heart starts beating faster. It's a bit like the day when Craig and everyone started coming at me in this very park, all jeering and demanding answers about the Queen, when I stumbled outside just in time to see Steve in his wheelchair.

I open my mouth to say something – but there's a commotion at the park gates.

'Is it her?' someone cries, and we all turn with bated breath.

But instead of the Queen, two burly men bound

through the gates and march up to me. 'We're not too late, are we?' one of them asks, gazing around the park. 'When do we show her?'

I frown. 'Show her what?'

They both look at me like I'm mental. 'Our tattoo,' the first one states.

I roll my eyes. 'We're not having *three*,' I say, and jerk my head towards Craig. 'He's bad enough.'

'But I lost a pint of blood!' the second one replies. 'That's nearly an armful!'

Nobody has a clue what he's talking about, so they both lift up their white vests and show off bulging beer bellies.

'Omigosh!' I blurt out. I have to stop myself from laughing — it's the most ridiculous thing I've ever seen. They've got tattoos — actual tattoos, like sailors and David Beckham and Kirsty. One has a blue anchor right across his stomach with today's date underneath. The other has a massive hand grenade. 'They're our military tattoos,' he says — and frowns because, by now, the whole town is laughing at them. 'What? It took fourteen hours! I fainted three times!'

I wipe tears from my eyes. 'It's not that sort of tattoo,' I say, gesturing to the colliery band and the WI. They take in the participants, and their shoulders slump in disappointment. One of them starts crying.

As the laughter dies down and the two men merge into the crowd, anticipation fills the air once more. I feel in the pocket of my cardigan for the two hundred pounds I've stashed in a brown envelope. *Come on, Janice*, I think to myself. *Don't let me down now.* And just as I'm remembering all my shouting about miracles and how I'd quite like that miracle to happen now, thank you very much, there's the sound of an engine approaching.

'She's here!' someone cries, and a man with a moustache lets out an excited squeak. It echoes around the park and everyone glares him into silence.

The noise is getting louder and louder and I cross my fingers that it's Janice.

'That's definitely a car!' Craig shouts, but no one seems to mind *his* outburst. 'Any second now!'

We wait. And wait. And wait a bit longer. The engine's getting louder but, for a car, it's taking an awfully long time to reach us. The seconds tick by until finally—

'It's the Queen!' little Amir Aban shouts out in excitement, unable to contain himself.

The knot in my stomach tightens. *Oh God. This is it!*

Everyone opens their mouths to start cheering, but then the Queen pooters into view.

On a motability scooter.

With a basket on the front. And a toy corgi inside.

'Uh . . .' Sarah stutters next to me, and I turn round to meet her gaze, panicked.

'Does the Queen normally ride a scooter?' someone whispers.

'Austerity Britain,' I blurt out, thinking quickly. 'She's trying to show we're all in the same boat . . .' I stumble forward to the park gates, keen to meet Janice before things go completely, utterly, horribly wrong.

'Billie, I presume?' Janice asks as I reach her.

'Shush!' I reply — because I'm not being funny, but Janice looks a lot more rubbish in the flesh than she does on the Lookalikes website. Her long white dress is frayed, and bits of the lace trim are missing. The fact that it's hitched up around her knees while she's riding the scooter doesn't help. Nor does her distinctly northern accent. 'You're meant to be posh!' I whisper.

Janice looks a bit put out. She reaches into the basket and, underneath the corgi, finds a carrier bag. A tatty old Asda carrier bag. She takes out her tiara and pops it on her head. I peer at it closely. It's silver all right, but it's chipped, and parts of it are rusted, and one of the spikes is missing altogether.

'Got my cash?' Janice asks as she positions the tiara in place.

I hastily take the envelope out of my cardigan pocket and shove it in her basket, under the corgi.

'Pleasure doing business with you.' Janice grins. 'Now, curtsey.'

'What?'

She nods at my knees. 'You're meeting the Queen, darling,' she says rather grandly. 'Keep up.'

I roll my eyes but curtsey nonetheless. And just as I'm getting up from the bobbing-down bit, Janice scoots forward a bit. Everyone gives a collective gasp because now they see her properly for the first time.

I turn round with a million tonnes of lead in my heart – I'm sure everyone's worked out what's really going on. I can't bear to look Kirsty or Mark or Sarah or Jake or Tamwar in the eye.

I help Janice off the scooter, and together, we make our way forward. Craig peers closely at Janice and his eyebrows twitch. Nobody says anything for a moment.

Then the man with the moustache lets out another squeak. 'Doesn't she look wonderful?' he exclaims.

And suddenly, everyone bursts into applause.

'Your Majesty!' they cry. 'We're so honoured!'

I gulp. *Hang on a second*, I think. *They're buying it! They're really buying it!*

Janice holds up her hand and does a Queenly wave. The applause gets louder. 'How do you do?' she asks in her poshest accent. It's not half bad, I'll be honest. Cameras start clicking away; Union Jacks are waving.

The WI woman who kept telling everyone off steps forward, but she's so excited that she mucks up her words. 'Ma'am, Your Ham, I'm arm as in Pam,' she blusters.

Everyone laughs, but Janice tactfully ignores her.

'Where's her security?' a man whispers to his neighbour, but luckily everybody's too busy cheering to hear him.

I motion for Janice to walk up and down the crowd lined up by the tattoo pitch, accompanying her all the way. This is really working!

'Almost there, Billie!' Kirsty gestures to the laptop. 'Your dad's going to be so proud!'

Linda's standing next to her, and the pair of them blow their noses hard as they watch me with Janice. Mr Law's standing next to Kirsty: he's got his arm outstretched like he's thinking of slinging it around her shoulders. I have to move quickly before I'm sick at the feet of the pretend Queen of England.

Then Craig bustles forward and positions himself directly in front of Janice. 'Your Majesty,' he says in the most ridiculous voice, and he dips from the waist, his nose almost touching his knees as he bows. 'I'm the leader of the other tattoo,' he says when he finally straightens up.

'There are two?' Janice enquires.

Craig smiles, but it's not a proper smile because it doesn't reach his eyes. 'There *are* two tattoos,' he replies, 'but one could say there's only one worth watching.' He looks over at me with a smirk. 'Theirs'll be over in minutes. They only have five acts.'

The crowd parts as I show Janice to a seat – away from Nana May, because I don't want people to realize how much like any other old lady Janice looks.

Craig jogs off to get his tattoo ready, and the Yorkshire Colliery Brass Band and pirates and Mike and the window cleaners and footballers all get into their positions. Then one of the tiger handlers takes a crowbar and starts prising open the wooden box, while the other picks up the iron chain poking out of the box and stands at the ready, whip in hand. Everyone shuffles back a little as they wait for the tiger to emerge.

After a few moments it gingerly sticks its head out. It's a stonking big, white stripy tiger. The handler cracks his whip and tugs at the iron chain as the tiger takes in its surroundings.

'I say!' Janice exclaims when she sees it. 'What a delight!'

Craig beams from ear to ear, and I frown as I take my position in front of *my* motley crew. I'm not being funny but Merchant Stanton Junior School Marching Band and a bunch of guys playing Scrabble pale into significance when you see a tiger.

I turn to see Sarah and Jake and Tamwar and everyone looking at me like they're expecting some Churchill-style rallying war cry, just because I'm the one who happened to get the Queen to Merchant Stanton.

'Ready, troops?' I give them a tight smile. The Yorkshire Colliery Brass Band starts up, and the crowd claps enthusiastically as they march along.

Darren looks like he's going to burst into tears. 'How can we compete with them?' he sobs.

Just then, there's *another* commotion outside the gates. Everyone turns to stare as yelps and whoops and war cries ring out.

'What's going on?' Craig asks, his face darkening. The colliery band stop mid-number.

A low hum sweeps through the park, and there, at

the entrance, marching slowly towards us, are seven old men, five old women and a chap with an IV drip pole. Their walking sticks are propped against their shoulders like rifles. Derek's hovering at the back, trying to stop the blind man from wandering off, while right at the front, leading the charge, is Mr Featherstone.

Riding in on Mr Clewson's tank.

Mr Featherstone's wearing a blue blazer with medals attached to the left breast, and a red beret. As his troops march closer, we can hear what they're singing. '*Old soldiers never die,*' they trill. Mr Featherstone's singing his heart out, struggling to keep his balance as the tank rolls on in. '*They just fade away.*'

When they eventually reach me, Mr Featherstone motions for them to stop and salute. He allows Derek to help him down from the tank and painfully raises his hand to salute me himself. 'Hope Springs Marching Corps at your service, Ma'am,' he says.

Well, this is unexpected.

'Why are you doing this?' I whisper.

Mr Featherstone gestures to Olive and Basil and

Cyril and the rest of the old folk, all dressed in their finery, all with massive grins on their faces. 'You were right. You've given Hope Springs a new lease of life.'

He looks down at the ground. 'And you were right about me. No man is an island.' His grey eyes fill with tears. He gestures to his jacket pocket, and I reach inside and take out the comb with GRANDAD written on. 'If you'd do the honours,' he says, smiling.

I take the comb and run it through his straggly hair. He doesn't flinch once. 'I'm even going to let him call me Mr F,' he whispers, nodding his head in Derek's direction. 'But don't tell the others.'

Then he catches sight of Janice. He peers at her closely but doesn't say anything. He motions for his troops to join the others. Out of the corner of my eye I see Nana May give a little wave to Cyril. Honestly, she's as blinking boy mad as Kirsty is.

There's a smattering of applause as the Yorkshire Colliery Brass Band march off. 'Your turn,' Craig sneers at me.

I take a deep breath and usher Darren and the

rest of the school band onto the track.

But just as Darren's about to strike up the opening note of 'When the Saints Go Marching In' on his tuba, there's a loud trumpeting sound.

We all gasp in amazement as Tamwar's uncle rides through the gates, clinging for dear life to the saddle on top of the elephant. He's rocking from side to side and doesn't look all that stable. We cheer as he sets off round behind the crowd. He brings the elephant to a stop and we all stare at it, waiting for its next trick.

Nothing else happens.

'Is that it?' someone cries after a moment.

Tamwar's uncle looks put out. 'What more do you want? She's not going to breathe fire or anything.' The elephant starts munching on a bag of peanuts, so we all turn back to Darren and the band.

Just then, there's *another* commotion at the back of the crowd. 'Can't we get on without all these disruptions?' I cry. The longer Janice is here, the more chance there is of someone spotting she's not real. I just need her to watch, sign the note, and then get the blinking heck out of Merchant Stanton.

But I'm drowned out by a shriek.

'Watch out!' a voice cries out in panic. 'He's got free!'

'Who?'

'The tiger!'

Nobody says anything as the words sink in.

Then all hell breaks loose.

The crowd parts as townsfolk and children and spectators and pensioners scramble towards the park gates. Cyril wheels his IV drip pole along and grabs Nana May. Darren drops his tuba onto the big toe of a Morris dancer. Scrabble pieces go flying as the players head for the gates. A gymnast barges into the table and the laptop falls off.

Mr Featherstone grabs Janice by the arm and yanks her towards the exit. 'Best come with me, Your Majesty,' he cries.

A single voice carries over the shrieks of the crowd. 'Where are you all going?'

It's the tiger handler. He's standing under the oak tree, a look of confusion on his face.

'The tiger's loose!' I yell over my shoulder, still heading for the gates. 'It could kill us all!'

A look of panic flashes across the man's face, but

then he curls up his whip in defeat. 'It's OK!' he cries. 'You can come back. The tiger won't hurt you.' He gulps. 'It's not real.'

Fighting the urge to flee, I ask, 'What do you mean?'

By now, everyone has stopped running. Most are turning towards us, panting for breath.

The handler lets out a sigh and turns towards the tree. 'Dave? Al? You best come out now.'

Two men shuffle out from behind the tree, and it takes me a moment to work out what's going on.

Dave's – or maybe Al's – bottom half is covered in tiger-print trousers. Al – or maybe Dave – takes off the tiger head. They both look sheepish. 'I just nipped back to go to the loo,' Dave – or maybe Al – says. 'I was desperate.'

I can't help giggling. 'You're wearing a tiger costume?'

The two men stare down at the ground and nod.

Craig's face starts to go red. 'I paid good money for you!' he cries in outrage. 'I want it back!'

The crowd lets out a sigh of relief, which turns into a wave of laughter. Then, after everyone's got their breath back, they start to head back towards the tattoo field, chattering and joking away. Sarah, Jake and I can't stop giggling. I let out a huge puff of air; my stomach doesn't feel fluttery or nervous any more. If that's the only thing to go wrong today, well, that's fine by me. People seem to have bought Janice as the real Queen, Craig's not as clever as he thinks he is, and everyone seems happy and excited now. Things are going to be blinking brilliant after all.

Mr Featherstone guides Janice back to her seat. 'Sorry about that, Your Majesty,' he says. 'Things aren't normally this mad.'

'Yes they are!' someone in the crowd shouts back, and everybody laughs. We're all in a brilliant mood now. It's the best day ever!

'That's quite all right, love,' Janice replies, smoothing down her dress. 'Most fun I've had in ages. Mind you, I've not run that fast since I had that loan shark looking for me.'

She beams up at the crowd, but they've stopped laughing.

Oh God.

Their faces are frozen. Time seems to stand still.

The WI lady frowns at Janice. 'What did you just say?'

Oh no. Oh God. Please, no.

I step forward and try to get everyone's attention. 'Shall we just crack on?' I say, trying not to panic.

'Did she say *loan shark*?' someone at the back of the crowd asks.

'She was joking!' I cry, frantically trying to bluff my way out of this. 'Weren't you, Your Majesty?'

'Oh aye!' Janice replies, still smiling.

I look at her, horrified. '*Posh*,' I mouth silently, turning so the crowd can't see me.

Janice lightly taps her head, like she's just remembered she's meant to be playing a role. 'I mean, oh yes!' she replies in her fake posh voice. 'Golly gosh, yes.'

Except that now it sounds totally ridiculous, even to me. People are starting to whisper. Craig strides over to us. 'Was that a *northern* accent?' he asks Janice.

'No!' I look at him like I think he's crazy.

'What's going on?' he asks, squaring up to me. 'You'd best start talking, young lady.'

I shrug my shoulders. 'I have no idea what you

329

mean.' I try to sound calm. 'Now, I suggest we get a wriggle on because the Queen doesn't have all day, you know.'

I start to move towards my tattoo participants, but I hear a scuffle behind me, and turn round to see Craig wrestling with Janice's tiara.

'What are you doing?' I cry, launching myself at him. 'She's the Queen of England! You can't rugby tackle her!'

Janice is desperately trying to keep the tiara on her head, but Craig's got a firm grip. I'm tugging at his tuxedo tails, but he won't let go. Just as I'm about to kick his shins, he successfully pulls the tiara off Janice's head, and brandishes it aloft to the crowd. 'Just as I suspected,' he cries, a look of triumph on his face. 'It's made of tin.'

He turns to me. The whole town – the performers, my schoolmates, the spectators – along with Mr Law and Kirsty and Mark and Nana May and Sarah and Jake and Mr Featherstone, stares at me too.

I shrink back. 'Austerity Britain . . . ?' I whisper, but even as I'm saying it, I know it's no good.

The jig is up.

CHAPTER TWENTY-SIX

I want to run. Just turn round and peg it out of the park and never come back.

I gulp as hundreds of pairs of eyes stare at me. So, this is it. Everything I've been worrying about has finally happened. I search frantically for the elephant, certain I'm about to be trampled.

And then I hear his voice. It rings out in the silence, loud and clear. 'Billie?'

I start to blink – my eyes feel hot and tears well up. I look over at the table: Kirsty and Mr Law have finally got the laptop connected to Skype.

And there he is. Dad. His face is right up close to the webcam, and even from here I can see the confusion in his eyes. Confusion and disappointment.

'How – how much did you see?' I stutter.

Dad shakes his head. 'Craig took off the Queen's tiara – except she's not the Queen.'

Everything, then.

'I'm sorry, Dad,' I whisper, and on the screen behind him, all Dad's army colleagues and mates start talking about what's going on.

It's finally time to come clean.

I wipe my eyes with the back of my hand and sigh, then turn to the crowd. 'I'm so sorry, everyone.' It's funny – I've heard everyone else say that word a million times over the last few weeks, and I never thought they meant it. But it still doesn't seem to sum up just how bad I feel about letting everyone down.

Craig's arms are folded across his chest. Out of the corner of my eye I see Sarah and Jake and Tamwar look at each other in confusion. 'I lied,' I say.

Nobody says anything, so I go on talking.

'I didn't mean to . . .' I hesitate – I don't know what I'm going to say, or how I'm going to say it. What is there to say, really? 'It's just – I wanted the Queen to send Dad home, and then everyone started coming on board with the tattoo, and I couldn't say no, because they were so excited, and then people were pointing and jeering at me that day here in the park before we saw Steve's missing legs – sorry, Jade – and then everyone started to believe that the Queen really was coming, and I saw how hard they were working – and I couldn't say that she *wasn't* coming, so I made it up and then, after I saw something about lookalikes on a chat show, I hired Janice and I had to raise two hundred quid, which Mark gave me instead of birthday presents for the rest of my life, and she was a bit rubbish – sorry, Janice, but it's true – but you all believed it was her, and things were going really well until she forgot to be posh.'

I take a big breath because that all came tumbling out in one go. Weirdly, even though I know everyone hates me, it feels kind of good to have it all out in the open at last. And if I'm going to be trampled by an elephant, Dad may as well know why.

Still nobody says anything, so I carry on. 'I just wanted my dad to come home.' My voice sounds all small and scared. 'I said it was so we could do the three-legged race, but the truth is, I was going to get the Queen to send him home early so he wouldn't get blown up or shot like the others, because it's her Armed Forces and she can do that if she wants to.'

After another moment of silence, I look up to see Kirsty and Linda standing with their arms around each other, blowing their noses. Then I force myself to look at Dad. And the funny thing is, he's all teary and blowing his nose too. I've never seen him do anything like that before. Even when the hamster I had when I was five died and I tried to flush it down the toilet because I read somewhere that that's what you should do with pets, and Dad got all stressed and thought I was a murderer – until I told him why I did it and he said it was only fish that you flush.

I can't bear this. I just want to know what he's thinking.

'I'm still keeping the money,' Janice states, breaking the silence.

I stop myself from glaring at her because, even though she forgot to be posh, I know deep down that she's not to blame for all this.

I am.

'Dad?' I say after another minute of silence.

Dad composes himself and puts his tissue in his pocket. He clears his throat. 'I'm the one who should be sorry, Bill.' He gives me a tight smile. 'You did all this for me?'

I nod. Dad's mates go quiet in the background. It's so silent both out there and in Battlefield Park, you could hear a pin drop.

'I didn't realize how much you'd miss me,' Dad continues. Everyone is looking at him on the screen, but it feels as though it's just me and him there. 'I mean, I knew you would, obviously, but I had no idea just how much pain my going away would cause you. But this is my job. I have to be here, to fight. You understand that, don't you?'

I nod again. I understand it, but I don't like it.

'The Queen wouldn't send me home, sweetheart, early or otherwise . . .' Dad gives me another smile. 'And even if she wanted to, I wouldn't let her. Life here's not like life there, Billie. These people need our help.'

Everyone looks down at the ground, and I can guess what they're thinking. Because I'm thinking the same thing, about how lucky we are not to have to worry about being shot at every time we pop to the shops. And even though Mrs Hussein's really annoying and Mr Law hates me for kicking midday supervisors, at least I get to go to school, unlike some children around the world.

Craig gives a big sigh. 'I guess we can all go home.' He starts to storm off. Darren and the Merchant Stanton Junior School Band pack up their instruments. The Scrabble players put their boards away.

Most of the spectators start to head towards the gates, and *everyone* throws me horrible looks.

'Not only did he miss out on a cruise to Egypt,' one Scrabble player huffs, jerking his thumb at his mate, 'but I had a free day pass to Longleat Safari Park.'

And that just makes me really angry. Not about the Longleat Safari Park day pass, but because of how everyone's behaving. 'All right, so I lied,' I blurt out, 'and I did stupid things, but I'm not the only one.'

Craig glares at me. 'What's that supposed to mean?'

'Who marks out a pitch to show that their tattoo is better than ours?' I cry. '*That's* stupid. And I'm just a kid, but you're a grown-up and you're meant to know better. You've been nothing but a big bully.'

Craig doesn't say anything, but he shifts uncomfortably from one foot to the other. Out of the corner of my eye I see the old people whisper to each other in confusion.

'And take Hope Springs,' I say, running over to them. 'I used to think the residents were all just hopeless and old, but they've got wonderful stories to tell – even if they're all made up, like knowing the Pope. They actually *want* to have fun, yet we just shove them in a cold dingy home where no one bothers to visit them because we think they smell of wee.' The old folk all look a bit sad at that.

I remember Derek and Mr Stephens' painting exploits. 'And there's no money from the council to spruce up the care home.' I glare over to Craig, who's standing next to his council official mate. 'Yet you were happy to help with his tattoo.' The council man, at least, has the decency to look ashamed.

'And take Tamwar and his family'... I say,

gesturing to his fifteen relatives. I stiffen a bit as I realize his uncle is still on top of the elephant. 'Even though they're the best dancers we've ever seen, nobody wanted them in the tattoo because they didn't think they were properly British.'

I know my little speech is working because people are starting to look uncomfortable. There are a few 'Sorry's from the back.

'This is meant to be an army town,' I say, gesturing to the British Legion chaps, getting into my stride now, 'and we've been fighting over who gets to do what in this tattoo or who can impress the Queen the most, which is ridiculous.' I turn back to Dad and his colleagues on the computer screen. 'Especially when there's a real war going on. People are dying and getting their legs blown off, and *we're* worried about whose band has got the best tuba.'

The Yorkshire Colliery Brass Band look a bit shifty at that. Darren leans in to Aria. '*Our* band, by the way,' he whispers.

'We don't have to listen to this,' Craig says, looking at the crowd. 'You're just a silly little girl who's caused a lot of trouble.'

'Hey!' Dad says on the screen, but Craig ignores him and heads towards the exit, a large gaggle of spectators in tow.

'This whole thing has been a *complete* waste of time,' he mutters.

Yet despite everything that's happened, and even though everyone in Merchant Stanton hates me right now, I don't think it *has*.

'If it wasn't for the tattoo,' I say in a clear voice, 'we wouldn't have known how good the gymnasts really are, or that Tamwar's uncle can ride an elephant, or that the Scrabble players are really good with long words, or that the WI make lovely bouquets, or that Jake *can* do things, despite his allergies, or that Sarah Knowles is really nice, or that Andy Nelson isn't such a bad person.'

Sarah and Jake both give me a little smile. Andy frowns, but he doesn't look too annoyed. 'So, all right, we've had our ups and downs,' I continue, 'but now we know how many talented people we've got in this town.'

Craig shrugs. 'So? It still doesn't make up for

the fact that you lied.'

I nod. 'I know, and I said I'm sorry about that. But you had fun, didn't you? I saw you. When you and Mike were changing your pub sign, you were laughing.' I think back to the other things I saw that day. 'And you said business has never been so good.'

Craig narrows his eyes at me. 'Business *has* been better,' he says slowly. But then he shakes his head. 'Doesn't matter . . . We came for the Queen. Nothing less.'

Suddenly a small boy comes bounding through the park gates. He staggers up to us, and we all stare at him as he sticks his head between his knees, desperately trying to get his breath back. He pants a bit more, but then straightens up. 'She's here!' he cries.

'Who?' I ask, confused.

The boy doesn't have a chance to respond. Just then, two men in suits stride into the park. They're both wearing sunglasses and holding their wrists up to their mouths and talking. 'Copy that,' one of them says. 'Kittyhawk's on the move.'

'What's going on?' Craig blusters.

'We're clearing a path for the motorcade,' one of the men replies. 'Mind your step.'

Craig almost trips over his feet as they shoo him away.

'What motorcade?' I ask, but my voice gets lost in the sound of the car that's coming from outside the park. Several cars. And sirens.

Everyone is rooted to the spot as we watch the events unfold. The two men in suits take up positions as a police car heads in through the gates and onto the grass in front of us. Behind them is a long black car like a limo. It's got blacked-out windows so we can't see who's inside, however much we all peer in. Behind that is another police car, its sirens blaring.

People in the crowd start whispering to each other.

As the limo comes to a stop, one of the men steps forward and opens the back door. We wait with bated breath. First of all, a blue satin shoe emerges. The second one swivels round to join it. A white gloved hand appears on the car frame. We see the blue coat as she gets out the car. The diamond brooch. The white set curls. The little blue handbag.

I practically faint as the lady takes in the crowd before her. Sarah and Jake nudge me in the ribs. 'Did you do this?' they ask. I shake my head, still too stunned to speak.

Craig glares at me. 'Not again . . .' He strides over to the car, his hand outstretched. 'Let's have a look at that tiara.'

Quick as a flash, the two men in suits are by his side. 'What are you doing, sir?' one asks, his hand hovering over the gun holster on his hip.

Craig steps back a moment. 'Uh, n-nothing . . .' he stutters. 'I was just going to check that she was real.'

'Of course I am,' the lady says.

That's when we know. Her voice is so distinctive, so familiar. Clipped and regal. We've heard it a million times – in every Christmas speech and every Royal Variety Show.

'Your Majesty!' I whisper, and the Queen of England smiles right back at me.

CHAPTER TWENTY-SEVEN

The Queen! I step forward hesitantly. 'How come you're here?'

Before the Queen can answer, Mr Featherstone marches over to her. He stops in front of her, and raises his hand in a salute. 'Your Majesty,' he says, nodding to her.

The Queen beams at him. 'Len,' she replies. 'Lovely to see you again.'

The other residents at Hope Springs all gasp in surprise. Derek looks utterly baffled. My mouth is wide open in shock. 'You know Mr Featherstone?' I say, and the Queen looks at me.

'For forty years he tended the gardens at Windsor Castle,' she says.

'The Queen was your VIP?' I think back to our conversation yesterday. My mind races as I try to remember Mr Featherstone's other mad claims. If *that's* true, then what about Lassie? And the Pope? And the Prime Minister telling rude jokes?

Blimey.

'I don't have long,' the Queen whispers. 'I'm planting a tree in Harrogate this afternoon.'

'Right you are,' Mr Featherstone whispers back. And with that, he ushers the Queen over to the chair beside the pitch. Out of the corner of my eye I see Janice looking a bit miffed. It was, after all, *her* chair. But Mr Featherstone sits the Queen down and then turns to the crowd.

'Come along then,' he barks as we stand there, still in shock. 'The Queen's not got all day. Let's put on a show!'

His words seem to stir something in us: all at once, everyone starts running around like headless chickens. Darren and the Merchant Stanton Junior School Marching Band grab their instruments; the Morris dancers pull up their socks. Dave and Al start putting on their tiger-print costume, even though we all know the truth. People collide in their haste to get ready, not even caring if they've caused an injury. As they're pulling their swords from their sheaths, the pirates nearly overturn the table set up for the WI bouquets; they don't bother to say sorry, even though a vase fell onto an old lady's foot. Mike and his mates pick up their ukuleles, and one almost whacks Derek over the head with a ladder as he's hurrying into position. And I just manage to leap in front of the Queen in time to stop the little girl in the gymnastics team from roly-polying into her shins.

'STOP!' I yell before I know what I'm doing. Even without the megaphone, everybody stops right in their tracks and turns to face me.

'Didn't you listen to a word I said?' I fix everyone with a stare. They all look a bit blank, so I have to remind them, even though it was only a few minutes ago. I guess the real Queen turning up unexpectedly tends to make your brain go a bit fuzzy. 'We're still fighting – we should be ashamed of ourselves.'

Dave and Al and Mike and the football team and the gymnasts and the Extreme Scrabble players all look down at their feet, red-faced. I swear the elephant does too, but he may just be snuffling for food.

'We've got a golden opportunity here,' I say, gaining momentum, even though I'm completely winging it, 'to show the Queen just what Merchant Stanton is made of and how brilliant and talented we are. The Queen! We don't want half the town marching one way while the other half is doing something completely different.'

Some people are nodding, so I plough on. 'Why don't we just work together, hey? No man is an island. Working together is going to make a better tattoo than anything two different teams will come up with.' I look over at Mr Law and he's positively beaming at me. 'Let's all be team players,' I cry. 'Let's stop all the arguments and jibes and sniggers and just get on together. All right?'

Nobody says anything for a moment. Out of the corner of my eye I see the Queen raise her eyebrows and exchange a glance with Mr Featherstone.

'All right?' I repeat. I'm looking around the park wild-eyed now, because I'm conscious that I may have just made a complete and utter idiot of myself in front of Her Majesty.

A few more seconds pass. 'Right!' comes a voice from the back of the crowd. I crane my neck to see who's spoken and my mouth drops open in shock again.

Craig emerges with his hand outstretched and walks towards me. I lean back a bit in case he's planning to punch me.

But then the strangest thing happens. The corners of Craig's mouth start to twitch, and his mouth slowly – slowly – curves into a smile. It stretches all the way to his eyes this time. 'Billie Templar . . .' he murmurs. 'Who'd have thought a ten-year-old girl would get the better of me?'

'I'm eleven,' I reply, but that just seems to make him smile even more. He clasps my hand and pumps it up and down vigorously.

'So you're happy to combine tattoos then?' I ask.

Craig nods. 'You're right,' he tells me. 'I've been an idiot and I should have known better. Ready?'

'Ready,' I say firmly. I don't even need to do

anything – all of a sudden, the tattoo takes on a life of its own.

Mike and the George Formby Appreciation Society prop their ladders on the back of the Motorcycle Club's bikes, and as they zoom round the track, they balance precariously at the top, plucking their ukuleles. The spectators gasp in delight and start clapping appreciatively.

After a few moments the motorbikes ride off and the footballers jog on doing keepie uppies. But as they're kicking the balls high in the air from one player to another, the little gymnast starts doing her roly-polys through the gaps. Her timing is brilliant, because as the ball goes up, she does a roly-poly and then catches it and balances it on her head when it comes back down. The rest of the gymnasts leap and cartwheel around the track at the same time, all perfectly in time with the footballers.

On the other side of the field, the Extreme Scrabble players are frantically picking letters out of the little green drawstring bag and placing them on the board. With sweat pouring down their faces as if they've just completed a marathon, they grab the board and carefully carry it over to the Queen. WE'RE SO PLEASED YOU'RE HEAR, YOUR MAJESTY, it reads.

Sarah gestures to the board. One of the men looks at it, then smacks his hand to his head. 'Shivers!' He scrabbles around in the bag for another E. 'There aren't any left!' he cries in panic.

Another Scrabble player glowers at him. 'You said they were all there!' He scoops some letters off the board.

'Sorry,' the players say to the Queen, as the board now reads: WE'RE SO PLEASED YOU'RE HERE, YOUR MAJ.

After they've finished, Darren picks up his tuba, ready to lead the Merchant Stanton Junior School Marching Band. He glances nervously at the Yorkshire Colliery Band. 'We only know "When the Saints Go Marching In",' he says, downcast.

The leader of the colliery band pats him on the back and smiles. 'That's all right, son. It's my favourite.'

And together, the two bands march along in perfect time. Mrs MacLean, the music teacher, is practically bursting with pride.

I look at the Queen and see that her foot is

moving slightly to the music.

As the swashbuckling pirates come on, the ladies from the WI set up their table and start their flower-arranging. The pirates help by hacking away with their swords at any unwanted stems. After a few minutes of swords swishing and petals flying, they've knocked together some lovely bouquets. The leader of the WI comes forward and curtseys as she passes the biggest bunch of flowers to the Queen, though she doesn't attempt any of the 'Ma'am ham' stuff this time.

Tamwar and his family run on and launch into their perfect dance routine. The whole crowd claps along as they show off their moves, the ladies' costumes fluttering in the wind. I look at the Queen again, and this time her foot is positively tapping. As the routine nears its end, one of Tamwar's relatives leads the elephant forward – and on top of it are seven ballerinas, all twirling away *en pointe*.

Next, Dave and Al lumber on in their tiger costume. They look ridiculous, but everyone cheers them anyway. The tiger weaves in and out of the Morris dancers as they knock their wooden blocks together. In the background, the tiger handler gets carried away and cracks his whip like he's Indiana blinking Jones.

And because he's joining in the tattoo – even though he's not meant to be in it – everyone else wants to be a part of it too. Mrs Hussein reaches into her handbag and produces a pair of spoons. She starts thwacking them against her thigh. 'What?' she cries as the other teachers exchange looks. 'I take them everywhere with me.'

There's a low drone overhead, and we all duck as a little toy helicopter zooms over the crowd. One of the men from the British Legion stumbles forward, a remote control in his hand. 'It's a fly-past,' he explains as the helicopter jerks around in the air. 'Couldn't stretch to the Red Arrows, I'm afraid.'

Sarah nudges me forward. 'Go on,' she whispers. 'You should do something. It's your tattoo.'

I ignore her. I know it's mean after all she's done, but I don't know how many times I can keep saying I can't do *any*thing.

Before we know it, it's nearly over – just the grand finale to go. Jake grabs Tamwar's uncle, and they leave the field. Moments later, a series of bangs mark the start of the fireworks display. The crowd ooohs and aaaaahs as rockets and bangers go flying up into the air. There's fizzing and *pffffts* and I see the Queen smiling in delight.

Now the residents of Hope Springs, led by Mr Featherstone, march on, walking sticks over their shoulders, and everyone claps and cheers. They look incredibly smart, and even though some of them are shuffling along, and Cyril's IV pole keeps getting caught up, they all march in time. There are looks of such pride on their faces. My eyes feel all hot and prickly because I've never seen them this happy.

The crowd cheers wildly as the last firework fizzes out and the marchers come to a halt. They salute us and we salute them back.

It's as we're all still whooping and cheering that we feel the first drops of rain. Everyone looks up to the heavens and umbrellas open among the crowd. 'Typical English weather,' a Morris dancer tuts. One of the Queen's security guards rushes over and shields her with a giant golf umbrella.

But I love the rain, because it's given me an idea

of what I can do . . .

'Nana May!' I shout. 'Fancy a dance?'

She beams at me and gets to her feet. We link arms and together, we launch into her favourite song.

'We're siiiiiinging in the rain,' we yell at the top of our voices. 'Just siiiiiiinging in the rain.'

Kirsty edges over to us. 'What are you doing?' she hisses. 'It's the Queen! God, Mum, you're so embarrassing.'

I glance around. Everyone is staring at us like we're mad. Even the Queen looks bemused.

I stop dancing and detach myself from Nana May. 'Uh . . . maybe we should stop,' I whisper.

Nana May looks so disappointed it blinking near breaks my heart.

'I want to go on dancing,' I whisper to her, 'but everyone's looking at us as if we're mental.'

Nana May pats my hand. 'I understand,' she says.

The rain's letting up now, and people start putting down their umbrellas. The Queen is summoning her security guards when, all of a sudden, this electronic sound blares out around the park.

The crowd parts, and there, body-popping his

way towards us like a lankier, grown-up version of Justin Bieber, is Mark.

'What are you doing?' I laugh, because watching Mark dance is so funny. It's like a giraffe trying to roller-skate. 'You *never* dance!'

Mark just shrugs and continues doing his robotic dancing towards us. 'Chilllllllllax!' He beams at me. 'Yeah? Just go with the flow.'

'Oh my God,' Kirsty mumbles, rolling her eyes. But she can't help it – she starts giggling too.

'Come on, everyone,' Mark yells to the crowd. 'Let's just have a laugh.'

Nana May starts high-kicking, and this time even Kirsty joins in. I jump up and down as if I'm sploshing in puddles like Don does in the film. And before I know it, *everyone* is dancing. Cyril's linked arms with Olive and they're bopping away. The little kids from my school are sploshing in *actual* puddles while their parents snap away on their cameras. Those with umbrellas are twirling them round and round. Clearly they've seen the film too.

'What a glooooorious feeeeeeeeling,' everyone sings, 'I'm haaaaaaappy again.' I couldn't have put it better myself.

After what feels like for ever with everyone absolutely geeking off, the crowd calms down, the cheering peters out, and the Queen signals to her bodyguards that she finally wants to leave. The spectators applaud politely as the guards escort her back to her car. As one of them opens the car door for her, the Queen nods to Mr Featherstone and smiles at us one last time.

But just as she's getting into the car, a lone voice cries out from the back of the crowd: 'WAIT!'

It's Dad.

He's got a massive grin on his face. I've not seen him smile like that in a long time. I rack my brains to remember when I last saw him that happy but I can't think of anything. Well, except for that photo in his chest of drawers – the one with him and me and Mark. And Mum.

And just as I'm thinking, *Good, he must have enjoyed the marching, then*, Dad puffs out his chest and shouts, loud and clear, 'That's my daughter, Your Majesty! And my son!' First he looks at the Queen, and then he gazes at me with that big grin of his.

There's a lump in my throat. Because as well as that big old grin on his face, there's something else. It's . . . pride. Dad's actually proud of me.

'Proudest dad in the world, I am,' he shouts from the screen, as if he's read my mind. 'Well done, Billie.'

And behind him, all the men in his regiment start whooping and cheering and clapping me. And the clapping spreads through the crowd: before I know it, Darren and the Merchant Stanton Junior School Band, and the motorcyclists, and the Extreme Scrabble players, and the footballers, and Mr Featherstone, and Derek, and Cyril, and everyone at Hope Springs, and Kirsty and Mark and Linda and Nana May, and all the crowd are clapping me too. Even the Queen's two bodyguards are joining in.

'Three cheers for Billie!' Mr Featherstone cries. 'Bravo!'

'Bravo!' the crowd yells, beaming at me. 'Bravo!'

I'm properly blinking back tears now. I've been doing that a lot these past few weeks, but I honestly, genuinely can't remember when I've done it for being this happy. 'Thanks,' I manage to say, but my voice cracks a little.

The Queen gives me the royal wave and then gets into the car. The engine revs, and the limo and the police cars head out of the park.

After a few moments the clapping stops, and we all sort of look at each other because we can't believe that actually happened.

'Come here, Billie,' Dad says, breaking the silence, and I run over and put my face right up to the computer screen.

'What you did, organizing all this,' he goes on, 'is amazing, love. Tickety-boo fantastic.'

I start to smile at him, but then I remember something. 'I only did all this to get the Queen to sign my note.' My voice shakes a little. 'But it wouldn't have been any good, would it? You wouldn't have come back early anyway.'

Dad hesitates. 'I'm nearly halfway through my tour,' he says after a moment. 'You know that. I'll be back before you realize.'

'What if you get shot?' I whisper. 'Or blown up?' I've never said this to Dad before. I've always been too scared.

He smiles at me, and then at Mark and Kirsty and Nana May. And Linda. 'I've got too much to live for.' He starts blinking really hard too. Perhaps it's a bit dry out there and it's hurting his eyes. 'I'll be home soon.'

I knew he wouldn't be gone for ever, but hearing Dad actually say it is the best news I've had all day. All week. All month!

Mark comes over and squeezes my shoulder. 'In the meantime,' he says, 'reckon you could put up with me for the three-legged race?'

I beam up at him, because I'm so surprised he's offered to help. 'No thanks,' I say.

Mark's face falls, so I quickly explain. 'I'm not fussed about the carnival any more,' I say. 'I was only banging on about it because I wanted Dad home as soon as possible. But he's coming home soon anyway, I know he is, so it doesn't matter any more.'

Mark nods slowly. 'Right.'

I peer into the crowd and spot Sarah, chatting with Tamwar. 'But I know someone else who might need a partner.' I grin at him. 'As long as you're better at running than you are at dancing.'

Mark laughs at that, and I laugh right back, and the laughter goes all the way through my belly and into my soul because I'm so happy. I'm happy that Dad's coming home, even if it's not immediately. And I'm happy that Mark's started being nice to me, and that he and Kirsty are going to carry on being nice to me, because they promised. And I'm happy that Mr Featherstone's nice – and I'll make him promise to keep being nice. And in return, *I'll* go on being nice to Jade and Sarah and Jake and Tamwar, because that's what friends do. Be nice to one another.

'Right, come on, everyone,' a voice rings out, and we all turn to see Craig marching towards the exit, a determined look on his face. Mike and the window cleaners march behind him, carrying their ladders. 'Follow us.'

'Where are you going?' I yell to him.

Craig gestures to Mr Featherstone and the other old people. 'Hope Springs. We're going to spruce it up. There's enough of us.'

Derek's eyes light up. 'Really? You're going to

help us?'

Craig nods. 'Me and whoever wants to be in my DIY army. Let's go!'

Mrs Hussein practically faints with excitement. 'This is what I'm talking about, 6H!' she calls. The spectators start to stream through the park gates, chatting excitedly to their neighbours.

Suddenly Mr Clewson's tank rolls by. 'I'm selling the car,' he shouts, his head poking out of the hatch. 'This is much more fun!'

And as everyone laughs, jokes, whoops and cheers, arms slung around each other — even Mr Law's got his arm around Kirsty, but it doesn't make me feel sick — I smile to myself.

Guess my Christmas miracle happened after all, I think, *even though it's the middle of July. Tickety-boo fantastic, Billie. Tickety-boo fantastic.*

Acknowledgements:

My heartfelt thanks to all at Random House Children's Books for their help and support in developing and publishing this book. Particular thanks to Annie Eaton and Sophie Nelson, and to the mighty and marvellous Natalie Doherty and Becky Stradwick for being all-round good eggs.

A massive thank you to Jodie Marsh at United Agents for her encouragement and skill and congratulatory box of cheese.

Thank you to Rhiannon Jones and Tom Smyth for their insight into a soldier's life on tour and for patiently answering my questions.

Thank you to the staff and pupils of Fair Field Junior School, especially Nicola Worsley and Aria Braden.

Thank you to Frank and Amy for putting up with my cries of 'Does this make sense?' while you were trying to watch *Masterchef*. Thanks to all my friends for their all-round brilliantness.

And last but not least, thanks to Mum and Dad, as ever.

Also by Ellie Irving:

Loudest burp?
Freckliest face?
Fastest time to superglue hand to head?

Luke loves world records. He knows everything about them – the hairiest man alive, the woman with the most tattoos, even the world's most venomous snake. But he never imagined that his strange hobby would come in useful one day.

When Luke finds out his tiny village is going to be bulldozed to the ground by developers, he knows he's got to try and save it. His brilliant plan? He'll make Port Bren famous – by getting the eccentric villagers to break fifty world records. In a week.

The clock is ticking.

And the records just keeping getting crazier...